THE PHOENIX INITIATIVE

By

Mark Reddan

This book is dedicated to my sister, Abi.

Thank you for all your hard work.

Also available from Mark Reddan;

The Company Books;

Agent Red

PART ONE

1

She opened her eyes.

Jane Doe awoke, sat up and looked around the room. It was a familiar sight and one that she had been waking up to every day for the past six months or so.

She was lying on a single mattress cot that was pressed up against the wall. Opposite her was another identical bed that had a man sitting on it. The walls were white, the floor was black, and there were prints of artwork from famous artists throughout the years decorating the walls. There was a small bookcase filled with literature and two big comfy armchairs for reading in. It was a nice room, as far as rooms like this went, and no matter how hard she tried, she couldn't ever remember a morning where she didn't wake up here, in this room with John waking up opposite her.

"Morning," he said as he got off his cot and stretched. He had an American accent and short hair that was shaved at the side, a military-style haircut that had been allowed to grow and brown eyes. He was wearing grey jogging bottoms and a black t-shirt. Jane was dressed the same.

"Morning," she replied. "Sleep well?" She was British.

"Good, thanks, you seemed restless again; everything OK?"

"Yeah, fine," she lied, "just weird dreams."

For the last couple of weeks, Jane had been having bad dreams. Places and people that she couldn't quite place but yet felt familiar, so real she felt like she was there. Running through forests, assaulting a house with a breach team and fire fights with her unit, a unit that she had no recollection of, yet she recognised all of them but couldn't place a name to a single face.

She got up, stretched, and put it out of her mind. There was a cost to what she was doing and what they were both doing, and if the worst that happens is some bad dreams about life before, that was a price she could live with.

They both left the room. The corridor they walked out into was long, narrow, and also painted white. Everything about where they were felt clinical. They walked down the hall and entered the bathroom. They both entered the shower bay and washed under shower heads at opposite ends of the room. John had a large phoenix tattoo on his back, it flowed down the left side, and the tail feathers curled up at the lower back. Jane knew she had one identical on her right side. After showering, they both used the toilet facilities and brushed their teeth. Once back in the room, they changed into fresh clothes and got ready to head to training for the day.

Jane looked in the mirror. She had a round face, long brown hair that she put in a ponytail, piercing blue eyes and a figure that had been shaped by years of hard training, even before she had come here.

She finished tying up her hair, and once she was happy it wouldn't get in her way, she left the bunkroom.

She walked down the corridor and into the next area of the building. It was like a giant warehouse; it had different training scenarios and building layouts for training and had a firing range at the bottom. She couldn't remember her life before being here, but she knew the training simulators and how to do them. It was muscle memory that was ingrained in her. It was reflexes and reactions. Those had never left.

Her or John.

John was waiting for her in a small seating area that faced the training areas. Four metal chairs were surrounding a metal-topped table.

A locked weapons storage cupboard waited eagerly to be opened and have its contents unleashed on the simulated enemies in the runs.

"You ready for today's fun?" He asked.

"Absolutely." She smiled back.

They waited a few minutes; they knew they could come a bit later as the man they were waiting for always arrived at the same time every morning. However, they both liked to be punctual, and one of Jane's mottos was always:

Punctuality is king; if you're early, then you're on time. If you're on time, then you're late.

There was a comfortable silence around the room, and the faint smell of gunpowder hung in the air. There was no ventilation in this area, so all the aromas from the drills and timed runs lingered in the air, reminding them both of what they had done and how much more was expected of them.

A door to their left opened with a suck of airlock pressure, and a man in a white laboratory coat entered the room holding his usual electronic tablet.

2

The routine was the same. Each morning they would be given new medication and a simulated mission to undertake. It would involve a scenario that would usually entail collection of information – a laptop or USB drive – rescuing hostages or taking down a specific target.

The hostiles would comprise pop-up paper targets as well as actual personnel moving around and firing back.

The man in the laboratory coat joined them, sat, and placed the tablet on the table. He was young, in his thirties with short blonde hair and always regarded both Jane and John with an air of cautiousness. He was swift to set the task, and then he would leave.

He took a small case out of his coat pocket and placed it on the table. He opened it up to expose the four small tablets sitting inside, two blue and two white.

Jane and John took one of each colour and swallowed them down. Every time she did so, she expected to feel different. Like a magical wave would wash over her and suddenly, it would all make sense like this would be the one that worked.

This morning, as with every other morning, she felt no different.

"Today's scenario," the man in the white coat said once the pills had been swallowed, "is a retrieval one. The course has once again been redesigned and re-arranged, and you will be going in blind. There will be no layout provided, no intel on how many targets you will be up against. You must enter, retrieve the laptop and exfiltrate without being shot. Understood?"

Jane and John both nodded.

"Good, run begins in ten minutes. As usual, you will be monitored and timed," the man said. "Good luck." Then he simply got up and left the room through the door he had entered by.

Jane and John moved over to the weapons case; a beep sounded as the locks disengaged and the door popped open.

Jane looked at John, and as she had every other morning, she said, "pick your poison."

3

All the weapons in the holders in the closet were retrofitted for paintballs. This allowed the experience to be as authentic as possible with the weight and manoeuvrability of an actual weapon but eliminated the risks associated with live fire. Only the firing range used live ammunition.

Jane selected the C8 SFW Carbine; it was her go-to assault rifle and a Sig Sauer P226 pistol for her side arm. She checked their mechanisms, knowing that they weren't live and had been adapted, but she did it every time. It was in her subconscious, and when they were live, she didn't want to get out of the habit of checking and maintenance. John had selected his usual M4a1 rifle and the Glock 19 for his side arm. Same as every other time and performed the same checking ritual as Jane had. They both placed ear wig communication devices in their ears and checked they could hear each other.

Once they were both happy, they closed the door but not far enough to lock it so they could put their weapons back at the end and moved to the starting position.

There were a few different setups, and they were regularly changed and re-arranged so that they couldn't get used to a layout, and it would constantly be new for them. There was a green light over a start point so they knew which one to go to. They lined up next to each other and got in their action stances, knees slightly bent and poised, ready to move when the light changed to red.

The light changed to red.

"Go!" Jane said, and they pushed off and moved towards the entrance.

They pulled the front door open, Jane was crouched low, aiming left, and John was aiming high to the right making sure all the area was covered in case there was a surprise waiting in the first section.

It was clear.

"You go right; I'll go left," Jane said.

"Got it," John replied and pushed off, moving down the right corridor.

The scenario house was like a maze of tight corridors and blind corners. There were open rooms with furniture such as beds, chairs, desks, cupboards, and bookcases – many things for enemy combatants to hide behind. There was no roof on the single floor areas and only a thin layer to support the parts made to be two stories, the lighting was dark, and there were flashes streaked across the walls designed to distract and disorientate.

She paced her way cautiously down the first corridor, keeping her footing secure and her senses tuned for any sight or sound that may be a hostile. She reached the door; it was on her right, and she put her body next to the wall, crouched down and, keeping her barrel at her eye line, looked around. She was tense, her body was like a coiled snake ready to pounce and attack, but the room seemed clear.

There were options for her; carry on down the corridor and make the right turn at the end, or cut through the room and use the door on the left side to come back out in the hall on the other side of the corner, or from the room, she could use the other door to push to the next room, further into the maze structure.

She moved into the room, keeping her weapon trained for any anomaly and went to the door leading back to the corridor. She swept round and checked the hallway. It was clear.

She turned back into the room, took a micro-second to make sure nothing had changed. Same chair, same bed, nobody here, everything as it was. She moved to the other door.

She pressed up against the frame, bent her knees slightly and again raised the barrel and pushed on. This room was darker, there was a ceiling, and it was robbing the space of most of its light. She kept her rifle trained, sweeping the room checking the corners. Clear.

Two doors in front of her; one straight ahead that was closed and one to her right that was just a frame. She moved to the open-door frame, but as she approached, a paper target swung out, filling the space, she fired two shots that hit the silhouetted man in the heart, and the target swung back around.

She stacked up against the corner, again repeating her process and again sweeping around and checking the corners while keeping the bulk of her body secure behind the wall.

Clear.

She turned and moved to the door, dropping her rifle, and letting it swing on the strap to her side and seamlessly drawing her side arm pistol to replace it.

It was logical when going through a closed door by yourself to have a small easy to raise and use weapon, you didn't want to open the door, and there be a hostile, and you need to raise and steady a large rifle before you can release a round. That's how you end up dead. So it was a habit to enter a closed-door room with the side arm as the primary weapon.

She gripped the handle, took a breath, and braced herself. She turned and pulled the door open, releasing it halfway and letting the momentum carry it as she moved her hand to secure the pistol two-handed. There were two chairs and a desk in this room, and from her position behind the wall at the open door, it was empty. She stepped in and cleared the spaces behind the frame that were not visible from her position, and moved forward. Then a man appeared, not a paper silhouette man, a real man. He came up from behind the desk and was wearing a grey jumper, black trousers, a paintball mask, and was wielding a paintball gun. Jane fired twice and hit him in his chest armour before he could pull his trigger, he fell to the floor, simulating his death.

Then she heard a noise behind her, and as she turned, a man crashed into her, sending them both flying across the desk and landing on the man who had been 'shot'. The pistol dropped from her hand and the man was on her. She put her arms up to protect herself from the punch he tried to land, then he moved his hand to his side and drew his converted pistol. She reached up as he pointed it at her, grabbing the top of it with her left hand and his hand with her right. She pulled and twisted, and less than a second later, she was holding his weapon aimed at him, laying on the floor underneath him, next to another live combatant. She shot him twice and he dropped to the side. She lifted his legs off and retrieved her weapon. Putting the hostiles out of reach.

She turned, put her side-arm away, got her rifle ready, and then moved to the next area.

This large room looked like a welcome area with a large round desk in the middle and chairs and desks around the edge. There was a doorway leading to this room on each wall. Jane repeated her entrance checking as best as she could as she moved through. A paper target popped up from behind a desk to her left and she quickly dispensed of it and exited through the door at the other side. She was in an area that was a small hallway with stairs at the end. The only way into this area was through the large reception style room, and the only way forward was up the stairs now. Either she was close, or she had gone completely the wrong way.

It didn't matter; as long as either herself or John got the laptop and they both got out, it was a win.

She heard a noise behind her, she hid against the wall and swapped to her pistol, a man walked through, it was John.

"Hello there," she said.

"Hi, I thought I saw you come this way."

"Having fun?"

"Always," he replied. "Ready to move?" He nodded to the stairs.

"Lead the way." She said as she holstered her pistol and tucked her rifle into her shoulder, keeping it loose but ready.

They reached the stairs, and John went first. Jane turned back to make sure no one was sneaking up on them and once she was happy it was clear, she followed him up to the landing. There was only one door up here. This seemed like a short run, but that was fine as not every assessment would take hours and be a survival exercise. They stood on each side of the door, and Jane put her hand on the handle. John counted down on his fingers from three, and on zero, she pushed it open. John went first and she followed, covering the other half of the room. It was empty. There was a laptop sitting on the table. It was closed and had a red cross on the top. This was how the trainers marked the objective, so they knew they had it. John switched to his side-arm, picked the laptop up and tucked it under his arm.

"Should've brought a bag," he said.

"I did," she said as she winked at him. Then she raised her rifle and led the way back out of the room. The moment they passed the door threshold, an alarm sounded. They didn't even pause a beat to register it. They knew that it meant they had the laptop, and any remaining combatants still wandering around would be converging, so they needed to move fast. They reached the door and peered through; it was clear. Jane led the way into the room as she knew the way out, the same that she had come in, and it wasn't time to try and find shortcuts through the doors on either side. Two men appeared in the doorway and were moving towards them and firing.

Jane and John took cover behind the large round desk in the middle of the room. Jane waited a breath, waited for the right moment and then when there was a break, she raised, saw them moving to cover and fired, hitting one in the chest. The other took cover behind a desk and fired back. A paintball hit the desktop and exploded, sending paint residue onto Jane's top as she hid behind the cover again.

"Three o'clock!" John shouted, and Jane instinctively raised her rifle to her right and fired at the man who was running into the room, the bullets found him, and he fell to the floor 'dead'.

She saw movement out the corner of her eye to her left and shouted, "Nine o'clock!" to warn John, he fired and hit the man. More came through on Jane's side, and they were exposed. They kept firing and hitting as many as they could, but the numbers were against them. They were either side of the entrance gap to the desk, but she knew if they went in, they would be cornered. Then a paintball exploded next to her head, but its trajectory wasn't from the front or either side; it was from behind.

"Get in the desk!" She shouted, and John, looking behind him and now realising they were surrounded, out manned, and out gunned, nodded, pushed the flap open, slid the laptop in and gave cover fire as Jane crawled in with him following her and closing it.

They were trapped. Jane knew it. John knew it. That's why it had been so easy to do the run. The run wasn't the point. The point was to trap them.

"How'd they get in behind us?" John asked.

"That was the point," she said. "We're sitting ducks here now."

Paintballs exploded all around them. There was a constant sound of popping and banging as the enemy combatants bombarded their cover, never giving them a break to return fire, and little puffs of paint could be seen over the edges. They kept low, hunkered down, trying to make themselves as small as possible.

"Let's make it hard for them," John said, looking over.

"You read my mind."

She rose and fired at the nearest men advancing on their position. She managed to take two down before she retook cover. John was still up firing, and when he came back down, she stood up again and returned fire. There were more men in this scenario than she had ever seen; there must have been at least fifteen or twenty all in the one large room, all around them, all firing at their position. They were all dressed the same as the men she had encountered earlier. It was unnerving seeing them all identical. Their masks covered their face, so they all just looked like clones advancing on them.

They traded off standing and shooting for a few rounds, managing to hold the circle of men around them off. When they ran out of rifle 'bullets', they switched to their pistols and Jane regretted not bringing the gun she had disarmed from the hostile earlier.

After what felt like hours but must have been around thirty minutes, they were out of ammunition.

"Shit," she said.

"I'm out too."

"Still got our hands, screw it, let's go at it."

"I like the way you think English," he said, preparing himself. "Ready?... Go!"

They both leapt over the desktop, and Jane lunged at the nearest man, tackling him to the floor, bringing her elbow down, and cracking the protection cover over his eyes. She reached for his weapon:

Never give up. Never give in.

Then her body felt like it had been punched, and paint was covering her arm, then another shove of force as another hit her back, and then her chest, and then her back again.

She knew it was over.

She was 'dead'.

4

The rest of the day had been spent sparring with each other in the boxing ring and shooting at the range. After completing a run and achieving all their objectives, they never got a debrief, so they doubted they would get one now they had failed one.

That afternoon they were sat in their room, in the chairs on each side of the bookcase. Jane was reading a book from an American mystery writer about a detective solving cases, and John just sat there, staring into space, until he said, "you ever regret this?"
Jane closed her book, thought for a moment, and said, "no." Then she just opened her page again and carried on reading.
"C'mon English, seriously?"
"No," she said again, "I don't think I do. I mean, why would I? I can't remember who I was before I came here, so why would I regret it?"
"Ok."
"Why, do you?"
"Yeah, sometimes."
Jane closed her book and put it down on the floor.
"Why?" She asked.
"I don't know," he replied, "to be honest, it may not even be regret I'm feeling. I don't know, I just sometimes get this feeling, you know, in my stomach, that makes me question why I'm here. What did I give

up? Did I have a life before this, or was my life just like this? Do I have a family out there somewhere? Am I missed? Are people looking for me? You know?"

"Wow, Yank," she leaned back in her chair and pulled her legs up underneath her, "that's a lot to address and unpack."

"You ever feel like that?"

"I suppose, maybe…but to be honest, I just never really think about it."

"You never think if you left a family behind?"

"I suppose not. I think that I think if I had a family, kids and all that, then I wouldn't have volunteered to go through all this…but then again, am I, was I, the kind of person that would do all this to make sure that my family and kids were safe and protected…" She trailed off as her mind went down pathways of thought.

"Tell me about it," John said. "You know, I know why we're here, and I have seen my record of who I was, and it all makes sense, but I think it's a bit unnerving when I'm being shown a file, and a shrink is telling me why I'm here, and how I chose it and volunteered and all that crap; but it's so weird how they redact all our personal information. So, in reality, it could be anyone's file they're showing us."

"You've really gone in deep with this, haven't you?" Jane said as she got up and paced the room. "But I agree, I thought it was strange whenever we have our psych evals that we are told what we used to do, and why we chose to do this, and they tell us it all but never actually anything about ourselves, who we were. I always just thought it was so we would be committed. I assume somewhere there are forms with my old name and signature on agreeing to all this. One thing I do know, my name sure as hell wasn't Jane before I came here."

"Yeah, and mine ain't John, I know that much. I mean, they have named us after dead bodies they find and can't identify, for crying out loud."

"All I know is we are here, and we came for a reason, and for whatever reason that includes our minds being erased, being named after unidentifiable bodies, given pills, tablets, undergoing brain surgeries and being trained harder than I feel I ever have. Whatever we are being trained for, it must be big."

"Yeah, you got that right English, sometimes I just wish I knew. All they tell me is that we volunteered to become the best soldiers ever to set foot on a battlefield."

"Me too, must be their hook. That's how they convinced us." She chuckled and sat back down.

"Look," she said, "We came here to be the best, whatever our reasons, and it's going to get harder before it gets easier, but if it means I get the chance to make the world a better place, a safer place, then I'm all in."

"Me too."

"It'll get tough; today proved that, they set us up in there,"

"The only easy day was yesterday."

"Oorah."

"No, English, just no. Never, ever, do that again."

"You love it," she said as she smiled and picked her book up, found her page and carried on reading.

5

Close by, in another room in the facility, there was a
meeting taking place. This room was larger and had a
big round table in the centre. Each person at the table
was sat in a high backed leather chair. There was a
large whiteboard at one end, and a large pitcher of
water sat on a table with glasses to one side if anyone
required refreshments. Fifteen people all together sat at
the table, all wearing white lab coats, each with a file of
paperwork in front of them. Most sat quiet and listened,
the debate had been going for a few hours and most had
said their piece and then just remained silent, but two
were in deep discussion,

"…We need to keep trying. This is the furthest we have
managed to come so far," the first man was saying. He
was of average height with brown hair, brown eyes and
wore glasses.

"But it's not enough, and today proved that," the
second man said. He was slightly overweight, with
dirty blonde hair and blue eyes.

"You have to. We have to give it more time," the first
man said.

"It's been six months, and there are no major notable
improvements. It's time to call it on these two," the
second replied.

"Their bond is the strongest we have come across. They
are…"

"It's not a friendship experiment, Doctor; it's trying to develop the next generation of warriors, super soldiers."

"But what is a super-soldier to you?" The first man asked, "Captain America? It ain't gonna happen, you have set your sights too high, and the goals are unattainable. Look at the reports." At this, the first man opened the file again, but to a different page this time, the others followed. "They are faster, stronger, more reactive than when they arrived. This is development."

"But not enough," the second man countered, "I know you are soft on them; God knows why, but they are here to undergo major changes, and they just are not showing the right signs."

"The signs are there!" the first man said, raising his voice. "Look at the data!" He pointed to a page in front of him showing graphs and numbers, all were rising in the direction he had wanted.

A third man spoke, "clearly, Doctor Jenkins is against proceeding, and Doctor Conners is in favour. Does anybody else have anything else they would like to add?"

The table was quiet.

"Really?" The third man said again, "this affects us all. This is all our work. Our lives are dedicated to this programme, and we need to be in agreement or at least a majority as to what we do going forward."

The second man - Jenkins - spoke up again, "we need to cancel these subjects, terminate them and move on."

"No," the first man - Conners - cut in. "We can't do that. These subjects show so much more progress and have so much more potential than any of the others we have tried here. We can't just terminate them and start all over again; it would be folly to do such a thing."

Another man spoke up from down the other end of the table. "How much more can these subjects take?"

"Enough, Doctor Howard, we still have different types of medication to try and other injectable substances to test. There is still a lot of viability to continuing," Doctor Conners said.

"Is that enough?" Doctor Simms interjected. She was around forty years old and had long blonde hair tied up in a high ponytail. "Is there anything else invasive we can do?"

"No," Jenkins said. "It's too risky, they have undergone so much already that it would be dangerous for them to do anymore."

"But you want to kill them anyway, so why not at least try?" Conners pressed.

"It's a waste of money."

"This is crazy!" Conners was getting agitated. He rose from his chair. "These are human beings, and these are the closest we have ever come, what you want, what they want us to create, is impossible to their standards, these subjects are performing twelve to fifteen per cent better than what they did when they first arrived."

"That's not enough."

"Are you out of your mind?"

"Please sit down, Doctor Conners," Doctor Howard said, and after a deep breath, Doctor Conners returned to his seat. He placed his hands on the desk. His head was hung as he breathed deep and composed himself.

Once he was ready, he continued. "These subjects, all the subjects, we use are already considered to be the 'best of the best'," he said. "I, we, work tirelessly to make them better, to make them stronger, faster, smarter, better in every way. These are not just people we have picked from the street; they are already trained to the highest level of the best military units worldwide. Don't you see how that affects the numbers? The people we use are already basically super-soldiers, and short of making them invincible, we are limited to what we can achieve. Don't you see, twelve to fifteen per cent better than already being the best is amazing, and they are special. We need to keep going."

"Then how do you explain today?" Doctor Simms asked, "they failed. They died."

"They're human, Doctor Simms; we gave them an enclosed space, limited resources and over fifty men ready to pile into that room."

"They should have won."

"How? The point was for them to lose. We set it up for them to lose so that they could learn. Not all improvements come from a pill or a bottle."

"That's all very well and good, Doctor Conners," Doctor Jenkins said, "but that won't be acceptable to the higher-ups. The military, not to mention our private benefactors and investors, they expect better."

"Just give us more time. I know we can do it." Doctor Conners said his voice was now soft. He knew he was fighting a losing battle and almost pleading with the room.

"I'm sorry, but I disagree," Doctor Jenkins said, "I don't think we will get much more out of these subjects, and I feel we should take what we have learnt from them and apply it as a base to the next ones and build from there again. Just like we have done with all of them leading up to these two."

"I agree," Doctor Simms said. "These subjects are the best we have achieved; I agree with you, Doctor Conners, but I also believe we have pushed them as far as they will go, and it doesn't make sense to pour countless more millions into them. We should do what Doctor Jenkins says and proceed to the next batch."

"I disagree. The results speak for themselves."

"Look, Conners," Doctor Howard spoke up. "Twelve, fifteen per cent is good, as you say, it's the best we have achieved, but at the end of the day, we can use what we developed with them and pass it on as the base, as Doctor Jenkins says. He is speaking sense. When we started this batch we had a seven per cent improvement, and now we have twelve to fifteen, think what we could get the next subjects too, it won't be long before the soldiers we are training will be twenty-five per cent better than normal soldiers. That's incredible, and once they are out there, it will change everything. How long before we are at fifty per cent better, or seventy-five, or one hundred?"

"I know the goal, Doctor Howard," Conners said, "I just believe that we can go further with these two, this John and Jane are the best yet, and I believe that we can go further with them before we need to move on."

At the far end of the table, a woman rose from her chair, "the best way to resolve this disagreement will be with a vote."

"Agreed, Doctor Francis," Doctor Jenkins said. "A vote is agreed."

"Majority vote wins," Doctor Francis said. "No arguments, the final ruling stands."

The fifteen scientists around the table prepared to take the vote. Although Doctor Conners feared he already knew the outcome, he hoped that enough of his peers would side with him; but doubt was creeping through his mind, spreading its dark tendrils around his thoughts, and he knew, deep down, that this was unlikely to go the way he wanted it too.

6

Unaware of the conversation happening in another part of the facility, Jane and John Doe were sitting in their room. Jane was still reading her book, but John had left and gone for a walk. As he returned, he sat in the chair opposite her again, browsing the bookshelf, humming to himself as he did so, scanning the titles lazily. When he couldn't find anything that tempted him, he turned back in his chair and slumped down into it.

"Bored?" Jane asked.

"Yep," he replied.

"Go to the range and shoot something?" She suggested, not taking her eyes off the page she was reading; she had her legs tucked up under her and was happily getting lost in the book's world.

"Not feeling it."

"Run?"

"No," he said as he sat there, making noises with his mouth. After a few minutes, it became too annoying, and Jane closed her book more forcefully than she needed to, but it was more for effect, and she said, "seriously, Yank, that's very annoying."

"Sorry," he said, "I was thinking."

"I doubt it."

"Rude."

"Although it does explain why you needed to sit down, and the noises, I thought it was your mouth, but they must have been your brain trying to work."

"What's up with you? Annoyed much?"

"Yes," she said, "I am. I'm trying to read and enjoy this book and all I can hear is noise coming from your face, and it's irritating me."

"You always this short-tempered?"

"How would I know? Have I always been this short-tempered in the time you have known me?"

"Yes."

"Well then, clearly I am, or maybe it's just you that annoys me."

"Sorry, English."

"Whatever. What's on your mind?"

"Doesn't matter, keep reading, go back to your book."

"I've stopped now, so talk to me. What's up? Still thinking about what we talked about earlier?"

"A little," he said as he rose from the chair and moved over to the bed, sitting on it and resting his back against the wall.

"So, go on then," she prompted him.

"We've been together, what, six months now?"

"Something like that, but we ain't 'together' together, Yankee."

"God no, couldn't live with that posh accent the rest of my life, drive me insane."

"You don't exactly sound like a songbird yourself there, sweetie."

"You crazy? I sound like an angel, anyway, how much do we really know about each other and all this?"

"Enough," she said as she got out of the chair, put her book on top of the bookcase so she could go back to it later, walked over to her bed, got on and mirrored his position, looking across at him. "But I'm up for a round of *twenty questions if you can remember the answer,* if you are?"

"You're on."

"Ok, you go first."

"Alright, age?"

"No idea, but young, 'cause I look this good. The file says I'm 38. You?"

"File says 41."

"Where you from?"

"File says New York."

"Whereabouts?"

"No idea it just says 'New York' that's all. You?"

"Lincolnshire."

"What's that, a town, city?"

"No idea, I think a city, but I can't remember."

"Well, this is going well then."

"Absolutely."

John thought for a moment before asking, "what unit you serve with?"

"Special Boat Service, again, courtesy of the file. You?"

"Navy Seals."

"File tell you that?"

"Yep, absolutely right."

"So how does a 38-year-old female English Special Boat Service member and a 41-year-old male American Navy Seal end up in a room together, doing all this training, with severe memory loss?"

"Beats me," John said. "But I gotta say, as far as people to undergo major potential life-changing surgeries, taking unknown pills and injections and spending my days doing training with, you're alright English."

"Oorah," she smiled back at him.

"What have I told you about that?"

"It's what you do, isn't it? I'm just trying to make you feel more comfortable."

"No, it's a Marine phrase; I'm not a marine. Would you like me to always ask you if you would like a cuppa' tea? Or some fish 'n' chips?" He asked the last part in an English accent, a terrible English accent, but Jane didn't mind.

"Actually," she said, "if you would then go and get me some tea, or fish and chips, then, by all means, ask."

"Get your own shit."

"Oorah to that baby."

"I hate you so much sometimes," he said as he got off the bed and left the room.

"No, you don't!" She shouted after him, "you love it!" Then she chuckled to herself, got off the bed, retrieved her book, sat back in the chair, and carried on reading, a small smile on her face.

As much as she enjoyed annoying John, or whatever his real name was, she knew that no matter what, she would protect him. It was strange as they had only known each other the short time they had been together here, wherever here was, but he was all she had, and they were partners now. Not romantic partners, she didn't see him like that, and she saw no indication that he had any romantic feelings towards her. Still, they were each other's family now, and most of what she could remember, almost all her memories, bar the occasional flash back, had him in them.

She didn't know what her name really was, or what his really was. All she knew was that John and Jane Doe were family, and this was their home. Sometimes she would have fleeting moments of wondering about her old life, not that she would mention them to John, but deep down, she was happy with her life at the minute. She didn't know where it was going, but she was training, and it would only be a good thing once she was finished, and she knew that with John by her side, they could achieve anything.

She heard shots fire in the next room over, they were far away, but the echo amplified them and reverberated around the open space, seeping through the door John had left open into the corridor and through the open door into their room.

She chuckled to herself again as she imagined John standing there shooting, pretending the target was her. At least it meant he was gone, and she could get back to her book.

7

The votes were in, and it was final. It had been settled.
The decision had been made to proceed on to the next
batch of subjects, this John and Jane Doe were to be
replaced, and the data that the men and women had
learned would be applied to the next batch of recruits in
order to try and develop further.

This wasn't the first time this had happened. Every
subject batch pairing before this had also reached this
stage. Some sooner than others, some had developed
more than their partner. Still, it had been decided before
the development had begun that the decision would
always be made as if the pair of candidates were a
single entity. This meant that no matter what, when one
was to be removed, they both were.
It had been decided this way because of the mental and
physical development stages of the candidates. They
had decided that bringing another subject into a partner
that may have already undergone weeks, or months of
training and development could unsettle the balance. It
was easier and better for the work if both participating
members were developed at the same stage.

Doctor Conners had got the result he had been
expecting, but not the one he had hoped for. Once the
results had been tallied and announced, he had once
again tried to reason, plead, and beg with the board to

reconsider, but there had only been a handful of votes to continue, and a considerable majority had outvoted them to move on and have this John and Jane removed. All the pairings before these had been removed, destroyed, eliminated, whatever term you wanted to use, and he knew that it would be maybe hundreds more before they got to the point that they were aiming for.

He had lost count of the number that had come before, but they had been working on this for years. How many lives had they taken trying to achieve this holy grail of a target?

Doctor Conners was brought back to the room by the sound of a voice saying his name.

"Doctor Conners, are we all agreed?"

"No, I still think this is a mistake, but it is the way it has to be."

"Ok, the subjects will be removed tomorrow, and the next batch will be prepped to begin next week. This will give us a few days to prepare, make the adjustments we need and be ready to proceed. Agreed?" Doctor Francis raised from her seat as she finished talking, leaned over and placed her hands on the desk. Everyone nodded their agreement, some more reluctantly than others.

"Good," she said. "We are making great strides forward, people. You should all be so proud of yourselves. Together, we will make this country safer and stronger than ever. Good work, all of you." With this, she straightened up, picked up her files from the tabletop and walked out; her high heels clicking on the ground as she walked was the only sound in the room. *This is madness*, Doctor Conners thought to himself. He knew it was how it was going to be, and he knew this wouldn't be the last time he felt this. His whole life was devoted to this study, to this mission, and he knew getting attached was a bad idea, but seeing these people develop and improve filled him with such pride that when they had to be terminated, it almost felt like it broke his heart.

He knew he would feel this way about the next batch too, but these subjects had shown so much promise and had come so far that it felt like such a waste just to throw it all away.

He put these thoughts to the back of his mind and concentrated on how he could improve the work they had already done and make the next pairing batch stronger, faster, smarter, better. He picked up his file from the table - he was the last person sitting as everyone else had already gone back to their work - and left the boardroom, returned to his office to set about making his adjustments.

Things were still on his mind when he finished for the day, it was late, and darkness had fallen. He usually finished late and started early. In fact, he couldn't remember the last time he saw actual sunlight that wasn't through his office window. He drove his Citroën home, and as he walked through the door, he kissed his wife and wrapped his arms around her. She always had this way of making him feel better just by holding him.

"Is Elise still awake?" He asked as the embrace finished and he slipped his shoes off and placed them on the mat by the door.

"No, she's asleep, she had a busy day and was tired, so I put her to bed an hour or so ago." His wife, Molly, replied.

"I'm just going to go and give her a little kiss,"

"Ok, I have some dinner in the oven for you. I'll heat it up."

"Thank you," he kissed her and made his way upstairs.

His daughter Elise's room, was pink. Very pink. Pink bed spread, pink curtains, pink wall paint, everything was pink. There was a little desk against the wall that she used to draw – princess related stuff mainly – and the wall around it was covered in her drawings. She had posters of Disney princesses dotted around the room, and there was a little princess outfit hanging over the back of the chair sat at the desk.

She was a typical six-year-old, and she had told him many times about how she wanted to be a princess when she grew up. She already was to him.

Conners leaned down and lightly kissed his daughter's forehead, she didn't stir or move and as he quietly backed out of the room, he looked at her, sleeping.

He knew that everything he did was for her, Elise and Molly were all Conners had, and he wanted to help develop the next generation of soldiers to protect this country so that they would be safe. He dreamed of moving his research from the military over to the emergency services once it was ready. Police officers that were smarter and better than any criminal could be.

Fire fighters that could stay in a burning building longer to save people. Paramedics, nurses, and doctors that could be able to save more lives. This, this is where he was heading, the military was the first step, he knew that they always were with this sort of thing, but he knew that eventually, once it's perfected, he would be able to move it over and allow the whole country to benefit from his research. Maybe the world.

He went back downstairs; Molly had plated up his dinner, a lasagne with potatoes and vegetables. It smelled fantastic as the scent entered his nostrils, and he sat down and tucked in. It tasted amazing, and once again, Conners marvelled at how lucky he was to be married to this truly magnificent woman. For the first time since that meeting, he could push out the thoughts of the day and just what he had.

8

Meanwhile, back at the facility:

Doctor Francis knocked on the closed door and awaited a reply. A man's voice beckoned her to enter, and she opened the door and went into the large office of Mister Daniel Knight.

Daniel Knight was the CEO of Knight Security, and Knight Security was a private contractor with accounts with the American military. He was the man in charge of the development of the subjects as per his contract and was responsible for the programme. He was not a pleasant human being.

"Do you have something to report?" he asked flatly as Doctor Francis entered the room.

"Yes, the subjects are at their limit, they are to be removed from the programme, and we will push on with new volunteers from next week," she said.

"Right," he paused. "How much further did we get?"

"Twelve to fifteen per cent improvement from the initial evaluation."

"Not enough."

"We understand that, but we are working as hard as we can, and we are seeing improvements. We just need to keep pushing, and when subjects reach their limit, move on to the next one. I said this would be a long process, Sir, but we are moving in the right direction."

Daniel Knight was a middle-aged man, he was overweight and his hair was thinning and receding. He had a harsh voice from years of smoking along with eating and drinking poorly. He wore an oversized suit, that even though he was a large man, still seemed too big and didn't fit well at all.

When she had first met him, Doctor Francis had been told that he had once served; sitting across from him now, she couldn't imagine it, if he had served his country in a military capacity, it was a long time ago, and he had done nothing to maintain his health since.

"What are the next batch?" He asked.

"What do you mean?"

"Who are we using next? It's not a difficult question."

"Oh, OK, um, hang on…" She took out her tablet from her bag, loaded it up and logged in. After a moment, she had found the correct documents she was looking for. "One is Russian. He is former Spetsnaz, SFO to be more precise and…"

"SFO?" He interrupted. "What's that?"

"Special Forces, Sir, I would have thought you would have come in to contact with some of them over the years."

"I just shoot them; I never stop to ask what their units are called, who else?"

"Ok…" she said as she opened the next candidate file. "The other is from Sayeret Matkal. She is Israeli and…"

Once again, she got cut off. "A woman." He said, rolling his eyes.

"Well, yes, sir, obviously, every batch is a pairing of a male and female. That's the parameters of the experiment, the development. It's always been a male and female."

"And that's why it's taking so long."

"Sir?"

"Use two men. That will make it go a lot faster, and the results will be much better."

"I...I don't follow that logic," Doctor Francis said, a confused look spreading across her face.

"Really? Isn't it common sense? Men are superior to women. It's natural, it's biological, they always have been, and they always will be. A man at his prime will always be able to beat a woman at hers. Men are stronger, faster, smarter. Why do you think for decades men have held all the highest positions? Been the leaders and done all the important things? If you remove the girl from the training, then the results will get better faster. Men work well together. They are better together, and they will push and help each other instead of having to try and drag a girl along and get her through it. That's just logical, isn't it?"

"Um... Well, sir, actually, in almost all the subject pairings we have had, the woman has shown greater improvement and have consistently beaten their male counterpart's scores. This Jane, for example, has shown a fifteen per cent improvement, but our current John has shown twelve."

"Yes," he said, raising his voice. "And you know why that is, don't you? It's because the John has to dumb himself down, has to help the girl get through it, has to make her feel special and make her think she is better because it's what people think today. There are more and more girls doing men's jobs. Are they as good at it? God no! It's just a front because people are scared of upsetting them. They don't want to be known as being mean or victimising girls because of their 'lady parts'." He used air quotes as he said it, "it's all ridiculous. If men could be allowed to do what they should, then everything would get done faster."

Doctor Francis, a woman, sat in the chair in that office dumbfounded. She couldn't believe what she had just heard. She was the head on the project, she was the one he came to for answers and reports, and he had just given her that speech that made her feel uncomfortable and, quite frankly, offended. If this job hadn't meant so much to her, she might have just left there and then. She had worked for just over two decades to get to where she had, and she had beaten out many males for promotions and career development, and it wasn't because of her 'lady parts'. It was because she was better than they were. She wanted to say all this, but instead, she calmed herself and pushed forward.

"How do you want me to proceed?"

"Isn't it obvious, get two men. Keep the Russian one and get another man in there. Then you will see results faster."

"But I really think…" she started.

"I don't care. Are you dumb? You asked me how to proceed, and I have told you. I have been suggesting it for long enough now and it's time people started listening to me. I've been paid a lot of money to do this, and I will get paid a hell of a lot more once I deliver the finished article, so hurry up and get it finished. I'm done playing these happy family lovey-dovey pairs, and I want to see actual results. Do I make myself clear, or do I need to simplify it for you?"

"No, Sir, I will make the changes going forward."

"Good." He said as he pulled out a pack of cigarettes and a metal flip lid lighter from his desk. "Anything else?"

"Actually, there is one more thing, Sir, some of the team have come to me with concerns about Doctor Conners, they are saying he is becoming too attached to the subjects, and it's clouding and compromising his judgement, and from what I saw today, I'm inclined to agree."

"Doctor Conners." He ran the name around his head as he lit and began smoking the cigarette. "With the glasses? I think I have seen him around. He seems alright to me, is it the girls, Simms and the others, just want him out the way?"

"No, Sir, it's not. He may become more conflicted and against the programme. I think if this is left unchecked for too long, then he may end up turning against us."

"Turning against us?"

"Yes, Sir."

"Then fire him."

"But he may expose us, and we don't want anyone poking around this place; what we're doing here is breaking a lot of laws."

"I know, I'm the one at the top of this tree. Remember, move him to another department. It would be a shame to lose a man of his standards anyway."

"Then it would seem foolish to allow him to become a whistle-blower. I think he should be removed from the programme."

"Nonsense. Conners is a fine man. Just keep an eye on him and if anything else happens, then let me know. That will be all for today."

"Actually, Sir, I have other things I need to discuss with you. I need to talk about the investors, the…"

"Not tonight," he interrupted as he exhaled more smoke into the room. No windows were open, and the cigarette smoke was filling the office like a cloud. Doctor Francis didn't smoke, and the smell made her want to cough, but she stifled it and took her instruction to leave, gathering up her things and leaving the office. *Daniel Knight,* she reminded herself as she walked down the corridor, past the other vacant offices; all the occupants had gone home for the night, *was not a pleasant human being.*

9

Jane awoke the following morning, the dreams that had filled her mind as she slept, the subconscious thoughts and memories that tried to reassert themselves as the conscious mind was not in the driving seat and not suppressing them, raced through her mind.

It had started out as her in a room with a group of others, the same or similar age to herself, around eighteen or nineteen, all dressed in the same uniform, a training uniform, with the same logo - *what logo was it*... Then it flashed to what seemed like a cinema reel of different places around the world. Cities, mountainsides, jungles, deserts, and countryside, all with her and the others fighting and shooting.
Many different images came and went in a flash, and it seemed like they were all vying for the centre stage of her recall. Signs and phrases in other languages flashed up and disappeared as she rode through this journey, like she was on a rollercoaster zooming past it all at a hundred miles an hour, her mind trying to grasp onto the images and feelings as they whipped past her, but it was all too fast. She couldn't make sense of any of it. Then it suddenly stopped, and she was in a room, a living room, of a house, a house that seemed so familiar yet was distinctly new to her. There was a boy sat on the floor playing, he must have been around eight or nine years old, he was playing with toy cars, racing

them around the carpet, giving them life with constant *vrooms* and *crash* sounds when he made them crash into each other.

She could only watch, she couldn't move, couldn't speak - although she hadn't tried to – she was mesmerised by this boy, just sitting playing. She had never met the boy, yet felt like she knew everything about him - *what was his name, though.* It felt like it was on the tip of her tongue, but she couldn't remember. She felt it was the most important name in the world, but she couldn't find it in her mind.

The room they were in was beige; it had beige carpet, curtains, wallpaper and even the two sofas faced towards the old box TV were beige, but they had purple and blue coloured blankets on them.

She stood there watching this scene in front of her, at peace with herself. Then it all changed.

The walls started melting and the wallpaper peeled back from the walls, but there were no walls beneath it, no surface. It was just black, only darkness. The pictures on the walls began turning to liquid and pouring down before disappearing.

There was suddenly a door, there hadn't been a door before, she realised, it had been a perfectly square room, but now a door appeared at the far end, and a man was walking in. She couldn't see him properly. He was black, like he was only a silhouette, he didn't seem to have a physical form, and she couldn't make out his features. He seemed to be surrounded by shadows, shadows that moved around him like they were alive and rose from his form like black steam.

Fear struck her, and for the first time she tried to scream, to warn the boy that had no idea what was happening - *how had he not noticed the walls melting, the furniture melting and disappearing, the man in the room that shouldn't be!* She tried to scream out, she tried to warn the boy, she tried to move, but couldn't and as the shadow man walked, hunched over, to the boy, he slowly reached down. He picked up the boy and put him over his shoulder, it all seemed to happen in slow motion, and she was screaming, but no sound would leave her body. The scene around her was falling apart, and she couldn't do anything about it!

The shadow man turned and began to walk back to the door, now the only solid structure she could see left remaining. Jane tried to move again, she couldn't, she tried to scream, but she couldn't, it was all too much, and fear ran through her veins as she knew this was wrong. The boy over the shadow man's shoulder suddenly looked up, right into her eyes:

Help me.

His voice was soft, almost a whisper, yet at the same time, she heard it all around her as it echoed through her soul. As soon as he spoke, it seemed like whatever was holding her there, released, and she could move. Jane ran as fast as she could to the boy, but the world seemed to be in slow motion, and no matter how hard she ran, she couldn't close the distance.

Help me.

She ran and ran but couldn't get to him. The shadow man reached the door and passed through, evaporating as he crossed the threshold, leaving only the boy there, floating in the position he was over the shadow man's shoulders.

Just floating, suspended with no strings.

Help me,
Help me,
Hel
He
Hey,
Hey,
Hey, wake up,
Wake up!

This was when Jane woke up and bolted upright off of her pillow. John was sat next to her on her bed. He had his hands on her shoulders and looked like he had shaken her awake. She was sweating, a lot. She was drenched. Her heart was racing, pounding against her chest, and she had this overwhelming sense of being uncomfortable. She didn't know what it was, but whatever Jane had experienced in her dream - nightmare - had shaken her to her very core and unsettled her in a way she had never felt before. She was scared, more scared in that moment than she had ever been in her life, she thought. She had never had a dream like that before, and she couldn't get her head straight as she tried to make sense of what she had seen.

"You alright?" John asked, concern in his voice and a look in his eye she had never seen before.

"Yeah, fine," she lied.

"Bull shit," he said. "You were screaming, loud, and thrashing about. Who needs to run? Who was going to get you?"

"I'm, I'm sorry?"

"You were shouting 'Run, run, you need to run. He's behind you; he's going to get you.' Then lots of screaming. What did you dream?"

"Nothing, I don't remember," she lied again. "I'm fine."

John gave her a look, took his hands off her shoulders and gently said, "you ever want to talk, I'm here, y'know."

"Thanks," she said as she lay back down. Her pillow was soaked with sweat. She turned it over and rested her head on the cool, dry side. "I'm OK, though."

John rose from her side, and she heard him walk back across the room and get back into his bed. She pulled the blanket, wet from sweat, up under her chin and curled her body into a ball under the covers, like a child who was scared of the dark.

"Good night," John said.

"Good night," she said quietly back to him.

What the fuck was all she could think. She knew it was still a few hours before the sun rose, but she just lay there staring at the wall, afraid to close her eyes.

10

Mercifully, morning arrived. Jane hadn't slept another wink all night. This was not like her - from what she thought about herself, anyway - she was always of the belief to rest while you can, make the most of opportunities to recover your strength, you never know what the next day may hold.

Even though it was now acceptable for her to get up and start her day, she stayed in bed a short while longer, curled up, staring at the spot on the wall she had fixed her vision on since waking from her nightmare. She had been waiting for an excuse to get out of bed, to put the events of last night behind her and get back to herself, training and winding up Yankee. But now that she had the opportunity to, she hesitated. She knew as soon as he saw her, he would ask her how she was and ask more about what had happened, and she didn't want that. It wasn't that she didn't want him to know; she didn't want *anyone* to know. It freaked her out that it happened and how it had made her feel.

Would it come to light in the next mind exercise?
She hoped not.

She heard John leave the room, and after another moment where she tried to tell herself how stupid she was for feeling this way, she rolled over, swung her legs out and sat on the bed.

She took a few minutes to compose herself, her heart still felt like it was beating faster, and her breathing seemed strange to her, almost like she was breathing heavier.

Once she was ready, she got up and made her way to the shower room. She undressed in the changing area and went in. John was under his usual shower head, and she went to her usual spot on the other side. There were twelve shower heads in the room, but no dividers were separating each other for privacy. She had never been bothered by this or seen it as a bad thing; it was just what it was.

As John finished, he made eye contact with her, and every part of her wanted him just to give her a polite smile, and leave, just like every other morning.

He looked at her, and then he gave her a polite smile as he wrapped his towel around his waist and left the shower room.

She breathed a sigh of relief once he had gone. She didn't want to be dealing with his questions. She just wanted to forget about it all and move on.

She showered, taking longer than usual; she just let the water wash over her, cleaning her, washing away the sweat and hopefully the feeling of the night before.

Once she was done, she wrapped herself in her towel and used the bathroom facilities in the adjoining room. Then she grabbed her clothes and went back to the room.

John was ready for the day, and as she got dressed into the same clothes as every other day, putting her sweat-stained night clothes in the container to be washed, she told herself it was over. John was waiting outside as she tied her hair up into a high ponytail. Depending on how Jane did her hair, sometimes she could see or feel scars on her head from the surgeries. She ran her finger lightly over the raised, scarred skin and wondered for a brief second about how, why, she had done this. Then she put it out of her mind.

It's just from what the Yank was going on about yesterday, she told herself, finished her hair and met up with John. They walked together into the large training area and sat at the table, and waited.

"All good?" He asked once they were seated.

"All good." She replied. That was it. He hadn't asked a thousand questions, hadn't probed her for information she didn't want to give; he had simply, in those few words, let her know that he was there for her. She appreciated that.

A moment later and the man with blonde hair, tablet and the laboratory coat entered. He sat opposite them. He took out a small silver case and placed it on the table. Inside contained two small white pills. They both took one and swallowed it.

"Today," the man said once the pills had been swallowed, "will be endurance. You will be on the outside training area and will be asked to navigate the terrain as best as possible, getting from point A to point B. You will be given free choice of how you reach the objective, and you will be timed and monitored. Meet outside in ten minutes. Good luck." Then he got up and left.

"Easy day," John said after the man had gone.

"Yep, although don't you think the only easy day was yesterday?"

"Well, clearly they're giving us a break after that ass-whooping we took yesterday."

They both got up and left the room, and headed outside to the endurance course.

Jane had always suspected the training base they were in was a disused military facility. The endurance race seemed to have a lot of military-style courses and obstacles, including a disused firing range for testing missiles, but every time she asked about it, the answer was always vague.

After the endurance training was complete, it was an easy day, mostly just running and obstacles for a few hours. Jane and John retired to their room. However, they were told to make themselves ready for a possible additional session this evening just before they did. Once back in their room, Jane asked, "What do you think they got in store for us?"

"No idea," John replied absently, "but I thought this morning was a bit too simple. Just have to wait and see."

Jane could see he wanted to talk to her about last night, but she wasn't prepared to, and he obviously took the hint because no word about it left his lips.

A few hours later, that evening, they were summoned back to the room they got their tasks from. They sat at the metal table and waited, then the blonde man came back and sat opposite them again. He took out another silver case and placed it on the table. John opened it, and there were two pills inside. These were larger and looked silvery.

"What are these?" He asked.

"New medication," the blonde man said.

"Never had two in one day before."

"It's part of the programme John. It's the next stage."

Jane had sat quietly during this exchange. It was odd to get two doses of medication in one day, it had never happened before, and this didn't look like the ones they usually took, but who was she to question? She picked it up, placed it in her mouth, threw her head back and swallowed. John did the same next to her.

"That will be all." The man said and then left the table, then the room.

Once back in their quarters, Jane carried on with her book, and John had found one to read now, but he kept glancing over the top of it at her.

She had considered having an argument with him, telling him to knock it off, but she was feeling tired, exhausted, all of a sudden. She decided to leave it till the morning. She put her book down and crawled into bed. It was early, and she was never normally this tired, but she just put it down to the endurance course and the lack of sleep. She climbed under the covers and got comfy and a moment later noticed John doing the same, his eyes looked red, and he seemed just as tired as she was. She thought this was odd, but before she could finish forming the thought, she had fallen asleep. A deep sleep, so deep it was like she was dead to the world.

11

Jane awoke suddenly and found herself in a large square room. It looked like a warehouse, big grey walls surrounded her, and the ceiling was high, with a skylight in it. The whole place was dimly lit, but she couldn't see where from. No light seemed to be coming in from the skylight.

Jane slowly got to her feet, making sure she had her balance, and once she was steady, she glanced around. Her head felt light, and she felt slightly disorientated, but she took a shaky step forward. There was a door at the end of the warehouse room, so she started making her way towards it. Her body felt heavy, sluggish, and slow. Each step she took, the room seemed to move and shake like the way rising heat distorts vision, almost like it was all a mirage. She tried to gather her thoughts, but they seemed jumbled, and she couldn't focus or organise them in any way to make sense. She reached the door and opened it, expecting another room, or the outside world, but in fact, she was on a train. She should have been confused; the size of the room she was in to the size of the train cars didn't correlate, but then it seemed not to matter like it wasn't important, and she just let it go and moved on. Inside the train was simple; it was just rows of seats, as any commuter train. They were mostly empty, but a few were occupied. She didn't recognise anyone, though, and it seemed as if they only had facial features when she was looking at them; otherwise, they were just blank, featureless.

The train was rocking slightly as it made its way to its destination. Jane swayed with it, trying to keep her balance as she moved forward through the carriage. She reached the door, slid it open and moved to the next carriage.

Except now there was no train. Jane was stood in a wooded area. She could smell flowers and greenery – which made sense – but also diesel, like a car or a truck smell – which didn't.

She looked around but found no vehicles, let alone any that were diesel-powered and running.

She looked around again. She had no idea how she had got here, it was dark, and the moon was bright overhead, bathing the trees and the grass in a blue glow. She couldn't find the path that she had used to get here or a path to get out, but as she turned in circles on the spot, she saw a little girl standing before her and stopped. She looked about eight or nine years old and stood so still that Jane thought she may have been a statue. Still unsteady on her feet, like the ground was moving under her, she took a step forward towards the little girl.

Then the little girl was dressed in a powder yellow coloured dress, with an apron over it. *She looks familiar; where do I know her from?* Jane tried to place her as she looked up at her, directly into her eyes and whispered:

Help me.

Jane's stomach dropped. The girl's voice was soft and delicate, yet so loud it could be heard over everything else and seemed to be all around her.

She tried to take a step forward but couldn't move. She began to panic, and as a drop of sweat ran down her spine, she looked around, pleading that what she thought was going to happen next wouldn't.

But it did. The man appeared out of the woods behind the girl. He was a man wrapped in shadows. They pulsed with him as he walked and seemed to wrap themselves around him, yet also be rising from his body like steam. She couldn't make out any features, but she knew she recognised him.

He was the monster from last night, the one who had taken the boy. She shouted at the girl to run and tried everything she could to move forward, to get to the little girl before the shadow man did.

The girl wasn't moving though; she didn't turn around, she didn't scream, she just stood there, looking at Jane as the man came at her from behind.

Help me.

The man reached her, he moved slowly and strumbled, shifting awkwardly in his motions, but when he reached the little girl, he bent down, picked her up, put her over his shoulder and looked at Jane. He had no eyes, but she knew he was staring straight at her, then he said:
"We're nearly there now; get ready."

Then he turned back to the woods, ambling back towards the tree line. His voice was deep. It had a deep tone and seemed to boom as he spoke. The moment he had picked up the girl, Jane was able to move, she cried out and ran as fast as she could to catch them, to close the gap. She was sprinting, and he was barely moving, but she couldn't get close.

The girl looked at her:

Help me.

The whispered tone of her voice was sharper, scarier, more terrifying to Jane as she chased them, as if the girl had been screaming.

It's just a dream, she told herself, *it's OK, it's just a dream. Just a dream. Just a dream.*

Help me.

Fear bubbled in her body, rising through her. She knew it was a dream, yet she was still terrified. It was like her body was trying to warn her of something, and this was the best way it could. Terror gripped her, and she knew she couldn't catch up. Jane kept rocking on her feet like she was on the train again, but her body was on solid ground.

Help me,
Help me,
Hel,
Help yourself,

Help yourself, wake up,
WAKE UP!

12

Her eyes snapped open. Jane was instantly alert. While her body felt weird, she knew that now she was awake. This was no dream.

She was lying on the floor of a truck bed. The truck was driving down the terrain of an uneven path through the woods. She could see the trees pass above her as they moved. The truck was rocking over the rough track, and she was shaking and rolling slightly as the vehicle tried to traverse the terrain.

Was this why I was unsteady in the dream? She wondered.

She could smell the scent of the first-morning dew settling on the foliage around her as they drove, but also the repugnant smell of the diesel fumes coming from the exhausts.

Was this the mix of smells from my dream?

Men were sitting on the small ridges on each side of her like a bench, riding with her to wherever the destination was. She took a moment to assess what was going on, she tried to move her arms, but they were bound; it felt like a zip-tie restraint.

Whatever's going on, it's not good. Deep down, Jane knew this and decided to play dumb until she had more to go on, so she closed her eyes and pretended to be still sleeping as her brain tried to process what was going on.

Was this an exercise?

How did I get here?
Was I drugged?
Where's Yankee?

She had so many questions and no answers. She had clearly been sweating in her dream again as her clothes were once again damp and clinging to her. There was no rain on the truck, so she ruled out that they had been driving through rain, and that was what got her wet, so it was sweat.

Her head felt light, and she felt disorientated, just like in her dream. It was unusual for her. She was ordinarily able to think fast and be able to make concise thoughts and decisions. However, she definitely felt that something wasn't right, and every fibre of her being was screaming at her to get out of this situation. The more she listened, the more she doubted this was an exercise.

But why else would they be doing it?

Then a bad thought entered her mind, and one that once it was in there, she couldn't shake.

They're going to kill you.

But why? She wondered; she had done everything they had asked, without question, it didn't make sense. The thought stayed with her, though, nipping at the back of her mind, and she realised she would need to see where she would end up and then decide from there.

The truck tumbled on through the woods, bumping and swaying, and Jane let the movements and the motion take her wherever they would if she were unconscious. She needed everyone to think she still was.

Then she heard a voice, a deep voice that had bass to it and boomed as he spoke,

"We're here," it said, "everyone ready?"

The sound of his voice made Jane freeze, she couldn't explain it, but fear grabbed her and wouldn't let her breathe. The truck stopped, and the sound of the loading gate of the truck opening was heard. Then she was being moved, dragged along the floor of the truck bed, lifted up, and then settled on what felt like a man's shoulder, in a fireman's carry style of position.

She started swaying and bouncing as the man began walking; every second that passed, she was becoming more and more convinced this wasn't going to end well.

The terrain became tougher to traverse, and there were a few moments when Jane thought the man carrying her would lose his composure and drop her. Thankfully, he hadn't yet. She braved a glimpse to see what she could make out and opened her eyes just enough in the hope that the men behind her – if any – wouldn't spot her rouse. It was still dark; it must have been around one or two o'clock in the morning as night had fully settled in and dawn looked to be still a few hours away yet.

A man was walking behind her, he wore all black, and it looked to be tactical. She could only really see his boots and trousers, but they were black; the boots looked to be military issue or remarkably similar. The trousers were black with pockets halfway down – cargo style – and as she bounced, she caught glimpses of his torso, he was wearing a black polo or t-shirt with a black windbreaker jacket over the top. She gathered what she could and closed her eyes again.

They're not dressed like the combatants we have when we train, even when we do the outside and night exercises. This reinforced her doubt of this ending well. The niggling thoughts in the back of her mind were getting bigger, taking more space and occupying more and more of her theories. She began planning contingencies.

After a few more minutes' walk, they were deep in the wooded area. They had never come this far to train, and Jane's internal compass wasn't sure if they were still even on the base.

The night air was cold, and she was still only wearing her training gear from before that she had left on thinking there would be another exercise: the black cargo trousers and a dark grey t-shirt. The chill of the night bit into her skin, and the breeze felt like blades slicing as it brushed lazily against her. She could feel her goosebumps, but she wasn't sure if they were from the cold or the anticipation of what she feared was coming.

They stopped.

The man put her down, and she kept her eyes closed. There was shuffling around, and then she heard talking from a distance. She couldn't make out what was being said, so she strained and focused as she tried to pinpoint the voice, the deep, base filled voice that gave her flashbacks to her dreams and instantly put her on edge. She couldn't make out much, but then she heard:

"Kill her, bury her with the others; I'm going to check on the others."

Kill her, so this was the worst case scenario. Who were the others? What else were they doing out here? It was time to move.

She waited until she heard someone approach. She waited, praying she wouldn't wait too long and miss her opportunity.

The sound of the footsteps put him right in front of her, and she took her chance.

13

She opened her eyes as she rolled over and pushed herself up from her knees. The guard - her executioner – had his gun out of its holster and raised at her, but he was too slow to react and fire. She grabbed the barrel and forced it back, his arms buckling, and the gun was forced into his face, crashing against his nose. She put her right leg behind him and hit him again with the gun, using the momentum to push him back, tripping him over her leg and forcing him to the ground. As he tripped, she yanked his weapon from his grip, seamlessly turning it around, so her hands were now holding it correctly – if not very comfortably due to her hands still being zip-tied together – in front of her.

She took a second to survey her situation, including her would-be executioner; there were three men, the other two had shovels in their hands, and there was a third leaning up against a nearby tree. They were the grave diggers then.

At the sound of their friend falling, they both turned, both realised the new situation. They were both holding shovels and didn't have a free hand to draw their weapons, but they tried, both dropping their tools and reaching for their side-arms in perfect unison. Jane fired the pistol she had liberated from the guard, and it roared out into the night, cutting through the silence and announcing death in its wake. She fired twice per man, hitting each in the chest with both intended bullets, the blood from the entry wounds revealing they weren't wearing any body armour. Why would they? They were just here to shoot her and bury the body. The shots echoed out into the night, and after a moment, silence fell again, and she turned to the man on the ground. She lifted her hands above her head and brought them down quickly into her stomach, flaring her elbows out like chicken wings, trying to get her shoulder blades as close to each other as she could. The ties that bound her hands together broke at the weakest point under the pressure – the locking mechanism – and fell to the ground. She was free. She leaned down and put her knee on the man's chest, pointing her newly acquired Glock pistol at him.

"Why were you going to kill me?" She asked.

"Because we were told to," he replied; his voice sounded nasal, and she realised she had broken his nose. Oh well.

"Why?"

"I don't know."

She slapped his nose, and he cried out. "Why are they trying to kill me?"

"I don't fucking know!"

"Ok, fine, where's John? Did you bring him out here too? Is he alive? Is. He. Alive?"

"I don't know."

"You don't know much, do you?"

"I know what I'm ordered to do; that's what I do." Blood was running from his nose and seeping through his hands that he had put up to try and cover it. She knew he wasn't going to tell her anything. Hell, he probably didn't know anything. He was nothing more than just a grunt who just did what he was told.

She cracked the pistol across his face and knocked him out. His hands fell to his side, and his nose was revealed. Definitely broken.

She searched the area quickly for anything she could use. None of the guards had any keys to vehicles on them, but they all had the same Glock, so she stripped the magazines and put them in her pockets, releasing the bullets already in the chambers in case the guard woke up and got brave.

It was still dark, with only the moonlight for illumination, but as she looked around, she could see mounds of earth in areas that Jane thought would naturally be flat, but with her mind running through everything she had to do, she didn't linger on the thought. The man with the deep voice had gone to check on the others, and he would be back soon, especially if he heard all the shots. He would be expecting one, two at most to make sure the job got done.

She had to move fast. Get back to the truck, get back to the facility, find John, and together they could work it out.

Then she heard a gunshot ring out to her left.

It was too far away to be someone shooting at her, and then she realised that the others the man with the deep voice had been talking about were John's executioners.

She took off, sprinting as fast as she could, trying to shake whatever was in her system out so she could push harder towards the source of the gunshot.

14

Jane reached a clearing; it had taken her only a few minutes, but whatever was in her system was slowing her down. She burst through the bushes into the open space; it was almost identical to where she had been. It was a large circular opening with trees all around. John was there. He was wrestling with a guard who was dressed in the same uniform as the ones that had been tasked with disposing of her. There was a gun on the floor beside them, and a body lay motionless a few feet away with blood seeping into the ground around it. A man was standing between her and John and the man he was grappling with. The guard was holding a gun and was trying to get a clear shot, but John had put the man between them as a shield. Then she heard a voice say: "Just shoot him already. That's an order." The voice was a deep, booming, bass-filled one, and she recognised it as the man from before. She knew that when she had heard it in her dreams, it was just a projection of what she could hear outside of her sleeping state, but it still sent a chill down her spine. The guard followed his orders now and shot at John. The bullets hit the guard he was using as a hostage, and once he was dead, John couldn't hold his dead weight up.

Jane had to act. John no longer had protection and was exposed. She ran in from where she was standing on the perimeter; Glock raised and fired at the guard with the gun, the bullets found their mark and hit him in the back, one in the spine and one where the heart would be in the front.

There is always a risk when you shoot someone that is holding a gun that the body would react and twitch; if it does, and the finger was close to pulling the trigger, it can cause the finger to depress and the weapon to discharge. This is why Jane would always try to disarm first in those situations, but she was behind the shooter, and she was too far away to close the gap and take him down before he could shoot John, so she did the calculations and assessed the risk and deduced she had to take the shot. So, she had.

The body lurched forward and dropped to the floor. His weapon fell from his grasp and remained silent.

The man with the deep voice looked around, not shocked, more surprised from the look on his face, and he responded quickly to the change in the situation. He didn't have a weapon; he was clearly in charge, and with a group of armed soldiers around him, why would he have? They were only disposing of bodies after all. He turned and made for the tree line behind him as Jane aimed for him. He ducked and weaved, clearly trained, and made it as hard as possible for her to get a clean shot. She was still lightheaded, and she guessed with her shots without a good mass of still body to aim at. She fired, then again, and again. The man's shoulder was forced forward as he ran through the bushes and deeper into cover, and though she couldn't be sure, Jane thought she had hit him in the shoulder.

She made to chase after him, but the sound of a large diesel engine starting rattled through the trees, sending nestling birds fleeing at the sound of perceived danger. She knew she couldn't catch him, and as the truck drove away, getting quieter in the distance, she turned her attention to John. He was sitting on a large rock at the edge of the opening, catching his breath as Jane searched the fallen bodies for anything useful. There was more ammunition but no keys or phones.

Must have left the keys in the trucks. I should have checked.

She walked over to John, handing him a Glock for him to use and a couple of magazines relinquished from his fallen hit squad.

He was wearing the same clothes as her, the grey cargo trousers and the black t-shirt, but he had a cut on his face above his eye and blood was running down from it. He hadn't been as lucky as she had been when confronting their executioners. As he reached up to collect his pistol, he did so with his right hand, reaching across his body, and his face cringed. She looked down, and his left arm was across his body, putting pressure on his side, below his ribs, around his stomach, then she noticed the red on his hands, the black t-shirt in the night had hidden what had seeped into it, but his hands revealed the truth. He had been shot.

Upon looking at her face, he knew that she knew, so he spoke first.

"It's not major," he explained. "Went through my human shield and into me."

"We need to get you help," she said, gripping his arm. "Can you stand?"

"Yeah, I'm a bit woozy, I think they drugged us or something, but I'm good." He groaned as she helped lift him to his feet.

"We need to leave," she said.

"And go where?"

"Anywhere, for now, I have a fear that training is over, and we didn't pass to the next stage."

"Why? We did everything." He winced as he stepped awkwardly and lost his balance for a second. Jane took his weight and helped him stay up. "Where are we?" He asked.

They looked around; there were mounds of earth here as well, just like where Jane had been.

"Hold on," she said and helped him over to a tree that he could support his weight on and rest for a moment. She then walked slowly around. She was becoming clear again now and felt much more like her usual self. She looked at the raised mounds, their size, their shape, how they were all laid in almost unison, uniform lines, and mounds. Some fresher than others, definitely not made by nature. These had to be manmade.

But why?

Then she realised and took an involuntary step back in disgust, her hand raising to cover her mouth.

John spoke from his watch point.

"Are they what I think they are?"

Jane sank to her knees next to the mound she was standing by, it looked fresh, it can't have been much more than a few months old, and preyed it wasn't what she thought it was going to be.

"Let me help you," he said.

"No, stay there, it's fine, I got this," she said as she started digging, using her hands as shovels to claw through the soil as fast as she could, mud-covered her hands, it dug in under her nails, some worms and insects rose to the surface and scuttled off back into the night, looking for a new home.

"You know," John said, then groaned as he repositioned himself against the tree. "…There are shovels around." But Jane didn't want to use a shovel, she didn't want to use them and have the sharp metal dig into it if it was what she thought she was about to uncover. Her hand found resistance. There was something buried under the soil, in the mud. She tried to find the edge, find a place she could use as an anchor point to lever it up. She scooped and brushed as much as she could off the surface, thinning out the resistance weight of the soil and found what she feared.

The tip of a nose appeared at the surface.

Her heart sank, and her stomach rose, but she carried on. She brushed off more of the covering and lifted it up. It was a head.

She had just dug up this persons' grave.

15

In the truck, the man was angry. It was foolish to have not brought his own weapon. It was a mistake he wouldn't make again.

He picked up the radio and changed the frequency so that it wasn't what was on the soldiers' radios he had left behind and spoke.

"I need a containment unit to the elimination site. Targets are loose, over."

"Affirmative, on route," was the reply that cracked through the radio.

The containment units were his best chance of resolving this quickly. They were highly trained and specifically chosen by himself as his elite units.

They would round up John and Jane Doe and eliminate them. This was inconvenient, and he was not looking forward to telling Mister Knight of his mess up, but at least it would be a satisfactory ending if they were still dead. He would wait until morning and then report. By then, they would be dead, and he would be able to save face, and his job.

He carried on driving over the rough, uneven terrain tracks, and once he reached the main trails, the ride smoothed out a bit and he rode it all the way back to the facility.

16

Jane had laid the body back in the shallow grave that was its last resting place. She wanted to dig the rest of the body up, dig them all up and take them somewhere where they could be properly looked after and laid to rest with dignity, but she knew that was unrealistic, and they had already wasted too much time lingering.

She felt as if a piece of her humanity had just been lost as she looked around and knew that each grave held a body beneath it. There was an even number, and it didn't take long to realise that they would have been the next ones in the lines.

She was supporting John as they walked, he had his arm around her shoulder, and Jane was taking as much weight as she could. They were walking back the way Jane had come. She had reasoned that if the trucks had the keys left in them, and they were brought here in separate transports, then the one she was in would still be there and still have the keys in.

She hoped.

As they trudged their way through the undergrowth, trying to keep to the narrow path that was overgrown with greenery and at times almost impossible to see, they heard a vehicle approaching. It was behind them and seemed to be stopping around the same place they had heard the large truck start and drive off from.

They've come back for us, she thought.

"We need to move," she said.

In her mind, it wasn't that far, she had put how long it had taken her before down to whatever they had given her to make her lethargic, but this seemed to be taking even longer, probably because one of them was struggling to walk and in pain. John was hunched over, gripping his wound, sweat pouring down his face; she needed to get him help.

She heard footsteps behind her, crunching through the shrubbery. It sounded like a single pair. They had probably split up to search the immediate area. She expected they would have men further afield as well to make sure they didn't slip through.

She knew they couldn't outrun them, and if the men got to – and moved, the truck before they got to it, then they would have no way of getting out or getting John the help he needed.

"We need to stop," she whispered, "I think there is only one coming this way, and if we can take him out, then that should buy us enough time to get clear."

John shook his head. "Leave me in some bushes," his voice was strained and weak, his body was struggling, and it was only a matter of time before the gunshot wound became infected and then before his body went into shock. "You need to go, leave me; I can hold them off, draw them to me, and you can get out of here."

"Leave no man behind," then she looked at him, "no matter how annoying he is." She smiled at him, and they kept moving, the uneven terrain of the trail making an already difficult journey infinitely harder. There was a break in the trees and foliage up ahead, and Jane deviated from the path into it. They went in, just far enough not to be seen from the main trail, and Jane lowered John to the ground as gently as she could. "Alright, I'm going to leave you here and go hide over the other side. When you see or hear him pass, make a noise to draw him to you, then I can incapacitate him. That should give us a clear run to the truck. Got it?"

"Yeah." The word was so soft it was barely audible; if he hadn't slightly nodded his head at the same time, she might not have understood what he said.

She nodded back, gave him a thumbs up and then turned and headed back through the greenery, across the path and hid on the other side.

Ideally, she would have liked just to hide and wait for the searching party to leave, but she couldn't take that chance of how long that would take or the risk of being caught on the possible return sweep, so she would have to act.

It took a few minutes, but the crunching of footsteps got progressively louder as they got closer and soon, she had a visual on him. He was dressed in the same black uniform as the other men she had experienced that night, but this man wore a helmet and Kevlar body armour; he also wasn't only armed with a pistol, he had an H&K rifle in his hands, held loosely in his grip, but it was definitely ready to be raised and engaged at a second's notice. These were much more professional.

As he passed her hiding place, she held her breath, aware of every micro action of her body.

Jane had always been told to have no fear, to 'trust her training', but she had never removed that element of fear she had; she felt it made her a better soldier. Anyone can blindly stand up and shoot or run through a building with no thought or compunction to their own safety, but those people had a habit of being killed early in their careers. Fear is what made her question her actions. It was what kept her alert, it was what helped her expect the unexpected, and the tingle that shot down her spine right now was no different.

She held her body tight, and as the man passed, the moonlight that seeped in through the trees reflected from his helmet and made him seem almost like a robot.

He was walking at a good pace, looking eagerly for any clues that may help him in his search; he was proficient, he didn't dwell, and he didn't rush. She admired his tradecraft.

He caught sight of where they had entered to hide John and paused, looking at the broken shrubbery with interest. Then the sound of a twig snapping caught his attention; it was coming from the same direction as the broken bush. He raised his weapon, and she could see that instantly his light, the loose grip was now taught and ready to fire.

In her mind, it seemed like all this was a horror film, them hiding in the woods in the middle of the night, the man stalking them, hunting them like prey, the tense moment of hiding as the monster stalks past her.

The only difference was she was the hunter in this scenario, and he was the prey. Once he started making his way to John's position, she moved, as silently as she could back to the path and followed him in, following his path as best she could so that he didn't hear her creeping behind him.

The man reached John's position and aimed his gun square at him. There was no talk, no mention of going back, or being under any sort of arrest, nothing. He was just going to kill him.

Jane knew she had to move, and as she pushed herself forward to close the gap, she actually did step on a twig that snapped.

Fuck!

The soldier turned, and Jane just launched herself at him, tackling him to the ground, the weapon falling and landing next to them. The soldier used his elbows and lashed out with his left that Jane blocked, but it was really just a feint for his right, which struck her in her head, and she was rocked back. She managed to stay on top of him, though, straddling him and returned with a punch of her own to his throat, he instinctively raised his hands to his neck, and he could be heard choking as he tried to clear his airways. Jane reached over, grabbed the rifle, and used it as a hammer, bringing the butt end down into his face; the first time failed, the second broke his eye protection, and the third blow knocked him out.

She stayed on him for a moment, and then she pivoted off and helped John up. She knew it would only be a matter of time before either he woke up or someone realised he wasn't coming back and came looking for him. She picked up the radio and put it in her pocket, picked up the rifle, hoping she wouldn't need to use it.

Back on the trail, they inched closer to the truck, praying it was still there and that they could get out before anyone saw them.

Then the radio crackled, and a voice said:

'All sectors check-in,'

There was a brief pause and then:

'Sector one – clear'

'Sector two – clear,'

'Sector three – clear.'

Then a long pause, Jane held her breath as she walked. She considered using the radio and pretending, but the soldier they disabled was a man, so she would never pass for it, and John was in no state to speak with enough conviction to fool anyone.

The radio crackled again:

'Sector four, report…. Sector four, report, do you copy? Over…Sector five?'

'Sector five – clear,'

'Sector six – clear.'

'All units move to sector four immediately.'

Five repeats of 'copy followed this,' and she knew soon the area would be blanketed by at least five more men, and realistically that significantly reduced the chances of getting out of here.

They kept pushing on, Jane supporting John as best as she could, moving as fast as they could manage and eventually, they reached the clearing. The bodies of the men that had been sent to deal with Jane were still where they had fallen, and as she followed around the edge and down a small path, she managed to find where the truck had stopped and dropped them off before they had started walking.

She breathed a sigh of relief.

"We're getting out of here, Yankee. You'll be OK." According to the badges and stickers, the truck was a Ford Ranger Raptor in black and looked nothing like the kind of vehicle the military would use. It looked like the sort of vehicle a civilian would buy for the 'outdoor lifestyle', but in fact, the most off-roading it would ever do would generally be through a puddle or up a curb.

She didn't care right now, though, as it was a vehicle, and it would get them away so they could get John help and regroup.

She helped John get in the passenger side and then heard rustling; she picked up the rifle she had put down to help John manoeuvre into the vehicle and held her breath, listening hard for any more disturbances. It was either just an animal or a soldier. She hoped for the animal but was expecting the soldier. Another rustle came from the same area, and she hid behind the side of the truck for cover. She laid down on the ground, looking underneath the Ford and saw a set of feet emerge out, moving forward cautiously towards where they had come from until something caught his attention, and he stopped.

He's seen John, shit!

As he turned to face the truck, she shot his foot, and he howled out into the night, but no one could hear him over the crack of the H&K as it unloaded. The soldier fell to the floor, and she shot him in the head. He died instantly. She wasn't a fan of head shots, but he was wearing armour and the only place that she could remove him as a threat without giving him the chance to return fire was a clean shot above the neck. The sound of the discharge travelled; it was still hanging in the air, echoing through the stillness of the night. It wasn't silenced, and she may have well just made an announcement where they were. Soldiers would be running to this location, and soon they would be overrun. Normally she would take the odds, but John was wounded, and she wouldn't be able to take them all down in a straight gun fight by herself.

She got up, ran around the Ford, and climbed into the driver's seat; the keys were in the ignition. Finally, some good luck. She turned the engine over, and the diesel engine came to life. She dropped it into drive and pulled away just as bullets started hitting the bodywork and shattered the rear cab window overlooking the truck bed. They kept their heads down as she barrelled as fast as she dared down the tight, narrow trail and soon, mercifully, they were out of immediate danger as the gun fire was drowned out in the distance behind them.

17

The man with the deep voice had been waiting for a call in from his unit. He was in his office, but the work he had tried to do had failed due to his distracted mind. He had had his shoulder seen to once he had returned, the bullet had gone through his shoulder, and he would be live, but his left arm was now in a sling, and he had told the medics not to ask questions. They hadn't.

It wasn't like this was the first time this had happened, a lot of the subjects that get removed from the programme wake up before their termination, but they are dealt with at the moment. This was the first time one – actually two – had woken up and been able to get the advantage over his burial detail.

He got up from his desk and looked out of his window on the third floor of the facility, out over the woods that flanked the back of it, the deep woods that held the bodies of the previous subjects – and many more to come – he guessed.

His office faced the back of the building. He preferred that. The offices at the front looked out over the old military space, most of which was concrete for the vehicles and the soldiers that used to reside here to walk on. Out past that was the old town. He much preferred the tree line to looking at buildings.

The night was quiet until he heard the distant sounds of what could have been gunfire; this made him smile in anticipation of good news. It was a few moments later when his radio crackled into life with static background noise, and a voice said:

"They escaped, Sir. They got away."

This was not the message he was looking for, and he was not happy. He snatched up the radio from his desk and replied:

"Find them; they can't be that hard to track. I think the male is wounded." He spat as he spoke, anger in every word.

"They got to the truck. They got away."

"Track them down and find them. The truck has a tracker. I'll send you the number, and I want this resolved by morning. Quietly. Understand?"

"Yes, Sir. Over." The radio went dead, and the room returned to the quiet of before. He sat at his computer and logged into the vehicle database they had. All their vehicles had trackers implanted as a standard protocol, so as long as they could catch them before they ditched it, this could still be resolved, and he may be able to deal with it all and keep it off of Knight's radar. He sent the vehicle's tracker details to the unit, and then, with his annoyance and anger bubbling inside him, he slammed his fist down onto the table.

There were still a few hours until the sun rise.

Still time.

18

John and Jane followed the trail until it became a larger, more open track, it was much smoother compared to where they had come from, and they soon reached a junction. There were tracks that looked similar to theirs going right, and there were fewer tracks to the left, and the ones that were there looked aged and dusted over.

"Thoughts?" She asked as she turned to look at him.

"Right… right, seems to… to go back…" John said in between heavy, deep breaths.

"So, left? Put distance between them and us, hope we can find a doctor. Or go back? We know they have doctors and medical supplies at the facility, but we may also be killed instantly as soon as we set foot back inside."

"Left."

"You got it boyo, that was my thought too." Jane turned the Ford down the left track and accelerated. She glanced over at John, he was getting paler, and his breathing was becoming more shallow; he was getting worse, and she needed to get him help.

They followed the track left. Jane pushed the Ford truck as fast as she dared, bobbing and crashing over the bumps. After a while, the trail ended, and they looked to be at the back of a village or town. The track entrance looked to be at the end of a side road, hidden from most passing traffic. *Maybe that's why it's so rarely used?* She wondered as she edged the truck out onto the tarmac, the sweet, smooth tarmac. They drove down the side road and arrived at what looked like the main road through town.

She thought for a moment that she had gone back in time. It looked like an old American town from a film or an 80's TV show. The buildings looked old, and although it was all modern shops down the main road, they looked like they were decades old, and the fronts had never been modernised.

She didn't realise places like this actually existed in the real world.

The main road through town was small, you could drive from one end to the other in about ten minutes, and there were houses off down the side streets and set further back, but not a great many of them. This seemed the kind of place you moved to, to retire from the big cities, to live in peace and quiet and see out your days. The type of place that once you're there, you never leave.

Daybreak was still a few hours away, and they drove around looking for a doctors or an emergency place, but they couldn't find one. John was getting worse, and there was a veterinary clinic on the main stretch that would have to do. They parked near the clinic, a few buildings down and down a side street; they wanted to get the truck out of sight in case anyone came looking for them.

"Wait here." She instructed as she climbed out and started walking. She went to the village store, it was locked, but no shutters or anything were protecting the windows. She hadn't even seen a police station as she had driven round looking for a doctors.

Probably not a lot of crime around here, she thought as she braced and forced her elbow through the pane of glass nearest the lock. *Until tonight anyway.*

Once inside, she knew what she was looking for and went straight for it. She hoped the veterinary clinic would have most of what she would need to stitch John up, but not everything. She grabbed a couple of bottles of Vodka and made her way back out of the store.

The veterinary clinic was across the street, and a few buildings up, and also locked. No surprise there, though. She walked around the back, hoping for a rear entrance. She wanted them focused on the village shop, not the clinic, so a more subtle back entrance would be perfect if someone were looking for them. There was a back door, but it was a heavy fire door, and no way would she be able to open it. There were no windows back here either, so it looked like it would have to be the main door and hope.

This didn't make her feel comfortable. It would leave them more exposed than she was comfortable with. She smashed the glass nearest the lock, reached in and turned the latch. She waited for an alarm, she couldn't do anything about it, but she was expecting one. None came, no sound.

She placed the vodka on the reception desk, rushed back to the truck, helped John down, and supported him as he stumbled down the path and into the clinic. She took him through to the back and found the 'operating' table. It was only a small building and easy to navigate.

Inside was modern and everything they needed to perform all kinds of procedures on the animals that came into their care. Jane helped John onto the table, lying him down and then went back and got the vodka and placed it on the worktop. She rummaged through the drawers and cupboards, collecting a scalpel, forceps, needle, stitching wire, and other items. She ripped John's shirt, exposing the wound, it was raw, but she couldn't see any signs of infection yet. She looked at it, rolled him slightly and he grunted. She looked at his back, no exit hole.

The bullet was still inside him.

"It's still in there," she said, unpackaging the equipment. She found a box of purple surgical disposable gloves on the counter and put some on. "I need to take it out."

John grunted his agreement.

"This is going to hurt," she said as she took a swig of the vodka, he held his hand out, and she passed him the bottle. He took a deep mouthful and gave it back. "You ready?"

He nodded and placed his head back, straining it against the bed and gripped the sides.

"Do it." He muttered.

She grabbed the scalpel and prepared herself.

She poured the vodka over his wound to sterilise it – she was pretty sure if she looked enough, she should be able to find something better in here, but this needed to be an in and out job. John cried out but managed to keep his mouth shut to stifle the noise of his pain. She cut along the wound, giving herself more room to work with and then she put the forceps inside, feeling for the bullet. John was writhing on the table in agony, but he tried to stay as still as he could, his knuckles white as he gripped the table. She found the bullet, gripped it, and slid it out. Instantly John stopped moving and breathed out a deep sigh of relief.

"I bet that hurt being in there." She said as she placed the bullet in the metal tray at the end of the table.

"Not as much as you rummaging around looking for it," he muttered, "I thought you knew what you were doing."

She threaded the stitch and began sowing him up.

"I did, it came to me what I needed to do, but you're the wimp who couldn't sit still," she smiled down at him.

"I thought you were playing fucking operation in there, trying to get my damn nose to light up."

"Always so dramatic, Yankee, and I think the words you're looking for are 'thank' and 'you'."

"Thanks, English."

"You're welcome."

After Jane had finished stitching him up, she helped him off the table, he was still weak, but without the bullet inside him, he could stand much better and had more mobility.

They gathered up their stuff, grabbed some painkillers and left. There was a room at the other end of the building marked 'Kennels', and it seemed that the back door was the other side, thankfully none of the animals – if there were any in there – had been disturbed and they slipped out, back into the night.

There had been a vacant office building a few streets over, and they decided it would be the best place to lay low for the night and allow John to recover. She had taken cash from the register and some pins and tools and once they reached the office, she was able to make a makeshift lock pick and, after a moment, she heard the tumblers fall and the lock disengage, the door was open.

There was a massive 'TO LET' sign in the window, and no furniture, only the grey carpet on the floor. They moved to the backroom, and Jane eased John down to the floor.

"I'll be right back," she said, "rest now." Then she left. She walked back to the main street, went back to the store, and put some food in a bag, sandwiches, drinks, a few other supplies. Then she walked further down and found a charity shop. She picked her way in and rifled through the racks, looking for something they could change into. She found a new t-shirt and a jacket for John, but the only thing that would come close to fitting her was a dress in deep purple. It was a nice enough dress, but it was cut a little low at the front for her tastes, and it exposed too much skin, but it would have to do as they would need to try and blend in tomorrow and combat clothes seemed like they would stand out a mile around here.

She sighed, resigned herself to the dress and found a small black leather jacket she could put over the top. It was short; it came up just under her ribs, but the arms were long enough, and it would help keep her warm.

They weren't the clothes she was expecting to be in here, they were younger than she would have thought, but Jane took what she could, reset the lock as she left and started walking back to the office.

It was nearly sun rise now, and once John was rested, he would be at least semi-operational, and they could plan their next move.

Then she heard a sound that made her spine tingle, and then she saw the van turn the corner and drive up the street.

19

Jane was lucky that she was near a walk-through between two shops, she had been aiming for it anyway as a cut through to get back to the vacant office, but the sound of the vehicle had set her on edge, and as soon as she saw it, she ducked in to cover.

She watched the van drive slowly past her up the street, and then it stopped when it arrived at the Ford Ranger.

Damn it, she cursed.

Then all the doors of the van opened, and she counted seven men as they disembarked.

Shit.

They were dressed in all black and wearing the same armour as the soldier she had incapacitated during their escape in the woods. She retreated back down the alley and let the darkness envelop her.

The office that John was in was a few streets away and set back from the main drag. Hopefully, she could get back there undetected, and the soldiers wouldn't look that far back into the town. Worse case, they would take the Ford Ranger back, and while that would make transport more complicated, she would much rather they take the truck than herself and John.

She heard orders being barked and then the sound of one of the soldiers reporting in the broken shop glass. Hopefully, between that and the clinic, they would focus their search in the area and not look too much further afield.

She exited the alley at the other end, the next street over and stalked across the road. It was quiet, and she could still hear the soldiers on the other side of the buildings. This side of the road could have been on a brochure for the American dream. It was a perfect row of picture-esque houses, all symmetrical and detached from each other. Each one had a small but perfectly kept lawn out front – some even literally had the white picket fence – and looked amazing, even in the moonlight.

She kept low, trying to contain the sound of the bags rustling and brushing against her. She heard orders being given and could make out most of it. Some men were going to search the street, while the others fanned out and searched surrounding streets for any signs of them. Jane picked up her pace and made it to the next walk-through just as two soldiers rounded the corner up ahead of her, looking for anything to indicate where the escaped had been.

She ran as fast and as quietly as she could. She had belief in herself that up against one or two, she could prevail, but it wasn't one or two, and even if she engaged a single soldier, they would know they were still around, and it would be impossible to escape.

She felt like a mouse, running a gauntlet, or that old game – Pacman – running through the zigzag of streets trying to avoid the things trying to get her.

Jane remained as quiet as she could as she ran deeper into the town, always expecting a shout to say she had been seen or to hear the sound of weapons firing at her suddenly, but she didn't. Soon enough, she was far enough into the maze that she thought she would be safe. She was tense. Her nerves were on high alert as she made a big circle around, making sure it was safe before heading back to the office.

She had almost made it, she could see the building across the street, and she was about to cross when she heard a radio crackle and a voice speak:

"Unit 2, all clear. Over"

She sank back into the shadows, behind the large bins, and waited. She was careful not to let the bags rustle or make noise; she was so close and didn't want to raise any attention to her or the building.

The soldier walked into view. He looked around. She felt like he knew she was there, but his gaze didn't linger, and he turned. Then he started walking towards the vacant office unit.

Jane's heart both stopped and felt like it was going to burst out of her chest at the same time. She prayed John didn't walk out of the back and expose their hiding place to the soldier that was now up against the window, peering inside.

Time seemed to stop. Every second felt like an hour, and all she could do was wait. The soldier looked at the handle, tested it, but it was locked, and Jane sighed a silent sigh of relief that she had put it back on the latch. After a moment of looking around, the soldier moved away from the glass, looked up and down the street, and then carried on past on his original path. She was surprised that they were going this far into the town to search, she would have thought once they found nothing at the shop and the clinic that they would have moved on, but clearly, they were determined to search everywhere before they would try the next area.

She waited another few minutes, making sure the coast was clear. She edged her way out of the alley entrance, looking around, making sure nobody was waiting for her, and only once she was satisfied that it was safe did she return to the bags, scoop them up, cross the street, pick the lock once again and snuck inside. She went to the back room, and when she entered, she dropped the bags, and the contents spilt out onto the grey carpet. John wasn't there.

20

It wasn't morning yet, but the man with the deep voice had decided to get ahead of the situation and call Mister Knight. He took a deep mouthful of the whiskey he had poured himself, picked up the phone and dialled. It was about to go to voicemail when it was answered:

"This had better be important." Knight said.

"Sir, the subjects have escaped."

There was a long silence, he never said a word, and the man with the deep voice decided to get ahead of it and said,

"I have a containment unit out now searching, we have found the truck they used to escape, and we are searching the area now," he paused, waiting for a reply.

"This is unfortunate," was all that Knight said. Then, after another pause, he continued, "you say they both escaped?"

"Yes, Sir."

"Ok, this is a problem... Have all personnel removed from site, move everyone to the backup location immediately. Go to relocation protocol. If he comes back, I don't want anyone here who can give him anything to lead him back to us. Then I want you to upload everything – or download – or whatever it is that needs to happen and erase all the computers. Take whatever you can and move it all. Once they have been found and neutralized, we will move back in and carry on."

"Sir, we have units here, combat-capable units that we can leave here if they come back, they will be able to neutralize them."

"No, make sure all our data is secure and escort our teams to the backup location; they are the most important. If they get compromised, then the years we have spent on this programme will be jeopardised. Understand? Your units are now protection details but leave the one you have out there and a second one to find them. I mean it, Mister Wells, you find them, and you find them soon, and when you do, you eliminate them. Is that clear?" His voice became sinister as he finished the sentence and the man with the deep voice – Mister Wells – knew he needed to resolve this fast.

"Yes Sir, Mister Knight, clear and understood."

"I will meet you at the backup location in the morning. I want this resolved by then."

"Yes, Sir."

Wells hung up the phone took another drink, gulping it down until the glass was empty, then he poured himself another and drank it down in one pass. Then he picked up the phone and started putting the relocation into motion.

21

Jane searched the vacant office building, panicking, praying each room she went into John would be in there, waiting for her.

He wasn't.

Have they found him and taken him? She considered, *no, because there would be signs of a struggle, and the door was locked.* She reasoned with herself.

He had to be outside, and while she thought of all the possible reasons he would have had to have gone out into the night, she knew that the reason didn't matter ultimately, he was out there, and she needed to find him. She checked there wasn't an ambush waiting for her and then left, locking the door behind her, and once again made her way out into the night.

It was starting to get light now, and she felt like this night had lasted forever. She would welcome the relief of daylight as she was sure that the fully armoured men would be a lot more reluctant to search for them in the day hours and draw attention to themselves.

She crept through the streets, checking the shadows of each corner, moving fast as she searched. She was making her way back to the Ford Ranger and knew that she was basically walking back into the lion's den right now, but her will to find John overpowered her common sense to get distance between her and her pursuers.

She had been searching for around an hour or so, she had had to hide a few times as soldiers passed her hiding places, and she was just starting to worry that she wouldn't be able to find him when she turned down an alley and heard shouting. She froze, taking a micro-second to allow for her body to register the sounds, looked around for the threat, but couldn't find one. Then she saw John stumble into the alley she was in at the other end. Her heart skipped as she saw him, realising he was ok. He was stumbling, his hand still pressed against his stitched-up wound, and he seemed to be sweating.

Then the world stopped.

A loud crack split the air as the bullet hit John in the leg. He stumbled and got up, then another bullet hit him in the back, and he fell, slumped to the floor, leaning against the wall. Jane's heart stopped as she watched. Everything seemed to be in slow motion, she started forward towards him, and then she saw the soldiers come into view, and she ducked in behind a recycling bin as cover.

Her heart was pounding and demanding that she rushed to help him, but her head and all her training knew she was too far away. She could call out, distract him, and run, but if they were like the other one they had met, he would simply kill John and then begin pursuit. She searched her surroundings, looking for a way of gaining an advantage over the situation.

None presented themselves.

She was still trying to find a way when she was surprised by a voice drifting up the alley; the soldier was talking:

"I will ask you this once, scum," he said, his rifle pointed down at John, who seemed to be doing the same, looking for a way to gain an advantage. "Where is the other one?"

"No deal," John muttered as he shook his head and tried to drag himself up the alley, there was a bottle lying on the ground next to a bin, and it looked like he was trying to reach it.

"Ok." The soldier said.

He fired three shots into John, and he slumped to the ground and stopped moving.

Jane wanted to scream. She wanted to burst forward from her hiding spot, charge down the alley and kill the soldier. Kill all the soldiers that have been searching for them; her training and her sense stopped her, however, but rage and anger flooded through her, and she could feel her emotions boiling, her fists clenched, and she could feel her nails digging into her palms.

John was the only family she had. He was the only one in her life she knew and trusted. The only human she felt love for.

The soldier who had killed John clicked his radio:

"One down, male. Send extraction team to my location to retrieve the body. Over."

"Copy that. Over." Was the reply.

Jane peered around the dumpster. The soldier had turned and was walking down the alleyway towards her. He had just left John's body there, with the rubbish, like it was garbage.

She felt her heart beating faster and faster, the thoughts racing around her head, she would kill him.

He came into view; she was hidden back and had the jump on him. As he drew level, she pushed herself up, grabbed him and slammed him into the wall, kicked him in the back of the knee, and when he buckled, she turned around and threw him to the floor. His rifle was on a strap, but not across his body; it slipped off his shoulder and skidded across the floor.

Jane mounted the downed soldier. He threw a punch, she caught his wrist, rage and anger swelling more and more inside of her, faced with the man who had just killed her only friend, all of her hesitancy drained from her, she wasn't going to incapacitate him, she was going to make him suffer and then kill him.

She broke his wrist. The soldier cried out in pain. She knew someone might hear and come for her, but she didn't care. All she cared about was causing this man as much pain as possible. John was dead. She would avenge him.

She grabbed his other wrist, broke it, sending another cry from beneath the helmet.

Her teeth were gritted. Jane was snarling as she punched him in the throat, then she climbed off of him, grabbed his rifle, stood up and looked down at him. He was coughing and spluttering, his hands limp from his wrists. She pulled his helmet off, revealing his face.

He was generic. He wore a balaclava around his face under the helmet, framing his face, so only his eyes, nose and mouth were visible. He looked to be in his forties. He had dark eyes. He was putting on a brave face, but a tear escaped his eye. She looked him dead in the eye and pulled the trigger, shooting him in the knee. He screamed now, and his whole body recoiled.

She wanted to tell him why she was doing this; she wanted him to understand what he had just done, what he had just taken from her, what the costs of his actions were, but she was too mad; she had no recollection of ever feeling like this. Rage, anger, hatred, and so much aggression was all she could feel, and it was all aimed at this man.

She shot him in his other knee. He screamed again, and he began to whimper.

She steeled herself, controlling her breathing so she could talk.

"You know what you've done?" She asked through gritted teeth. "Do you have a family?"

The soldier nodded in between the writhing on the floor, it seemed involuntary, and when he realised he had done it after, his eyes widened.

"I'm going to return the favour," she snarled, "I'm going to kill your family."

The soldier's eyes widened even more. Fear etched on his face as he shook his head, silently pleading.

"Call for help, scream, tell everyone where you are. Then I can kill all of them too."

The soldier found a last bit of resolve; he shook his head, trying to look defiant. He failed.

"An eye for an eye." She said, raising the gun to his face.

Then she fired.

The moment she pulled the trigger, it seemed a wave washed over her, and she realised what she had done. She didn't regret it, but she knew the gun shots would eventually lead others here, plus people were coming to take John's body away already.

She ran down the alley, knelt beside John, tears streaming down her face. The pain in her heart felt like it would never end. She looked at him and realised that in his death, the last of her humanity seemed to have faded and died.

"I will kill them all." She whispered her promise to him, kissed his forehead, then got up and ran back to the vacant office building.

The path back was clear, not that she cared, she had the rifle now, and she hoped someone would get in her way.

She knew what she would be doing with her life now. She knew her mission.

She reached the office and went inside, through to the back room, laid on the floor next to the spilt bags of food and clothes, curled up into a ball, and cried.

22

The next morning…

The sun in the sky signified the end of the worse night
of Jane's life.
She hadn't slept. She had just been lying on the floor,
alternating between crying and feeling the hatred
bubble up inside her. In the quiet of the night, she had
thought over her options of what she could do next.
She knew that her best option was to run, to get as far
away from here as possible and stay one step ahead at
all times until they gave up on chasing her.
But she didn't want to do that. She knew it wasn't
going to happen. Sooner or later, they would catch up
to her, and she didn't want to spend whatever was left
of her life looking back over her shoulder, making sure
she wasn't going to get caught.
Option two was to give herself up and let them kill her.
She had considered this option a few times during the
night as she laid on the floor but knew in her heart she
wouldn't just allow herself to be gunned down, no
matter what their reason for it was.
Option three was to turn the tables; kill every single one
of them. All the scientists involved, everybody she
could find relating to whatever herself and John had
been involved with. Burn it all down to the ground.
This was the option she had settled on.

She had nothing else in her life, nothing else to focus on or take into consideration. She waited until she believed it was safest, she doubted the soldiers would be walking around as brazen during the day, but she couldn't be sure. She ate the sandwiches and drank the water from the store, then she changed into the dress and jacket she had collected last night, put the clothes she had stolen for John back in the bag, and set out into the town.

She walked as naturally as she could, but she was aware of how a dress that showed more of her chest than she would have liked, the jacket and her combat boots looked like as a complete outfit.

It would have to do.

She looked around as she walked, checking for any stragglers that may have been left behind to look for her. She didn't see any.

The sun was warm, and there was no wind; it was a pleasant day for a walk, and Jane realised she found herself craning her neck up so she could feel the warmth of the sun on her face.

She arrived at the entrance to the alley where John had been killed. They had been taken, and all that was left was a patch of dried blood. Most of it had been cleaned up. The soldier she had killed had also been recovered. She paused, just looking at the last place she had ever seen him, feeling the guilt gnawing away at her insides that she couldn't save him.

Why had he even been out? She wondered, knowing she would never know the answer.

After a moment, she tore herself away from the spot she was rooted to and carried on back towards the main street. The nice weather had brought some people out, and they were meandering around, going in and out of shops, living their lives.

Living their lives… Don't think about him.

She went into the convenience store – the one she had robbed the night before – put on her happiest face, and approached the counter.

"Hi," she said, her smile wide and eyes bright.

"Hello there, how can I help?" The woman behind the counter looked to be in her mid-fifties, had a round face and gave off an air of having no idea that anything else in the world existed outside of this little town.

"Hi, I'm new around here an-"

"Oh, I should say you are," she interjected, "I've not seen your face before. Welcome to Willow Creek," then her smile dropped, "are you OK, my dear?"

"Yes, of course; why?"

"Oh, you have such terrible red eyes; you look like you've been cryin' for hours."

"Erm…ok I mean, yeah, I have… but I'm OK," she lied. "I was actually looking to move into the area, just thought I'd come in and have a look around, see what it's like."

"Oh, here? In Willow Creek? It's like a little slice of heaven," she chuckled to herself. "What's made you and your husband want to move here?"

"I'm, I… I don't have a husband."

"Oh my spuds and gravy, I'm so sorry, you and your," she hesitated, "wife?"

"No, no wife either, just me."

"Oh, oh right, Ok." She looked confused, almost like she was trying to work out how someone wasn't married.

"There was someone," Jane started, "but he's gone now. It's just me."

"Oh, of course, a widow. I'm so sorry, deary. How long ago?"

Jane couldn't be bothered going into it, so she let the woman think what she wanted. She just said, "recently," and then pushed forward with her questions.

"So, it looks lovely round here, it's beautiful, and everyone seems friendly."

"Oh yes!" The woman beamed. "Everyone is wonderful, which is why it's so strange what happened last night."

"Oh?" Jane leaned in, trying to act surprised and intrigued. The woman smiled again; clearly, she loved to gossip, Jane let her go with it.

"Well," she began, "I don't know if you saw, but I've had to put a cover over the glass in the door? Well, this is because last night, I only went and had a break-in for the first time ever, can you believe it? I surely can't. Didn't take any money mind, just some sandwiches, few drinks, and some odd bits 'n' bobs. I mean, who doesn't have a sandwich and water at home? I tell you, beggars' belief. Not only that," she continued, barely stopping for breath between each statement. "I heard from Margaret, that Jean got told by Rosemary that there were people on the streets last night making all sorts of commotion. Yeah, it's true," – Jane hadn't said anything to disagree with her – "an' you'll never guess what she said she saw when she looked out, only soldiers, military soldiers at that, in outfits an' everything. Can you believe that? I tell you, I can't, but then Jean's eyes have been going in her old age, getting a bit difficult to see things she is."

"Soldiers?" Jane said, grateful to get a word in. "What were soldiers doing around here?"

"Lord knows," the woman said, "I mean, I tell you, I mean, I ain't never seen anything like it, I lived here all my life and even when they was using the old base on the edge of town, we never saw much of anything like soldier related stuff, you know?"

"So, why were they here?" Jane asked.

"Maybe something to do with the break-ins. I'm not the only one you know; the vets up the road also had it. It looks like someone's been rummaging through their stuff. Hannah – the lady who owns it – says they stole some of her stuff, but why? I don't know, makes you wonder, doesn't it?"

The door behind them opened, and a couple walked in, around Jane's age. They looked her up and down before going to the shelves. Jane knew her time was now limited, so pushed her questions:

"What happened to the old army place then? They still use it?"

"Oh, no," the woman said. "It ain't been used for years. Although some people say you can sometimes hear stuff going on late at night or see lights or what have you, but I never have. But then again, I live up the hill, you know," she pointed over Jane's shoulder like it would illustrate her point. "So, I'm too far away to see or hear anything like that," she continued, "just ghost stories and whatnot, I think."

The couple were now standing behind Jane, and she felt it was time to leave.

"It was a pleasure to meet you," she said. "Can I have a lighter, please?"

"Yes, honey," the woman said, turned around and picked up a yellow disposable lighter.

"Terrible habit, y'know."

"I know, I'm trying to quit, maybe being here, away from the city, with all this lovely fresh air will help me, do me some good." Jane smiled. The woman began asking where she was from, but Jane cut her off, said thank you, placed the money she took from the soldiers down on the counter for payment, scooped up the lighter and was out the door.

Back out on the street, she moved away from the shop door and allowed herself to think.

The military base is shut down.

Was their training official?

Was the base not actually shut down, and it had just been converted to a private facility and the whole 'shut down' was just speculation from a group of local gossips?

What was going on in there?

She ran questions through her mind as she ambled down the street, trying to blend in, discreetly looking at everyone as they passed. Some were looking at her; most weren't. She believed the ones that were was because of her attire, the dress that was a bit too big, and the low cut at the top revealed too much, and as she walked, the motion gave risk to an accident that showed even more. She slowed her pace and tried to cover up as best she could with the jacket.

She decided she was going back. She would break in and find out what's going on. It was where everyone was anyway, and even though the lady had been charming – in-between all the ramblings – she was still set on her task. Her mood had not improved.
She wanted to kill everyone that was involved with their training. Logically, the best first step was to go back to where they had been trained.
She went back to the office, got changed into her combat clothes, kept the jacket to cover her arms, used the bathroom, collected what she needed and walked back to the Ford Ranger.
By a miracle, it was still there,
Must have deemed it not important enough to take back, she thought. The bottom half was covered in dust and mud, and now she could see the bullet holes peppered in the body work, but it still worked and drove fine, and that's all she needed it to do. She climbed in, started it up, reversed out and drove down the main stretch.
The bullet-riddled, window shattered Ford drew a lot more attention.

23

Mister Wells had received good and bad news. The good news, one of the escaped subjects had been terminated. The bad news, the other was still at large. They were in the backup location now. It was another de-commissioned military base a few hours away. He had been waiting the rest of the night for news from his containment unit, and when the call came, he had been hoping it had been dealt with. Now he had another call to make.

He dialled the number for Mister Knight and waited for it to be answered.

"Hello."

"Mister Knight, Sir, it's Wells."

"I hope you have some good news for me, Wells."

"Yes, Sir, one of the escaped subjects has been terminated."

There was a pause on the line before Mister Knight spoke again:

"One?" He said.

"Yes, Sir, we are still searching for the other one, but with daylight, it has slowed us down. We don't want to have too much presence about and draw suspicions."

"I want him found, Wells, I wanted him found by the morning, but now you have given me a problem."

"He has been, Sir; it's the female subject that is still at large."

"The woman?" There was a moments pause, and when he spoke, his mood seemed to be a bit happier. "That's good. I thought it was the male and would be a problem. This should be a lot easier for you to resolve now."

"Sir?" Wells asked, confused.

"What?"

"I don't follow."

"The woman will be easy to catch. A woman at her peak is always weaker than a man at his, so your unit, the men in your unit, should have no problem with her. I thought it was the man that had eluded you. I'm glad to hear you got the difficult one first; now just clean up and get back to me once you have."

"Erm… OK, Sir."

"I'll deal with this more when I arrive."

Mister Knight hung up, and Mister Wells stood for a moment, a bit taken aback by the conversation.

Why did he think the woman would be easier to find?

He shrugged it off and forgot about it, switching his focus to finding and fixing his mistake.

Elsewhere, Knight was sitting in his luxury home, in the big luxury bath, and as he hung up, he knew that Wells hadn't dealt with the situation as he had told him to. If it didn't get resolved soon, he would have to report to the investors, and he didn't want to do that. He wanted it sorted before it needed to come to that.

24

Jane drove the Ranger back the way she had come, through trail dirt roads and on until she was close to the military facility. She parked up a safe distance away and waited. She wanted to go now, to burst in and kill them all, but they were still looking for her, and there was a good chance they were expecting her to come back and would have precautions in place. She would wait for the cover of night. There would be a higher chance of success. Hopefully, many of the staff stayed on-site, if they had, and with a bit of luck, the soldiers would be out looking for her again under cover of darkness, so would be less risk.

She sat in the truck for a while. She drank and ate some more of the food from the shop and waited.

The day seemed to drag, and she passed the time by going for walks through the wooded areas, careful to keep a lookout for any cameras or security devices. She wondered how many bodies had been buried in this vast, endless sea of trees.

Would John be brought back here to be buried?

She put thoughts of him from her mind, they only made her sad, and then they made her mad, and while it can be a very motivating emotion, she needed to be level-headed right now, so she would allow herself time to grieve later.

As the day began to fade and the night drew in, she began moving towards the facility. It was easy enough to get on the base, most of the external camera's seemed to have been removed, and as she skirted around, she found what looked like a side entrance tucked away in a small alcove. A few chairs were positioned outside, and many spent cigarette ends littering the floor and overflowing from some old pots – a smoking area.

The door wasn't a security door. It had glass panels that showed a small canteen area inside.

She tried to pick the lock, but it was heavier than it looked, and bent her make-shift tools, so she decided to do it the old-fashioned way. She shattered the top glass panel, reached in, and opened the door.

She was in.

She had the rifle strapped with her, across her shoulder, and waited to see if anyone came to meet her. No-one did. No alarms sounded either.

Good start.

She walked across the canteen and out through the door, into the complex. She had never been to this area before and had no idea whereabouts she was or where to go.

She figured the important stuff would be on the higher floors, in an office, or a documents room somewhere. She began looking around for stairs.

The facility was massive. She knew it was large, the areas and training scenarios they had run while being here were in enormous rooms akin to warehouses, and the outside courses were like marathons, but she had no idea there was quite this much going on that she couldn't see.

Everywhere was painted white, and chrome door handles and signs directed you to the departments it had when it had been a 'functioning' base.

After a while of wondering, she found where she was looking for. It was like an accounts space or human resources. Jane hadn't come across anybody as she walked around, she thought this was odd, she had expected to see at least one person, either a security soldier or a worker, but she hadn't, so she had changed her plan, and she had gone looking for employment records. She wanted to find the names and details of all the people that worked on her and John. Then she wouldn't have to wait or hope. She could begin going on the offensive. She could go into attack mode.

It had taken her maybe another half an hour to find what she was looking for, but she had found it.

The room was simple; it was just like any other office. This one didn't have any of the fancy kit that some of the others she had searched in did, and it looked like a room that's only goal was to hold filing cabinets of various sizes with labels detailing their contents. There was also a small desk in the middle of the room, with a laptop sitting on it. Leads ran down and were plugged into a tower at the edge of the room, tucked in between the cabinets. It was a data hard drive stack and looked like it may have access to everything she would need. She took one last look down the corridor to make sure it was all clear, then she entered the room and closed the door behind her.

She searched through the unlocked cabinets and tried to force the locked ones open but failed, and when she was out of other options, she turned her attention to the computer.

She sat at the desk and turned it on. It took a minute to load, but then it lit up and came to life.

To her surprise, it wasn't password protected. That was a welcome piece of good luck.

But why would they protect it if the only people who know it exists are those who used it? She reasoned with herself.

She started typing and looking in folders for the staff details, she seemed to work most of it intuitively like it was muscle memory, and she figured she probably knew how to do it all before she came here. It was just her brain kicking in and remembering what it needed to, for which she was grateful.

She was looking through the folders when she came across one that caught her eye and sparked something in her mind. It wasn't a folder on the employees; it was a folder marked:

The Phoenix Initiative

She opened the file, and all the contents options flooded the screen, files and files, folders and documents on a programme run by the military.

She opened a document file and read.

The Phoenix Initiative, as with regards to the previous attachments, will begin in a few months, subject to appropriate recruiting.

The programme aims to develop advanced soldiers for military units that will be able to operate at a higher level than 'regular' recruits.

This will take place when suitable candidates have been found, and once we have found our volunteers, it will begin.

The candidates will have their minds erased completely. They will lose all memory of who they were before. We will give them new names and reveal enough of their previous lives to explain what they are doing and why they chose to undertake in this programme.

It is imperative that we are able to develop the next generation of soldiers before other interested parties do. If we lose the upper hand in this, there will be no way we will be able to keep our country safe. You have been chosen to lead this programme due to your service history and the recommendation of the people who have the final say on this programme.

We are expecting great things from this next step. The animal tests have proved successful, with an increase of 3% improvement in various fields, and we believe that it is time to move on to the human stages in the belief that with what we have achieved so far and the developments we are still making, we could have soldiers ready in as little as two years.

That was all she could see, it looked like it had more to say, like it was just a section that had been copied from an email, but she would need to find the original correspondence to get more information.

She looked through other documents she found, most of them similar, and they were all dated almost seven years ago. This has been going on for a lot longer than they predicted.

She found a folder marked:

Candidates

She opened it up and couldn't believe how many documents were inside. The list was longer than the screen, and she had to scroll down to get to the bottom. They were all named John and Jane Doe, but then had little tags next to each one, almost like nicknames. *Probably to help them distinguish which ones they're talking about.*

She expected hers and Johns to be the bottom ones, but they were the ones up from the bottom. The tag read:

Yankee and English
(self-given names.)

She felt violated. They were the nicknames they had given each other because they knew their names weren't 'John' and 'Jane', and they didn't want to use names until they knew what they really were, so they came up with the names due to their nationality. They weren't for these people to use. She wanted to punch the screen.

She controlled herself and looked at the file underneath, there looked to be a new John and Jane lined up.

She opened the file.

The first page was a service file for a woman, her picture was removed, and her name and personal details had been redacted. All she could make out was that she used to work for the Israeli unit Sayeret Matkal.

Jane was impressed as she read down her record. She was a very skilled, remarkably successful operative with an exemplary record.

She scrolled down to the next page. It was for a man; the picture had also been removed, and the name and details had the black redaction box over them. She could see he was Russian though, former Spetsnaz and again, a fine record. Except the woman's had NLS (no longer sanctioned) in red stamped across it.

She closed down the file and opened the one that pertained to herself and John – her John, Yankee – and started looking through it. John's was first. It was his service record, an incredible one. His face and all his personal details had also been removed. There only remained a few images of him in his uniform.

She moved down and found her file. It was exactly as she suspected. No image, no details, and the service record was everything she knew because it was everything they had told and shown her. She couldn't gather any more information from it. She cursed at it and closed the file down. She came out of the candidate's folder, and after a few more minutes looking, she found the file she was looking for, the one with all the details of the scientists that were assigned to *The Phoenix Initiative.*

She opened it up and did a quick look through, there were a good few names on here, and all had their personnel details. This was perfect. It was exactly what she needed.

She smiled to herself, a dark smile because she knew that now she had this information, it was only a matter of time for all the names on these documents.

The clock was ticking, and their time was coming.

She tried to see if she could take the computer but was aware that if she disconnected it, what she wanted may not be saved to the computer, and she would lose it.

She looked around, couldn't find what she was looking for, she left the room and searched the nearby offices, finally finding one, a USB thumb drive. She hurried back to the computer, plugged it in, looked at what was already on it – nothing useful to her – so she deleted it all and moved the entire file about The Phoenix Initiative onto it. Once it had all downloaded, she closed it all down and once again searched the surrounding offices until she found a laptop and charger sitting on a desk. It looked like there had once been a static monitor and tower too, but they were now gone. She picked up the laptop, retraced her steps back to the canteen, then back out into the courtyard, into the woods and back to the Ranger.

As she drove back to the town, she was pleased with herself, she had got what she had come for – in a

manner of speaking – and had got out without incident. She glanced over at the laptop on the passenger seat, felt the USB stick in her pocket. The satisfying sensation of the anticipation of what was coming next tingled down her spine.
She smiled.

It was still dark when she got back to town, and she parked the Ranger closer – but not too close that it was obvious – to the vacant office she had decided was now her home base. Her make-shift lock pick had snapped while trying to break into the base, so she had no choice; she went around the back and broke a window. She climbed in through it and sat on the thin grey carpet, plugged the laptop in, hoping the owners still had electricity going to the building – They did – and fired the laptop up, plugged in the USB, opened up the file on the team working the programme and began looking through them.
"Got you."

25

Jane was woken a short while later.

She had looked through the files and decided on the order with which to proceed. She wanted the people at the top, those who gave the orders, but they lived far away and travelled in, but she found a couple of addresses that were right here in Willow Creek. She reasoned that as they were all going to have to die anyway, she may as well start with the locals first, then expand out.

She had considered starting there and then, but she realised she hadn't slept properly for a couple of days now, and she needed to rest. She had also only eaten cheap store food, and while that was good enough short term, she needed to fuel herself and make sure she was ready for this undertaking, so she had talked herself into a good night's sleep, a good breakfast at the diner in town, and then tomorrow night she would start. Another twenty-four hours would be ok.

So, she had slept, but now something had stirred her; she didn't know what it was. It was primal, a sensation that warned her body and told her it needed to be alert. It needed to be ready. The hairs on her arms were on end, and her body tingled as if trying to sense the air for the danger.

Is this what animals are like in the wild? She wondered as her eyes searched the darkness. Then there was a noise, a crunch outside of boots on loose pavement. She tensed, straining to clarify the noise, allowing her whole body to reject anything that wasn't important. Was this a threat?

Then she heard a low grunt and glass breaking underfoot.

The shattered window,
Someone's in here!

She sprang up, grabbed her rifle, and hid up against the wall next to the door. Her breathing was steady. She was aware of the danger, she allowed it to make itself felt through her body, but she was in control. If it were an enemy combatant, they wouldn't be leaving here alive.

Jane waited, then she saw him enter the room, but he took her by surprise, he wasn't walking in stood up, he was crouched, and by the time she made the adjustments he had seen her, their bodies were close, and he decided instead of trying to reposition to get a shot he would attack. He let go of his rifle and let it swing to his side; at the same time, he pushed himself up, tackling Jane around the waist and forcing her off her feet. She rose into the air, her feet left the ground, the rifle slipping from her grip, and went tumbling. As they landed, she rolled free, and they both came up to their feet.

When she saw him, standing there in his uniform, a flash of an identical man shooting John came into her mind. Her body got hotter. She felt rage and hatred boil up inside her again as it had done before. She cried out in hate as she moved in to attack him.

It was dark in the room, but her vision had adjusted, and Jane could make out enough. She moved in, punching with her right. He brought his left forearm up to block. He returned with his own right, and she swept her left arm in to block and push the attempt wide. He was armoured, and not many weak points were available to her, but he still had some. She kicked the back of his knee, and he buckled, she moved around behind him and got him in a chokehold, but his helmet was making it difficult. The soldier rose and tried to shake her off, his hands grabbing at her arms. She brought her legs around and clamped herself to his back. He tried to break her free, but she held tight, then he moved back fast and threw himself against the wall, trying to dislodge her. She jarred as she hit the wall but was able to cling on. She needed to remove his helmet, she shifted her grip, and as the soldier threw himself against the wall again, Jane undid the clip, and as she fell off his back, she brought the helmet with her. She hit the floor and rolled, giving herself some space and rose to one knee. She couldn't make out his features well in the darkness, but they didn't matter. He was exposed.

He drew his side-arm, and she moved in, grabbed the nozzle with her left hand, his shoulder with her right and pulled him down with her. As they fell, she placed her feet on his stomach and flipped him over, removing his pistol from his grip as she did so.

Now he had no weapons, and the thought crossed her mind just to shoot him, but she was angry, and it felt personal. A bullet was too good for him.

She growled as she strode over to him, his armour slowing him down as he tried to get back to his feet, she moved behind him again, gripping him in another lock, crushing his windpipe, but before she allowed him to try and remove her, she twisted hard and fast. There was a loud snap as his neck broke, and when Jane let go, his body dropped from the kneeling position and fell to the floor.

She stood over him, her whole body tense and her fingers still taut in anger. She breathed deep and wondered if a person could feel pain after death. She kicked him hard, just in case there was any chance the body had residual pain reception for a short time after. She searched his body, no identification, but he did have a radio, so she had ears now and could hear what they were doing.

She hadn't heard him call in before entering, so hopefully, she had some time before anyone came looking for him.

She went to the broken window in the back and covered it as best she could. Hopefully, it now looked like it had broken a while ago and not recent, she may get lucky, and no one else will come looking inside. She hid the body out of sight and knew she would probably need to find a new place to hold up from now on.

Then she settled back down, hoping that she could get some more sleep before morning or before others came looking for their missing friend.

26

The morning came with no further incidences. Jane used the bathroom and got changed into the dress again. She hadn't showered in a few days now, and she was beginning to smell. She would need to find a place with a bathroom soon. But for now, she would just buy some deodorant and hope that masked it enough.

She went back out into town, it was once again clear of soldiers, but she wondered how long that would last if she kept killing them every night. Sooner or later, they would lose patience, and then they would just keep looking for her, regardless of the sun.

She went back to the local store, picked up a couple of things – including some deodorant – and went to the counter to pay.

"Hello again, dear," the round-faced woman said as she welcomed her, "lovely to see you're still here."

"Yes, it's just such a pretty place. It feels like I've lived here my whole life." Jane smiled back.

"Oh yes," the woman nodded, "Willow Creek, no place like it."

"Not that I can ever remember."

"So, are you looking at the house up by the old farm then, at the top of town? Because I think that's the only place that's available, yes, I think it is, is that the one?"

"Yes," Jane replied quickly, making a note to find it later. It may be perfect for staying a few days undetected.

"Yes, it's a lovely little house, that is, I think so anyway, but hey, what do I know? A lovely couple lived there before, I can't remember why they moved," she paused, "I mean, why would you?" She chuckled to herself.

"Why indeed."

"Oh yes, it must be that place," the woman continued, "I mean, the only place that's currently empty is the old estate agents offices, but they moved last year, and it just sits there now, I mean, y'know, what else would we need in a place like this? We have everything you could possibly want."

"Yeah."

"An' you won't be staying in an office now, will you? No way, no how, how silly would that be?" The woman chuckled again. Jane paused, considering the irony of what she said, then nodded and said: "Yeah, imagine that."

"Are you…are you wearing the same dress as yesterday? I mean, its lovely, and everything, but -"

"It's my favourite." Jane cut in.

"Oh, well, it is lovely, my dear. I can see… a lot of you in it."

"Thank you," She beamed back, trying to act like that was the plan with wearing it.

She paid and left the shop.

She moved down the street to the diner. It was more like a café, but it would have hot food, which she needed right now. As she pushed the door, there was a little ding of a bell. She stood, waited to be seated, then a young woman came to greet her, in a uniform dress that seemed reminiscent of the fifties, but only really due to the cut; it was yellow. She followed the woman to her seat and slid into the booth.

"What can I get ya?" She asked.

"Do you do English breakfasts? You know, sausage, bacon, egg, tomato, that stuff?"

"Yeah, we sure do; it has all those and black pudding, beans, mushrooms and comes with either toast or fried bread."

"Perfect, one of those, please. Toast."

"Sure thing, how would you like your eggs?"

"Runny."

"No problem, anything to drink?"

"Coffee, black."

"Coming right up." The waitress smiled and walked away.

She looked around, the diner seemed almost round, with booths around the edges and tables of various sizes dotted about separated by dividers with classic black and white images of New York among other cities, and musicians from decades past decorated everything. It was how Jane would have imagined a nineteen-fifties inspired diner would look, only smaller. She had been seated at the window, there weren't many people in eating, but those that were, were around the edges, making the place look busy – and therefore popular – from the outside.

It made sense to do it in big cities where you wanted to seem attractive to passers-by and get them to come in, but did it serve a purpose in a town where it seemed everybody knew everybody else?

The waitress brought the drink over and placed it on the table.

"Thanks," Jane said as she took a sip. It didn't taste great, but it was hot and strong and would help keep her awake and alert.

A short while later, her food arrived, she thanked the waitress, and it was only as she started eating did she realise just how hungry she was. The food felt warm in her belly, and she savoured every mouthful, letting the textures and flavours dance on her palette and rejuvenate her.

Once Jane was finished, she just sat there, letting her body take in the food, and drank the rest of her coffee. When the waitress came to clear the table, she asked: "Do you know where the old farm is?"

"The old farm? Erm, yeah, sure, it's on the edge of town." The waitress replied.

"Which way?"

The waitress hesitated before she spoke, "Right out of here, to the end of the road, then it's the left just before the end, follow the road, and you'll come to it."

"Great, cheers." Jane put the money on the table as she slid out from the booth and left the diner.

The money she had used to pay for breakfast was all but the last of what she had. She had around two dollars left in her pocket, and that wouldn't get her far. She went back to the office, changed again into her more comfortable clothes, collected the rest of her things, and locked the door for the last time as she left. She loaded up the Ranger and set off looking for the farm and the empty house that was somewhere near it.

It took her a while, but she found it. First, she found the old farm, the directions the waitress gave – seemingly vague at the time – were accurate. Then all she had to do was drive around until she found the empty house. The streets were almost identical, and each house was beautifully presented to the world. She eventually found it, it had a 'FOR SALE' sign hammered into the lawn, and the gentle breeze of the day was causing it to sway slightly.

She had come prepared. She had got hair clips and things from the shop to make herself another lock pick. She parked up on the drive of the house and picked her way into the back door. It took longer than it should have, but it eventually gave in. She unloaded the Ranger of her things – It was only a couple of bags – and then drove the truck and parked it at the old farm. Now she knew where she was going; it was only a ten-minute walk to cut back to the house.

Once back inside, she locked the door, and the first thing she did was go upstairs and turn the shower on. It took a second, but water came out, a dribble at first, but then it picked up to full. She breathed a sigh of relief that it hadn't been cut off. She undressed and stood under the warm water, just letting it run down her body.

27

The computer monitor hit the wall and smashed into pieces. Mister Knight shouted a curse at it to try and get his frustrations out. Mister Wells was standing in front of his desk, trying to remain calm.

"Are you fucking kidding me?" Knight growled, sitting back behind his desk.

"No, Sir, we still don't have her."

"How is this fucking possible?" Knight shouted. "It's one fucking girl!"

"Yes, Sir, but…"

"No! No, no buts. I don't care. You find her, and you kill her."

"Yes, Sir, my unit tracked the truck again last night and fanned out the surrounding area. One of our men didn't report back, and we haven't been able to locate him."

"So, she's taken out two of you?"

"Yes, it's possible, Sir."

"That's ridiculous. What's wrong with you people? It's one woman, you have a whole unit of men, and you still can't get her."

"Sir, she is highly trained and…"

"So are you!" He bellowed, spit flying from his mouth as he rose again from his chair.

"Yes, Sir, but she is no ordinary soldier. She is trained. That was the point of her."

"And the point of you is to keep them in check," he turned and paced back and forth. "You're making me look like a dick. You're making me look stupid. Am I stupid?"

"No, Sir."

"Do I look stupid to you?"

"No, Sir."

"Then why are you trying to make me look stupid?"

"I'm not, Sir."

"Find her. I don't care how. Find her now!"

"Sir, as you know, we are limited. We can't be seen just walking around the town. They will get suspicious. They will have questions, and we're not supposed to even be there."

"If you haven't found and neutralised her in twenty-four hours, I don't give a shit if it's daytime, I don't give a fuck if the god damn sun is shining the most shine it has ever fucking shined, I couldn't care less if the entire town is out on the streets watching you. You find her."

"Yes, Sir. Understood."

"Because if you don't, I will have to report this to our investors, and they were very adamant about it being kept under wraps. I can deal with the army trying to get up my arse. I don't want to have to deal with them."

"Yes, Sir."

"So, what are you still doing here? Go find her." Knight waved his arms in a motion to dismiss him.

With that, Wells turned and left the office.

Mister Knight sat back behind his desk and slammed his fist into it.

"Fucking dick."

28

Jane spent the rest of the day looking through the files on the employees on the laptop. She read and re-read them. She had a vague idea of where some of the places were but didn't know the geography that well. Two lived in Willow Creek, though, and one a few towns over, she figured only a couple of hours away. She would start with the ones here and then move on.
She circled back to the file she had decided would be her first target and once again looked through, it was for:

Dr Martin Reece

Doctor Reece was not a face she remembered. She didn't meet a lot of the scientists face to face. The most she knew was when they gathered around her while she was being operated on or in the background of some viewing gallery when they were running drills.
It didn't matter, though; his name was on the list. It was his time.
There were still a few hours left before she wanted to move, so she laid down on the floor and got some sleep.

The dream took her. It started out as just her, running around in pitch black. She didn't even feel she was walking on anything solid; she was just running and running, no matter which direction she turned or how fast she ran. She was panicked, looking for a way out, searching desperately for anything to cling on to. She was sweating, and her heart was pounding. She felt like she would never escape. Then there was salvation, a light faint in the distance, but it was a goal; she ran as fast as she could. It felt like it took forever, but eventually, she made it, and as she pushed through, the light blinded her. It took her a moment to get her bearings, letting her eyes re-adjust to the bright light from the darkness.

She was standing in an alleyway, it looked familiar, and she tried to place it. Then she saw John stumble into view, and it became clear that she was watching his death again.

A loud crack was heard, and the bullet hit him, identically to how it had before. Once again, he slumped to the floor. She wouldn't allow this to happen again, she tried to run to him, but she felt sluggish, slow, tired in her dream. Then she saw the soldier appear; only, it wasn't the soldier, it was the shadow man. The darkness was enveloping him once again, writhing and moving around his body like a living organism, rising like steam from his figure and not allowing her a chance to make out any of his features, because he didn't have any.

Jane knew what was coming, and fear paralyzed her. The shadow man would take him. He would pick him up and take him away. She couldn't let that happen. She screamed, but no sound came out. She screamed and shouted at the top of her voice for him to run, to just get up and run, but it was like she had been muted, and she couldn't get a single sound to leave her lips. She tried to move, but once again, she couldn't. She willed her limbs to act, to allow her to save him, but it seemed she was like a statue, cemented to this spot, doomed to watch but unable to intervene.

The shadow man reached down, took John by the wrist, and lifted him up with inhuman strength; it was like John was made of paper. This time though, the shadow man didn't pick him up and put him over his shoulder as once John was on his feet, they both turned to face Jane.

She felt her body release her and she ran, she could do it this time!

Every step Jane took, she felt she was the same distance away, John and the shadow man were walking slowly towards her now, and with every step, the buildings around them started to crack, break and crumble. Everything around them was falling apart, the buildings collapsing, the alley floor was cracking and falling apart behind them as they made their way towards each other, even the sky seemed to be fading.

John stepped away from the shadow man, moving towards her, she could do it, she could save him, he opened his mouth:

Help me.

Now he seemed to be melting. His skin seemed to be pouring from his body, then, when he was only nerves and muscle, that started pouring away too. She screamed at him, tried to push her body to reach him, to touch him, to hold him, to save him.

Help me.

She was getting closer, but now he was just a skeleton, his legs breaking as he crumbled to dust in front of her. He reached out his bone hand to her, she reached for him, but just as they were about to touch, his hand fell apart, and then so did the rest of him.

She stood there, shock on her face. She looked up at the shadow man, who just blended into the darkness that was taking over the scene once again. The buildings had all but gone, and the night was now empty of stars. The shadow man started coming towards her, this was new, and she was panicking, she tried to back away, but now he was running, and she was moving with slow, laboured movements backwards, what would happen when he reached her?

He seemed to scream as he approached, a high-pitched sound that hurt her ears, louder as he came at her. He looked to be flying towards her, and just as he was about to touch her, she woke up.

She woke with a start. She was breathing heavily and had been sweating. Her t-shirt was soaked. She looked around, looking for the man who now haunted her dreams, but no one was there. She put her head in her hands and rocked slightly on the floor, trying to get rid of the images that taunted her when she closed her eyes.

She shook herself off, tried to push it to the back of her mind, tried to move it aside so as not to allow it to cloud her thoughts of what she would do.

Whatever was causing it, though, whoever this 'Shadow Man' was, clearly it was something to do with her subconscious. John, she understood – as much as it hurt to relive it – but what was it about the children from before?

Did I have children? She wondered – a problem for another day.

One thing the dream had done, though, through reliving the events, had once again made her angry and made her resolved to make sure everyone paid.

Starting tonight.

It was getting dark now, and people should be arriving home soon if they haven't already. She grabbed what she needed, put them in her pockets and left the house. She started walking to the first address on her list.

29

It took her longer than Jane had expected. The night was quiet, but there was a strong wind that blew through the streets. She had to plan her route to her destination carefully, but thankfully, there was only one time she needed to duck into cover to allow a jeep full of soldiers to drive past.

It was a clear night, and the stars shone overhead like diamonds illuminating the black night. The moon looked big and bold, like a silent guardian watching over the earth, making sure everything was as it should be.

Jane arrived at the house just after midnight. It was easy enough to find. The nicely laid out grid of streets and the numbered plaques on most doors allowed her to follow a path almost directly there.

The house looked much like all the others. It was a two-storey, white building with a square of lawn at the front with flower beds around the edges, through the middle was a narrow paved pathway that led to the steps up to the porch area, which had a waist-high wooden border with a pattern carved out and painted white to match the house. The porch was a couple of steps deep to the front door. A planter and a stone statue of a lion on each side of the door marked the entrance.

Running alongside was a driveway that went all the way past the side of the house to a large garage set back at the end of the garden. There wasn't a gate or anything to block access, and she walked down and into the back of the property, looking for the best access point.

The garage was a stand-alone building, with a large access door the width of the front that rolled up mechanically to allow the car access to the space, and at the side was a small door for the occupant to enter and exit.

She picked the lock for the side access door, it took a while, and she feared the impromptu lock picks weren't going to last long, but eventually, she heard the last tumbler fall, and she opened it up and went inside.

Inside the garage was a Volvo parked in the centre, an older model, maybe ten years or so, but it looked to be in good condition. There was a workbench at the back, with racks of tools hanging above it on the wall. She looked through the drawers, found a roll of duct tape and some other loose items. She took the duct tape and a pair of secateurs from the rack, turning them over in her hand. She smiled.

She left the garage and went to the house's back door; it was quiet inside, and all the lights were off. She worked the lock until it clicked, then she slowly eased the handle down and opened the door, slid inside, and pulled it closed behind her. There was no alarm in the house; the only sound came from the wind howling around outside.

She took a moment to let her eyes adjust, scanning the room she was in. It looked to be a utility room, there was a washer and dryer under the counter along the right side, and a washing basket and detergent were on the top. She moved further into the house, through the door at the other end, and entered a kitchen – dining area. There were all the usual appliances and an island in the middle of the kitchen space. Everything was white, from the worktops to the cupboard fronts, and the floor was laminate with a pattern on it. She placed the duct tape and secateurs on the island. At the other end of the room was a small wooden four-seater table with chairs. She moved through, keeping quiet, listening for any sound he had heard her, but none came, so she continued moving forward. The next room she found herself in was the living room. It was carpeted with a little sofa aimed towards a small TV on a stand. A large bay window looked out onto the porch and then the road, and to her right, as she walked in were the stairs that led to the second floor. She made her way upstairs, the carpet cushioning her steps. She was aware of the risk of creaky floorboards. Her muscle memory kicked in, and she kept to the sides, knowing that the highest risk is in the middle of the step, the part with the most wear, the part that takes the most weight. She reached the top of the stairs and searched the landing for where the bedroom – the most logical place he would be – was situated.

There were three bedrooms and a bathroom, and they all had their doors open.

She moved silently, like a big cat on a hunt, testing each step before committing, her eyes constantly moving to make sure that there were no hidden surprises. She figured he would be in the master bedroom at the front of the house, so she aimed for that room first. She waited at the door, waiting for something to surprise her, but nothing did. There was only the calm of the night, with the wind rustling the trees outside. She peered inside the room and saw the bed. The door wasn't open enough for her just to walk in, so slowly, painfully, she inched it further open, involuntarily holding her breath as she did so, but it didn't squeak, and she was able to open it enough to get inside. She moved up to the bed and looked down at the man asleep inside it. He was lying on his side, facing her direction. His breathing was deep and rhythmic; he had no idea she was standing over him.

Two thoughts crossed her mind:
Kill him and leave.
Make him feel it before she ended his life.
She chose option two for no reason other than it would make her feel better to project her pain onto someone else.

Jane left the room and quickly scanned the other bedrooms; they were empty and mostly seemed to be used for just storage as boxes and items were laid about all over the place. She went back downstairs, she didn't try to stay silent, but she also didn't make a point of being as loud as possible – if he heard anything, his natural reaction would be to investigate first, especially if he were sleepy, and she would deal with him then – she grabbed a chair from the table and carried it upstairs and put it in the spare room overlooking the back garden. She heard him stir, but when she checked on him, he was still sleeping. He had just rolled over. She went back and retrieved her tape and secateurs and was walking back upstairs when she heard a noise, the bedroom door opened all the way, and a man was standing in the opening. His hand up against his face, wiping his eyes as he tried to wake his body up enough to see what was going on. Jane reached the top of the stairs, dropped her items from her hands and stood in front of him, waiting for the recognition to sink in. It took a moment, but the shock and surprise were apparent on his face, even in the low light. First, it was that someone was in his house at all, then he realised who it was, and that's when the real fear set in.

"Hello, Doctor Reece," she said. Then she punched him hard, and he fell to the floor.

She dragged him into the backroom, lifted him onto the chair. His skin was warm from being in bed, and he was only wearing boxer shorts. She used the duct tape to secure his wrists and ankles to the chair, then she went back downstairs and got a chair for herself. She placed it down and sat opposite him, looking at him as he sat with his head slumped. The feelings began once again rising through her as she thought of John in that alleyway. She pictured the same procedures that she had had, only this time it was like she was floating above it all, watching it happen to him, imagining how it must have been. The injections, the hypnosis, the mind-destroying procedures, the brain surgeries, the fluids, and God knows what else pumped into his – and her – body.

At its peak, she wanted to skin Reece alive, to try to find ways to subject him – and all the others on the list – to similar things to what they had done to them. It spiked in her mind, and in her anger, she slapped Reece hard across the face.

The shock woke him up, and he looked around when he realised he couldn't move, then his eyes found Jane, and the fear was easy to read across his face.

"Welcome back," she said.

30

The truth of the matter was that Doctor Martin Reece
didn't know anything.

He knew he didn't know anything; he was a low-level
guy who wasn't much more than a helper in reality, and
as such, he wasn't privy to anything worth knowing.

But now, somehow, he was taped to a chair, with Jane
Doe sitting opposite him. His brain couldn't work out
how this was happening; he had gone to bed as usual,
he had heard something that had woke him up. When
he had got up to look, he had seen someone in his
house – that was a shock – then his vision had cleared,
and he had realised who it was – that was when the fear
set in – he was about to speak, shout, scream, anything.
Then she had hit him.

Then he was woken by a shock, and Jane Doe was
sitting opposite him. This wasn't a dream; this was a
living nightmare.

She got up, picked up some secateurs from the floor
next to her, lifted the little finger on his left hand and
placed it between the blades.

She hadn't even asked him anything. Why hadn't she
asked him anything?

He would tell her everything he knew, but she wasn't
asking anything.

The look in her eye…

Oh God.

31

She sat there for a moment, just looking at him. Doctor Martin Reece was scared – he should be – and as he looked around, she watched him, then his eyes found her and opened wide as he let out a soft gasp.

He was secured to the chair, and after a moment of just looking at him, she slowly got up, the darkness shrouded most of her in shadows, but the moon caught her face. Picking up the secateurs from the floor as she did so, she moved around to his left side and slid his little finger from his left hand in-between the blades.

"No! No, please, please don't!" He begged, his eyes darting back and forth from her face to his finger.

She closed the grip and started clamping down, his skin cut, and blood trickled down, then dripped onto the carpet.

His face grimaced and contorted with pain:

"Please, ah, ow, argh… please stop!" He pleaded, "I'll tell you everything!"

She stopped, saw the relief wash over his face as he let his body relax. The cut wasn't even that deep.

"Everything?"

He nodded. "Yes, everything, please, just please don't hurt me."

"The thing is," she said, tapping the secateurs in the palm of her hand, "I don't want you to."

"Wha – What? What do you mean? I can…I can tell you about the programme, what I know of it anyway, and I will, I'll tell you."

He was sweating and twitching nervously.

"I have the files I need to answer any questions I may have. Well, enough anyway."

"What don't you know? I'll tell you. I'll tell you it all, I swear, I promise!"

"What's my name?"

"Jane, Jane Doe."

"Wrong." She put the secateurs on the chair and moved back to his finger, gripping it in her hand. "That's the name I was given; no one is actually called 'Jane Doe'. It's the name they give to unidentified bodies that they find murdered or washed up somewhere."

She forced his finger back and broke it. Reece yelled out in pain, twice, and tears streamed down his face. He urinated himself.

"So, I'll ask again, what's my name?" She gripped the next finger along.

"No. No, please, I don't know, Ok? I don't. All I know is what the file said. I'm a nobody really, basically an intern to the programme, I…I was just recruited as support…support staff, I swear. I swear, I honestly don't know anything more."

"Shame." She broke the next finger, and he screamed out again.

"How… how are you here?" He asked through deep, laboured breaths once he had stopped screaming.

"I walked." She answered abruptly.

"No, I, I…I heard you and John were no longer viable and, and…" He didn't finish the sentence. He thought better of it.

"…And…" She prompted, pulling his middle finger up and gripping it. He paused, trying to get the courage to speak, she applied a small amount of weight to his finger, and he tensed.

"…Killed." He finished, his voice low, barely above a whisper, a prominent tone of shame in his voice.

"They tried." She said. "They got John, or whatever his name actually was."

"I'm sorry," Reece said, tears rolling down his face. He began sobbing. "I know how much it hurts to lose someone."

"I lost everyone!" She shouted and broke the middle finger. Another shout of agony rang out from Reece, filling the house.

"You know nothing of this!" She growled through gritted teeth.

"I know enough," he replied through the pain. "I lost my wife two years ago, and I would give anything… to find the bastard… who was driving that car… and break every, bone, in his body, then kill him." His breath was short. He was speaking in short bursts through the waves of pain. Jane sat down opposite him. "So, maybe you do."

"I get it, and I'm sorry. I, I…I honestly thought you guys, you had signed…signed and agreed to this. I, I thought it was what you wanted. Please. Ju – just make it quick."

Her head tilted slightly, "What happened to answering all my questions?"

"I don't, I don't kn – know anything, and noth – nothing I can say will stop, will stop this from happening." He was getting whiter by the second. He was sweating, the moonlight causing it to shine on his skin, his breaths were getting shorter and shorter, and he was starting to slur his words more and struggling to keep his eyes open. His body was nearing shock. He wasn't trained for this, and his body had probably never experienced anything like this physical pain before.

"You're right." She said.

"I, I, I, know," he breathed, "you just wa – want revenge for Ya – Ya – Yankee."

"You don't get to call him that!" She roared as she leapt from her seat, striking him across the face. The chair toppled, and he fell to the floor. She knelt beside him and punched him again, and again, raising his head and slamming it to the floor. Rage and fury and anger fuelling her fists, all reason and sense were removed as she kept punishing him. Her mind flashed through images of John, the smile, the laugh, the training, his death.

When she finally stopped, she fell back onto the floor, panting hard. Her knuckles were covered in blood. So was the carpet, so was Reece.

Jane checked his pulse.

He was dead.

She sat back, elbows on her knees, head in her hands and just looked at him, what was left of his face, the mess she had caused. She had a moment of what she thought may have been regret, but it didn't stay. He had to die. They all have to die.

He's with his wife now.

It was more than could be said for her and John. She was still alone.

She went back to his bedroom and found his phone. It was locked, so she went back into the room and used Reece's fingerprint to unlock it. She changed the security to a password to take it with her, and it be of use. She grabbed the phone charger and duct tape and grabbed the keys for his car on her way out. Then she went to the garage, used the fob to open the large door. It was loud and rattled as it retracted. It sounded like thunder, even over the sound of the howling wind. She got in the Volvo, reversed it down the drive and set off down the street.

There was still more work to be done tonight.

32

The Volvo drove nice enough, it was a smooth ride, and the engine pulled well. Jane wasn't a car person – at least she didn't think she was – so she didn't really care as long as it worked. She had a rough idea of her direction but used the navigation on the phone to help guide her in. She found the house. It was practically identical to the one Reece lived in and was about a ten-minute drive away, on the other edge of town. It was an easy drive as there was little on the roads in the sleepy town at that time of night, and she didn't come across any soldiers.

Her adrenaline was pumping, and she had to try to control herself from shaking. She felt she had done it a thousand times before, but this was different. She had killed an unarmed man, a non-combatant. The rules had changed now. There was no going back.

She pulled up a few houses down and looked up at the address. This was home to Doctor Victoria Simms. The next name on the list.

From the outside, it looked the same as the house Reece lived in, same style structure, same side driveway running the length of the house to the back, but this one had a larger front garden but no porch, and the path led straight to the front door.

Jane knew she was in there alone; in her file, she had seen that she lived here during the week and would often fly home to Chicago to be with her husband and two children at the weekend.

It was a weekday, and there was a light on in the front of the house. She was up late.

Or just left the light on,

Time to find out.

She repeated her routine from Reece's house, but as she walked down the side past the windows, she glanced in, seeing if she could see any signs of Simms. She couldn't.

She carried on round the back to a door that was almost identical to the one she had entered through already earlier that night.

She picked the lock, but in the process, she bent one of the makeshift picks and knew that she would need to get something new to use once again. It took her a while, but she gained entry, gently pulling the handle down and slipping inside.

The room was much the same as the utility space in Reece's house; only this was much more sparse, the appliances were a lot older.

Probably takes most of the washing and things home at the weekend, she thought as she moved past them to the door. This would get her into the kitchen area, and from there, she would need to be quiet. She turned the handle, and as soon as the door popped off the catch, two bullets exploded through the door, forcing her to drop to the floor.

They had penetrated the door like it was paper and had gone over her shoulder, a millimetre over, and they would have hit her, a few more, and they would have killed her.

She looked up at the door, looking at the angle of the exit points. If the kitchen were the same layout as Reece's, then she would be by the island in the kitchen, only a few paces behind the door. She waited to see if anyone would come through, but they didn't. She looked around at what she could find, there were some old pans and kitchenware in one of the ground-level cupboards, and she grabbed a frying pan. She got up but kept low, anticipating another round of bullets. She needed to find out where the shooter – she assumed Simms – was, so she banged the pan on the side, a moment passed, and another three bullets spat through the door, this time over slightly. If she had fired there first, Jane would have been killed.

But now she knew where she was, and Jane took her chance. She crashed through the door and threw the pan at the shooter – it was Simms, she was wearing tracksuit bottoms and a vest top – the pan hit her and threw her off balance, the gun falling from her grip as she stumbled back.

Jane kept the momentum and ran into her, taking them both to the ground. Simms clawed at her face, forcing Jane to use her arms to protect her eyes, then there was a knee in her side, and she was forced back, then a foot in her stomach that was enough to wind her and give Simms enough space to scramble up and grab the gun, she aimed it at Jane but she pushed herself into a slide and dove behind the island before a shot rang out, hitting the cupboard door that was behind her.

"It's too late," Simms panted, standing up. "I called them when I saw you skulk past the windows; they're coming."

"Who are?"

"The programme," she said, trying to catch her breath, "the containment unit that's been looking for you, they're on their way."

"That's Sig P238, right?" Jane asked, getting herself into a crouching position.

"I think so," Simms replied, confused by the randomness of the question.

"Good."

"Why?"

"Standard?"

"I think so. I just got it for protection." Simms said as she started to circle the central island. Jane could hear her footsteps and the direction from where she was coming from, so she mirrored it to keep distance, and what she needed was at the other end of the kitchen side.

"Just come out, I don't want to have to kill you," her voice was now shaky; Simms had probably never shot anyone before, and how she scratched and fought meant that she wasn't well trained.

"You won't," Jane said, "not with that anyway,"

"What do you mean?"

"The Sig Sauer P238 standard magazine holds six bullets," she said, still moving closer to the other end.

Once she was there, she got ready before continuing, "…and count 'em, you've had your six."

Jane came up from behind the island, grabbing a knife from the butcher's block on the side. Simms was looking at the gun, trying to work out if she was right. By the time she looked back up, Jane had thrown the knife across the kitchen, over the island. It hit her square in her heart, and the momentum forced her to take a step backwards before dropping down onto the floor.

Jane walked around the island, mentally kicking herself for not bringing the rifle. She should have. She let her emotions of wanting to inflict as much pain as possible cloud her rational mind of the easiest way to kill someone.

Stupid and egotistic.

She stood over Doctor Victoria Simms's body, watching the blood pool out from her onto the linoleum floor, the knife still protruding like a victory flag of a mountaineering exhibition.

She wanted to search the house and was making her way to the stairs when she heard vehicles approaching and tires squealing as they came to a quick stop.

"Shit," she breathed to herself and turned back to the kitchen, there was a loud knock at the door, and just as she reached the kitchen, there came the crash of the front door being kicked off its hinges and boots entering the house. She hid behind the doorway, looked over at the exit to the utility space, sizing up if she could make it, but then the door opened, and a soldier walked in.

33

The soldier entered; he was wearing the same uniform as the others. His eyes were drawn to the body on the floor, and he hadn't checked his corners. He crouched as he reached for his radio, and Jane pounced from behind the door, lashing out with her foot to kick his hand away, then she brought her knee up to his chest, but the armour took the blow, so she struck again but to the bottom of his jaw, this rocked his head backwards and forced him off balance. She reached down to grab his weapon, but he grabbed her wrist and kicked her in the side, forcing her away, and she slipped on the blood and fell to the floor. She got to her knees, and the soldier rose to his feet, he reached down to grab his side-arm, and Jane pushed off, using the blood to lubricate the floor, she closed the gap and put her foot out, connecting with his knee, forcing the kneecap to crack and shatter as it was forced to bend the wrong way. The soldier cried out and dropped. The only part of their faces exposed with the helmet was the mouth, so she lashed out with an elbow once again connecting with his jaw, knocking him out.

She heard movement in the other room, grabbed his rifle from the floor and laid on the other side of the body. A soldier entered, weapon ready, but it took him a split second to assess the situation. There were three bodies motionless on the floor.

Jane leaned up and shot him twice in the chest armour and once in the face under the mask. He slumped to the floor as he died.

She scrabbled to get up, the blood on her hands and boots making it more challenging, she had blood down her face and side from where she had slipped in Doctor Simms blood, but once up, she made for the back exit. She heard the door open again and took cover behind the island as bullets shredded the cupboards above her. *"We've got her. Over."* A soldier reported. Jane knew she was trapped; the second she made for the door, she would be killed, but if she stayed too long, then she would get surrounded and then killed.

She looked around and saw the frying pan on the floor, figuring it was her only chance. The kitchen area was smaller in this house and walled off from the dining room. If she could make it hard to get in, then she could buy herself time. She reached and grabbed the frying pans handle, then she rested the gun on the top of the counter and blind-fired in the general direction of the soldiers, moving swiftly to throwing the pan and rising straight after it. As she rose up, she saw the pan distraction had worked; the soldier was looking at it and was just moving his gaze back when she fired, moving towards him, keeping the trigger depressed until it dry fired, and she was out of ammunition.

The soldier was dead long before she ran out of bullets, but anger kept her finger depressed. She pushed his body to the door to cause a block, there was movement on the other side, and a force hit the door, trying to open it. She grabbed the rifle and the side-arm, placing it at the small of her back and then turned and made for her exit. She moved into the utility space just as the back door opened, and she fired instinctively, aiming for the head. There were two soldiers outside. One was lying on the floor as she moved through, his eye visor shattered, and blood covered his face. The other was a few steps back. She raised and fired at him, hitting his armour. She dropped as he returned fire, the bullets missing her by luck more than by judgement, and she fired again, only this time at his knees. She found her marks, and his legs went from under him as he howled out in pain into the night. She ran to him, kicked his weapon away, looked down and asked, "How many more are there?"

He didn't respond, his hand went to his back-up, and she batted it away, taking it from his holster and pointing it at him.

"How many?" She asked again, kneeling next to him and pushing the barrel onto his knee cap.

He screamed in agony before finally relenting through gritted teeth, "I don't know."

She shot him in the exposed stomach that was showing as his armour had ridden up as he fell. He cried out once again and tried to reach for his radio. She took it from him and threw it away.

"How. Fucking. Many? I won't ask you again."

"Six-man unit," he conceded through gritted teeth, "but that's only one unit... we have many, and we won't stop." He sounded defiant as he coughed up blood and spat it onto the grass.

"Thanks." She said as she removed his helmet, stood up and shot him. He stopped breathing deep, trying to control the pain. He stopped breathing altogether.

She left the body there, removed the magazines and put them in her pockets. She used the side-arm, held it in a two-handed grip, nozzle pointed downwards, ready. She went back into the house; it was silent now. The orchestra of bullets had stopped, and there was only a ringing in her ears and the dead silence of the night remaining. Even the wind seemed to have been scared away by the noise.

She moved the body blocking the door. There was no man on the other side now, and she figured he was the one who then ran around the back. She killed the man she had knocked out and moved upstairs. She kept her weapon – a Sig Sauer M18, which she believed was standard military issue for this type of unit – trained on the corners in case any surprises came her way, but now her only company was silence.

Jane searched the rooms. They were all sparse and had little to no decoration in any way, clearly just a place for Simms to rest her head close to work before going home at the weekends. But she did find a rucksack. It was black with netting on the side and front. She decanted her extra ammunition into it, keeping a clip in her lower cargo pocket for quick access.

She looked through her jewellery and found some bobby pins and hair clips. She took those, a few more items, and emptied her purse of its $200 contents, putting them in her new bag before leaving.

She walked back to the Volvo, keeping an eye out to see if anyone were coming. She was expecting police sirens and lights coming at her at any moment, but they weren't, so she got in the car and drove away before they could.

34

Back at the vacant house, Jane pulled the Volvo to the back of the drive, uprooted the 'FOR SALE' sign and took it inside.

This many of their men dead, they would stop at nothing to search now, and no point advertising, she reasoned.

Once inside, she went upstairs, into the bathroom and started the shower running. She used the toilet and undressed, looking at the blood all over her clothes. She hadn't been wearing her jacket and was grateful because now it would cover the blood-stained t-shirt. She couldn't do much about her trousers, though.

She looked at herself in the mirror; the side of her face was covered in blood, as was her hands, and up her arm. She was grateful it wasn't her blood, but she still felt weird having someone else's smeared all over her. She reached up to the mirror and ran her fingers under the reflections of her eyes, like teardrops, as the steam from the shower began to cover the glass. She shook her head, wiped it off and climbed into the shower.

For a while, she just let the water run over her, covering her body, cleansing her of the night. She didn't have any actual soap, but she used the water to wipe off the blood. As she stood there, her thoughts wandered, first to John, then to the family of Doctor Simms; they would never see her again, and thinking how that would make them feel, made her feel the same about John.

She reasoned she would understand if they ever came looking for her out of revenge. But now those feelings of missing him were once again camped in her mind, and she couldn't shake them. She ended up sitting in the shower, her knees tucked up to her chest, arms around them, holding herself and her head buried, crying, her tears mixing into water that ran over her.

35

The following morning Mister Wells was once again stood in front of Mister Knight, and he was sure if he had anything else he could throw, he probably would have.

"...this is a fucking disaster!" Knight finished saying.

"Yes, Sir," Wells said, his deep voice calm. "But it's not over yet, I have dispatched team two, and they will find her."

"That's what you said about the first lot!" Knight shouted.

"Yes, Sir, she is proving harder than I..."

"It's one fucking girl!" Knight cut in, "one stupid girl who has shit, no weapons, out by herself, wandering around, and you still can't get her! How are you trying to resolve this? Hmm? By inviting her to a god damn tea party!"

"No, Sir, she is elusive and well trained."

"You're supposed to be well trained. It's your job to keep them in line! What use are you to me if you can't do that? I should just put you in the hole we dug for her!"

"No, Sir, I can...I will rectify this. As per your instructions, we are sweeping the town now; we will find her."

"She has killed two of our people, TWO! In one night!" Knight rose from his chair, his face was going red, and he wiped some spit from his top lip.

"Yes, Sir, but we knew that may be a possibility. That's why we moved everyone."

"How did she find out where they lived?" He asked, calming down a little bit.

"We don't know yet, but we are searching security footage. She must have done as you predicted and gone back to the facility. Maybe she found something and is using that. We haven't got anyone there yet, so we haven't done a full inventory."

"Fine, find out what she knows, where she got her information from. Maybe we can track it back to her."

"Yes, Sir."

"Leave now. I have things to do."

"Yes, Sir."

"Keep me informed of any developments."

"Yes, Sir"

Mister Wells left the room, and Mister Knight sat back in his chair and leaned back. He would have to make the call now. The military knew there was a problem and had basically washed their hands with the whole project, denying it ever took place with their approval – years of work down the toilet. Knight was on his own. He picked up the phone and dialled the number, it was answered on the third ring.

"Hello," the voice said.

"Hello, this is Knight."

"Who?"

"Daniel Knight, of Knight Securities."

There was a whirring noise, and then the voice came back.

"OK…how can we help?"

"The project I'm working with you on has got a problem; one of the subjects has escaped and gone native. I'm tracking it down as we speak, but it has proved elusive and killed a few of my men, around six."

"Ok, thank you for bringing this to our attention. We will be in touch."

"No, wait…" but the line went dead. "Fuck."

Elsewhere, the problem was reported higher up. The Chairman of the committee listened as he was told of the problem, then at the end of the conversation, he said three words.

"Get me Leo."

Then he put the phone down.

36

Thirty minutes later, the man known as 'Leo' was sitting at the long table in the meeting room. Most of the time when he was in here, there were twelve others, with the thirteenth sat at the head chair. Today was one of the times he was here by himself.

He sat looking out the large window that ran the length of the entire wall, looking out at the city, then there was a click, and a shutter rolled down, robbing the room of natural light.

Leo turned and watched the man walk in. The man was tall, just over six foot five, and had the figure of a man who enjoyed the finer things in life. Good food, good wine, lots of sun. His grey hair was covered in black dye in an attempt to still present as young, dynamic, and dangerous. He was in his sixties and wore a slate grey suit with a black tie. The Chairman took his seat at the head of the table.

"Thank you for coming." He said, his accent strong and every word he delivered was confident and precise, like his words were the most important ever spoken. In this room, they were.

Leo said nothing.

"I have called you in today because we have a developing problem, and I want you to take care of it."

"Ok," Leo said. He was from the south and had a drawl as he spoke. He wore a brown suit with a white shirt.

His tie was alligator print, and his boots were actual alligator skin.

"One of our projects has taken a turn and needs cleaning up. I want you to do it."

"Ok," he said, hesitation in his voice.

"Problem?"

"Oh, no, of course not, I can handle it, I just woulda thought this would be more Aries field."

"It would be, but he is still in England, looking into the man who killed Gemini," The Chairman paused, "do you have a problem with how I organise and assign things?"

Leo shook his head, "no, no, of course not, Sir, whatever you need."

"Good. The programme is based in the military station based on the edge of Willow Creek. You will start there."

"Yes, Sir. May I ask what it's about?"

"You will be hunting down and eliminating a rogue asset that has escaped the programme. The programme is called The Phoenix Initiative and is developing enhanced soldiers for the military."

"The military?"

"Yes, we were able to get onto the programme as shadow investors many years ago. We were poised to take the successful asset procedure once they had perfected how to do it. They have been feeding back results so we could use it for ourselves."

"Ok."

"This is for your ears only, you will be given the rest of the information after, but that's all for now. Track it down and kill it."

"Ok, Sir, but wouldn't it make more sense to capture it?"

The Chairman rose from his seat, Leo leaned back involuntarily, instantly regretting his question. The Chairman walked down the table and stopped behind him, putting his hands on Leo's shoulders.

"I don't want an uncontrollable one, and I don't remember ever needing to explain myself to you."

"No, no, Sir. You don't."

Leo had a memory of a man who had sat in a chair a few down from his about a year or so ago. He had failed, and had ended up with a letter opener in his neck.

"I'll make arrangements and leave immediately," Leo said.

"Good, this is now your responsibility. Whatever happens, it will come back on you."

"Yes, Sir."

The man known as Leo was a strong, well-trained man. He was ex-special forces and had spent a few years working for different agencies before being approached by the Committee. In every room he felt confident and in control, except that one.

He left the room and made his preparations for travel to Willow Creek.

37

Doctor Conners finished work early and went home as fast as he could. Like most of the senior scientists on the programme, he had been called into a meeting that afternoon and told of what had happened.
Like everyone else, he was shocked and scared, as the thought of Jane killing people involved in the project made him sick to his stomach. He wondered if maybe he had been wrong to try and keep them on as subjects if this is what they were going to do? Perhaps the whole programme needed to be shut down?
He didn't say any of this. He just kept it to himself and left as soon as possible.

He drove his Citroën home as fast as he could, he was sure he passed at least two speed cameras going above the limit, but he didn't care. Right now, he just needed to get home. It took him a couple of hours from the secondary facility, even at the higher speeds he pushed the car to do. He pulled into the driveway and jumped out of the car, fumbling for his keys as he ran to the front door, dropping them on the driveway. His wife opened the door, the light from inside bathing her in a glow like an angel stood before him as the relief of seeing her face washed over him. He picked up his keys, and looking over his shoulder, went inside.
The warm comfort of the house that normally welcomed him felt wrong tonight. Just being in their

home – the one place they should feel safe – was dangerous.

"We need to pack you a bag, and you need to leave," Conners said, heading straight upstairs to the bedroom.

"What?" Molly replied, confusion in her tone as she followed him upstairs, "Rich, what's happened?"

"I can't say right now," he responded as he dragged the travel case from the top shelf of the wardrobe in the bedroom, putting it on the bed. "Just get Elise, pack a bag and go stay with your sister."

"What? No," she grabbed his arms and turned him to face her, "take a breath, and tell me what's wrong." She said, calming reassurance in her voice; she had a way of doing that to him.

"Molls, there's no time. You're in danger. Elise is in danger. You can't be around me for a while."

"I don't understand…" she began.

"I don't have time, look, the project I'm working on, the one I can't tell you about…"

"Yeah…"

"Someone is killing the people that are working on it, and they won't hesitate to kill everyone in this house when they decide it's my turn, now," he took a breath, held her hands and calmed himself for a moment, "please, Molls, you and Elise are the only thing that matters, I can't lose you. Please, please go and stay with your sister, I'll call you once it's all sorted out, and then I'm done with all this."

"Done?" She questioned, "all you talk about is how important this is, how whatever it is you're doing is to keep Elise safe."

"Yes," he closed his eyes and dropped his head, took a moment, then lifted it up again and opened his eyes, "but keeping the world safe doesn't matter if you're not in it."

He turned away and started packing the bag.

"Please," he pleaded, "please, just trust me on this." She moved into him, took his hands, and put them around her, he put his head down on her chest, and she kissed the top of his head. She cupped his face in her hands and lifted it up, kissing him softly on the lips.

"Ok," she whispered. "Ok. I'll get Elise ready…But please, please stay safe, and come back to us."

"I promise." He said as his voice broke and a tear ran down his cheek.

Less than an hour later, Conners was watching his wife and daughter drive away, knowing there was a genuine chance that he would never see them again. Even once they were out of his sight, he still looked at where they had been in the distance, pretending in his mind's eye he could still see them.

He went back inside and walked into the living room. He picked up a photo from the small table next to the couch of the three of them, smiling for the camera in a field with blue sky above them.

He knew if he were going to survive this, he would need help. He knew of only one place he could get it with no questions asked or investigations into what had happened.

Conners grabbed a small bag of stuff; every noise he heard, he froze, thinking it was her, coming for him, but every time nothing happened, so he carried on as fast as he could.

He knew of these people from when they had been approached about becoming involved with the programme. They had originally tried to recruit members from them, amongst others, before they decided to rely on volunteers.

Once he had a bag packed, he got in his car and drove. When he was out on the motorway, he dialled the number.

He called The Company.

PART TWO

38

The thing he hated most about casinos wasn't the noise, the constant ringing and music from the slot machines barraging his ears with the wall of noise, even at the other end of the building, where he was sitting. Nor was it the lights, the artificial white lighting that hung from the ceilings. Even when they tried to make the place look fancy by using faux chandeliers, even when coupled with the strobing, flashing lights from the machines, designed to entice you in with their pretty colours, making you want to play. No, the worse thing about casinos for him was definitely the smell.

The place – not just this one, all of them – reeked with the stench of sweat and desperation; it was an assault on his senses. He was sat in a huge, enormous building that people swarmed into to try and turn their lives around, forever risking everything on a pull of the lever or believing they could beat the house. Some people played for days non-stop; you could practically see the sweat rising from them. The look in their eye as they hung on to the hope that the next pull of the lever, the next hand, the next turn of the wheel, would be the one that made them rich. Invariably it didn't, and yet, they tried again, losing more money and ending worse up off than when they started.

He detested places like this.

He was in a casino in Las Vegas called 'ZEUS'. It was a beautiful building. There was a large water fountain outside that had jets on a sequence to create shapes and patterns spraying into the air, and there was a giant statue of Zeus – or that's who he thought it was meant to be – on a large plinth in the centre of it.

Like many of the big casinos on the strip, there was a semi-circle drive up to it and a covered over valet parking area at the front to greet and take your car away for you so you could head straight in and start giving them your money – some people wouldn't see their vehicle again for days – and it was all done to make you feel special.

Agent Red – or Logan Taylor as he chose to call himself – was sat at one of the bars in the expensive part of the casino. He was 5"10 with brown eyes, dark hair and a scar in the rough shape of a crescent moon from his eyebrow round to his temple on his left eye. He was wearing a tuxedo comprising black trousers, a crisp white shirt, a deep crimson red smoking jacket with black lapels and a black bow tie. The suit was made bespoke for him and fit him perfectly. He wore Oxfords on his feet and a Breitling Superocean B20 automatic with a black dial and steel strap on his wrist.

The Zeus was in two sections, one for the tourists and the 'regulars' who just came to throw money away, and a 'VIP' section for the high spenders that preferred privacy and wanted to spend a lot of money on poker and other similar games. To get into the VIP section, you had to meet the dress code. Out front was tourist attire, but if you wanted to play at the big tables, you had to look like you belonged there.

He was watching the poker game across the floor, and one player, in particular, a woman named Mei Zhen – he believed it translated to 'Beautiful Pearl' – but she was not as alluring as the name suggested. She was part of an international group of people smugglers that used wars and famine around the world to pray on women and children who wanted to escape, promising them safe haven, but instead getting them addicted to drugs and selling them on to be used for slavery, and sex workers.

Taylor had been following her since she had arrived in America; he had flown out just before she had arrived. It seemed every few months she would visit Las Vegas, and this casino, in particular, renting the 'Presidential Suite' in the hotel that was above the casino floor for patrons to stay in. Then playing almost non-stop for a week or two, then leave and return to China.

After having watched her for a few days, seeing what she did and what would be the best way to approach his assignment, he had learned why she did it.

She was getting paid. The games were fixed. It was obvious after a while. She would only play at a few tables, and usually when they were quiet – when they weren't, the other players started losing quickly and soon left – often leaving her to play alone, and then she would proceed to win almost every hand – a lot of money. At first, he thought she was just that good; maybe she was counting cards or something similar, but it was while watching her play a few rounds of blackjack that he realised no matter what cards she had, the house would intentionally keep calling cards until they were bust. This led him to watch the other games with a closer eye, and sure enough, poker, the croupier would near enough always fold, as she put a lot of money on cards that were easy to beat.

She kept away from games of more chance – they were harder to fix – and soon, she was up over forty million dollars from when she had walked in.

After a few hours of watching, he was growing tired; he had normally used the time she was playing to sneak up to her room. He had downloaded the contents of her tablet and sent them back to The Company – the client had asked for proof of what was going on – he was now just waiting for the all-clear, and he would be back on a flight to England within twenty-four hours.

Maybe once it was classified as a completed assignment, he would play a couple of hands himself, make a mini-vacation of it before he headed home?

He doubted it.

Mei Zhen rose from her table, requiring a tray to carry the different coloured hard plastic gaming cheques that represented different amounts of money. One of her bodyguards carried it for her – she had two – and wherever she went, they went. This made it hard to get close to her, but also meant it was easy to gain access to her room and her things if her only security was always by her side – so it was a double-edged sword.

She began walking towards him at the bar. She was short, around 5"4, she had strong cheek bones, and her hair was tied up in a high ponytail. Her dress was gold and shimmered and shone in the light. It looked to be a form of sequined pattern and went down to the floor, trailing slightly behind her as she walked. It was strapped over the shoulders and was tight to her figure. She was a small, petite woman, but her eyes were a deep shade of green and held a look that, even from across the room, showed she was no shrinking violet; she would have you killed in a heartbeat. He imagined how the women and children she sold like old possessions she no longer cared for felt as they looked into her eyes.

He didn't like her.

She reached the bar, stood between the stools further down from him, and ordered herself a drink. Then she looked over at him. He casually met her eye, gave a wry smile, and went back to his drink.

She watched him for a moment, then moved up the bar and sat next to him, her bodyguards seated at a table a few feet away.

It was quieter in the VIP section at the back, behind the roped area and up the stairs to the second floor, and it only had a couple of dozen patrons playing, so it was a lot more intimate.

"I see you looking at me." She said as she slid herself onto the stool next to his, crossing her legs, exposing her thigh through the gap at the side and letting the dress fall and settle itself.

"It's hard not to," he admitted.

"I will take as a compliment," she smiled.

"Please do; it's how it was intended."

The bar tender brought her drink over.

"What's that?" Taylor asked, nodding to the drink.

"It is called 'Screwdriver'," she said, picking up the orange-coloured drink and taking a sip, "vodka and orange juice, all I drink while I am here."

"Ok," he nodded.

"What you drink?" She enquired, leaning over, moving in closer to him.

"Water." He replied, taking a sip, "just water."

She reached her hand out and introduced herself. "I am Mei Zhen."

"Pleased to meet you."

"And you are?"

He considered his options, the names he could give her, but he had been there a few times already while surveilling her, and The Company had set him up under his preferred name, Taylor, when they had set up his background to gain him access to the high stakes area. So, either she had made him and therefore already knew it, and it was a test, or it was information she could easily find.

"Taylor," he said, shaking her hand.

"Pleasure to meet you, Mister Taylor."

"May I say," he offered, "Your English is excellent."

"Thank you; I can speak many languages fluently."

"Impressive."

"How about you?"

"No, just English, and sometimes that's hard enough… You always been interested in languages? Or just travel a lot?" He enquired, trying to sound casual in asking a question he already knew the answer to.

"I travel," she replied, "for my work."

"Wow, what do you do, if you don't mind me asking?"

"Of course not; I help people relocate from countries that they would die if they stayed," she nodded slowly, shuffling on her stool to reposition herself.

"That's meaningful work. Where do they relocate to?"

"Wherever I can get them." She whispered, like the emotions had got the better of her. "I come here sometimes," she began again, "to get away from it all, to relax so I can do more."

"You need to have time for yourself. It's important," Taylor agreed, "and of course," he nodded to the tray of gaming cheques on the table between the bodyguards, "winning millions of dollars must help."

She forced a chuckle before she spoke, "It is not about money, but any money I get, I put back into my work."

"I bet you do," he forced a smile at her. Just looking at her made his skin crawl. He had images of the photos he had seen in her file of what had happened to the people she had taken while promising them a better life before they became modern slaves, beaten and raped before being moved on to have to have it happen again, then to be murdered and dumped when they are no longer of any use.

"I bet you do." He said again.

He took a big drink of his water and briefly wished it was alcoholic. He would be grateful when he could put this assignment behind him. He didn't know who had hired The Company to do this, but he hoped what he gathered would be used to arrest her, or maybe worse.

He was never generally bothered by the assignments he got. He wasn't worried about who hired him or why. He just did what he was asked, but she got under his skin and there flashed a moment where he wanted to reach out and kill her there and then.

His phone rang.

"Excuse me," he said, as he rose from his stool and walked out of ear shot, taking his Sony Xperia out of his inside jacket pocket. It was a number he knew, and once the little green circle completed and the green padlock symbol appeared, he answered, checking over his shoulder that he wasn't being listened to and spoke in a low voice, "Hello."

"Hello, it's Carol," the voice said.

"Hey, what do you have for me?"

"Client has received all relevant information and has upgraded contract to removal. Would you like to know more?"

The contract escalation seemed to mean that whoever now had the information couldn't do anything with it, or the people they reported to wouldn't. Either way, he had been given the opportunity to finish this himself.

"Yes," he said without hesitation.

"Client wants it messy, wants to send a message, think you can do that?"

"Anything specific?"

"Assassination, but no way to hide it. No poisons; she wants stabbed or shot to death. No chance of a cover-up."

"Ok, done. But I'll need you to call every police and sheriff's department and all the local and national news media, get everyone there. That way, it will give whoever less time to make it all go away. As soon as I've taken the shot, you need to be on it."

"Agreed. What if you can't get out?"

"I can take the shot far enough away. I can make sure even if they arrive before I can get away clean, they won't suspect me."

"What shall I tell the client?"

"Tell them it will be done as soon as she heads to her room later tonight. And stay active; I'll need you as soon as I'm ready to move. In five-ten minutes from now, set off the fire alarm in the Zeus."

"Ok. Bye for now."

"Bye."

Carol hung up, and he put his phone away, cleared his throat and moved back to the bar. Mei Zhen was still sat waiting for him.

"Can I have another bottle of water, please," Taylor said to the bar tender, "and a fresh glass, thank you."

"You have some water still left," Mei Zhen said, tapping the top of the glass,

"I like it fresh in the glass." He smiled back.

"You are an interesting man, Mister Taylor. You have a first name?"

"I do," he watched the bar tender take a fresh bottle of water from the fridge, "not that one, one two in from the back please," then watched as the bottles got changed, he kept his eye on it, and the glass as he brought them over,

"Can I have a bigger glass, please?" he asked, then watched as the glasses got changed and the new glass was put in front of him, a forced smile on the bar tender's face.

"Thank you very much."

"Very interesting." Mei Zhen repeated. "Tell me, what is first name?"

"Logan," Taylor said as he subtly ran his fingers around the bottle and over the cap. Once he was happy, he opened the bottle, poured a small amount into the glass, swirled it around, and let it sit.

Mei Zhen watched him as he did so.

"What you do for a job?" She asked finally.

"Securities broker," he said. "It's not fun but pays for trips to places like this, so it can't all be bad."

"You gamble?" She asked, "I never see you play."

"I only gamble on things that I know I can win."

"Then is it gamble?"

"No," he laughed, "I suppose it's not."

"Life is no fun if you do not gamble from time to time."

"I suppose it depends on the stakes."

"What you gamble on?" She asked, putting the glass up to her lips, taking a slow sip and moving in closer again.

"I suppose I gamble on the fact that if I don't do my job, bad things can happen." Taylor mused. "Or maybe life's a gamble, you do things and hope everything turns out OK, you gamble that if you do the right things you'll be rewarded," he paused, leaned in towards her, "and if you do bad things, you gamble that you don't get found out."

She smiled a big smile, showing her teeth, putting the tip of her tongue between them.

"Maybe we should carry this conversation in private?" She whispered, running the fingertip of her index finger down his arm.

"Maybe we should, but that phone call is something I have to deal with, so, maybe if you're here tomorrow, we can pick it up then?"

"I think I can be better than your phone."

She leaned in, and he tried not to recoil, then the fire alarm went off. He was grateful as the bodyguards leapt into action, springing from their seats. One piled the money cheques into a bag, the other moving and pulling Mei Zhen from her stool and ushering her away into the crowd.

Taylor got up and followed them into the crowd, blending in. As he pretended to engage in the panic, he sent a message from his phone and almost instantly, the alarm stopped. A voice came through the speaker system:

"We are sorry about that, folks, false alarm. Please head back to your seats. We will be with you shortly to take any orders you would like. Once again, false alarm, and thank you for playing at Zeus."

The floor was carpeted red with what looked like gold stars at equidistant intervals, the waist-high railings were gold to match the faux chandeliers, and the walls were white, but years of smoker's smoke had stained them.

Most of the patrons turned on their heels and went back to their games, but Taylor carried on out the front of the casino and into the night. The fresh air hit him like a wall, and he realised how cold it was outside as he handed the valet his parking ticket and watched him run down and around the building to get his car.

39

Taylor waited for his car to be brought around. He heard it before he saw it. The loud growl of the V8 rumbled as the valet brought the black Dodge Challenger around and parked in front of him. Taylor thanked him, passing a tip over as he climbed into the car and set off. He drove down the strip until he could move over to the other side and come back the way he came. The strip was wide, with four lanes on each side, plus the central divide, sidewalks, and valet parking inlets. All the casinos and buildings were set back from the road. He pulled up at the hotel-casino opposite the Zeus, thanked the valet who took his car and walked inside.

It wasn't as grand inside here; it was more of a one-stop, the kind tourists come to and never really leave for the whole trip kind of place. He walked through the lobby. There was navy blue carpet everywhere and chrome fittings and handles that showed all the handprints of those that used them. There were people sitting in the casino area, and even from the lobby, he could see the tourists in their loud shirts playing on the slot machines and the card tables. Waitresses walked around with drinks trays serving them, making sure they had no reason to get up and stop putting their hard-earned money in the machines. He approached the reception desk.

"Hi, any messages for me?"

The woman behind the counter smiled politely and asked, "What room number please?"

"2537," Taylor answered.

"Ok…" She tapped on her keyboard and then looked back up, "No, no messages."

"Thank you," Taylor smiled and moved to the elevators. Once inside, he selected the twenty-fifth floor and rode it until it pinged to signal its arrival, and the doors slid open. He walked to his room, checked no one was watching – a force of habit – swiped the key card and entered. The first thing he did was sweep the room. Taylor wasn't sure who – if anyone – knew he was here, but he swept the room anyway. It came up empty. The room was basic, with cream carpet, cream walls. There was a double bed, a TV on the wall, a table for his things under the TV. There was also a separate room to the left of the door with a sofa, a mini-fridge, and a larger TV on the wall.

He took off his smoking jacket, hung it in the wardrobe, then withdrew the large suitcase from under the double bed and placed it on top. He opened it to reveal the L115A1 sniper rifle and took the scope from its foam padding. He walked over to the window and looked through the magnification scope.

He could see into Mei Zhen's room. She was standing with her bodyguards in front of her, they looked to be arguing, she made to move past them, but one held his arm out to block her.

Good protocol, keep her contained, keep her safe.
Taylor smiled to himself.

He cleared the desk under the TV and dragged it to where he needed it to be, opening his window, so he had an unobstructed view. Then he called Carol and put it on speaker.

"How can I help?" She answered.

"It's going down; you ready?"

"When you are."

"I need everyone here ASAP."

"I know, I got this." She assured him.

As he was talking, he was assembling his sniper rifle, it didn't take long, and he was soon in position. He was laying on his belly on the table, looking through the scope down into Mei Zhen's room.

It had been difficult getting into this position, Mei Zhen usually held the top floor, and the Zeus was a taller building, but Carol had been able to hack in and cause electrical faults that meant the casino hotel moved her. Carol had had to do it twice more before the target was on a floor with a window facing the right direction.

He watched the room through his scope. He watched the bodyguards do a final sweep of her room and then leave. He watched as Mei Zhen walked from view into the bathroom. He stayed watching until she returned, a towel around her body and her hair. She sat on the bed, finished drying and then went to the mini bar and got herself a drink.

There were times when a shot was possible but not one hundred per cent definite. He would get one shot at this, and he had to be patient.

"Stand by." He spoke so Carol could hear him.

It took a short while, but then Mei Zhen opened her balcony doors and stepped out into the fresh air. Taylor felt himself smile.

She stood, looking out at Las Vegas, but he knew that even if she looked directly at him, she wouldn't see him, he was too far away, but he could see her. Through his scope, he could make out every detail of her. He could practically read the label of the towel she had wrapped around herself. He could see her eyes, see her perspiration from her shower roll down her face. He started his breathing, calmed his body.

It is often said that being a sniper is easier to disassociate yourself from the act of taking a life, as you only see it through a scope, so therefore it doesn't have as much impact. They are wrong. Through the scope, the marksman sees everything, all the small details of his target as the bullet flies towards its victim, they can see everything, like it's on the best definition TV money can buy. It doesn't disassociate you from the act of taking a life. It forces you to take a front-row seat and watch the consequences of the trigger you have just pulled.

Taylor knew all this, but still, he looked down that scope, waited for his moment, made his calculations to account for distance and wind… breathe in, breathe out, and when the times right, on the breath out…

He pulled the trigger.

He watched in what seemed like slow motion as the bullet soared the distance between them, it hit Mei

Zhen in the heart with such force that it forced her back through the balcony doors, shattering them and showering her with glass, blood pooling around her and soaking into her white towels. He saw it all like he was standing right next to her.

"Now." He instructed Carol.

"On it." She replied and hung up.

He looked again, confirming his kill, and he saw the two bodyguards rush up and kneel by her body.

It was time to go.

He dismantled the sniper rifle, put the unit back and closed his window. He slipped his jacket on, grabbed his bags, and as he left the room, he heard the soft click as it closed behind him.

Once back in reception, he approached the desk.

"I'm checking out." He said, "Room 2537."

The woman behind the desk frowned. "That's an early check-out. Is everything OK?"

Taylor smiled, "yes, fine, thank you, I really enjoyed my time, but I have been called away on business regrettably, never seem to get a vacation."

"Well, the room is all paid for and no extra charges, so thank you for staying with us, and we hope to see you again."

"Thank you," smiled Taylor as he handed the key card back, picked up his bags and walked out the front doors.

Taylor handed the stub to the valet, and he also ran to get his car. While he was waiting, he looked across the street. There were no sirens yet. He was half expecting to see the bodyguards running towards him, but he knew that even if they figured it out immediately and ran over, the roads are so wide and busy by the time they made it, he would be long gone.

The valet brought the Challenger around, and Taylor tipped him, loaded up the bags, climbed in, and when there was a break in the traffic, he pulled out.

40

As he drove away, he called Carol again.

"Assignment complete." He said, "tell the administrator I'll be on the next flight back home."

"Thank you. I will do that."

"I didn't retrieve the visual and listening devices. I want you to set off the self-destruct, destroy the hard drives – or whatever – but I want them to be found when local police search. It will be another thing that will make it hard for them to cover up; cameras in the halls and listening devices around the room always smell of conspiracy."

"Ok…Done," Carol said.

"Thank you."

"I'll inform the administrator right away."

"Thank you, Carol, it was a pleasure. As always."

"Yes, yes it was. Will you be returning to the safehouse tonight?"

"No, I'll b-" he broke off his sentence as he cursed and swerved to avoid a car that pulled out suddenly into the lane in front of him.

"Sorry," he grumbled, "people need to learn to drive. I'll find somewhere near to the airport to stay, less travel in the morning."

"Ok. Would you like me to organise a flight for you?"

"That would be great, thank you. Make it for the morning, though, or later tonight. I want to get a bit of shut-eye before I do anything else."

"Of course," she said. He heard her typing, and then she spoke again, "I'll send the details to your phone."

"Thank you."

"I'll see you when you get back for debrief."

"See you then." He hung up and settled in for the short drive back to the airport.

It was a twelve-hour plus flight back to England, and while he knew he could sleep on the plane, he wanted a moment of peace and quiet before dealing with the noise and the tight seating arrangements.

He found a motel chain a few miles out, with a 'Vacancy' sign lit and decided it was as good a place as any for a few hours, or a night. He turned the Challenger in, pulled it into a parking space and climbed out.

The building was two stories, with a desk booth at the entrance. It was old and had been painted white decades ago and never refreshed. The stairs were metal, and it looked like the windows were still single glazed. It reminded him of the kind of place that he would see in movies, where a sleazy character would take a call girl or where an informant would be taken and killed once he had been discovered.

It would do.

He walked up to the desk clerk who had his head down, engrossed in his phone, only looking up after he finished tapping the screen.

"Well, don't you look fancy?" The clerk whistled. He was being sarcastic. He was around twenty years old, and either; his family ran the place, or it was a job so he could save some money. Either way, he didn't care much about customer service.

"Thank you. Can I have a room, please?"

"Oooh…" He tilted his head back, "an' you British too, you real fancy. English, with a fancy suit like that…" He leaned in, mockingly looked around, and whispered, "you a spy or summit?"

"Yes." Taylor replied dryly. "I'm a spy. You figured it out. Can I have a room, please?"

"No need to be like that, mister, I just messing wit' 'ya…Sure, you have room twenty-four; it's just up the stairs."

"Thank you." Taylor took the keys, turned and started walking to the stairs.

"'n don't you worry mister spy, your secrets safe wit' me!" The clerk shouted back at him.

Taylor shook his head and wondered how some people managed to dress themselves in the morning.

41

Taylor didn't get to sleep long.

Once he had got in the room, he had checked his phone. The flight was in the morning. It was already late, but it gave him a few hours of sleep before he needed to be awake. He had taken his small bag to the room with him where he used the bathroom and took a shower – in a shower that looked like it hadn't been cleaned properly in a few weeks – and then gone and laid on the bed, letting his body relax and drift into sleep.

An hour or so later, he was woken by the sound of his phone ringing. He picked it up, hit answer and put it to his ear.

"Good evening, Agent Red." The voice said. It was a woman's voice, but it had a metallic sound to it, like it was being played through speakers that the phone was being held next to. He recognised it instantly. It was the voice he always spoke to when he was designated his assignments.

"Hello," he replied, sitting up and stretching.

"I have an available appointment; would you like to take it?"

It was weird hearing her say those words. They usually came in the form of a message to his phone; then, he would report in. This was different.

"Ok," Taylor said sceptically.

"There is an assignment in America. It will be assigned to Agent Orange in due time, as you are scheduled to return soon. But he is currently unavailable, and this is time-sensitive. It's a protection contract. Would you like to know more?" The voice stopped abruptly at the end of the question, and he sometimes wondered if all it was were just a recording that had parts added to it.

"Yes." He replied.

The voice started again. "Very well. The client has taken out a contract with The Company for protection from an individual seeking him out and aims to cause him harm. He is currently in Denver, Colorado, and you will rendezvous with him there. You are tasked to keep him safe until Agent Orange is able to come and relieve you. From there, he will take over the assignment..." There was a pause, "you will be compensated for your time and assistance in the matter should you choose to accept."

"Do you have any other information?" He asked, "who is trying to kill him?"

"We do not know. The client said it is a highly skilled and trained operative. He claims they have already killed two, and he fears he is next."

"So, he may not be?"

"Affirmative."

"So, this could be a waste of time? How long has he requested protection for?"

"That is not relevant. You will be responsible for him until Agent Orange can relieve you. He should be in your care no more than one hundred and twenty hours."

"Five days..." he mumbled, thinking it over.

"We need an answer, Agent; if you choose against it, I need to offer it to another Agent in country. This is time-sensitive."

"Ok, I'll take it."

"Very well."

"I need a change of flight."

"It will be done. The next flight is due to depart in two hours from now from McCarran International. Arrangements will be made for transport for you upon your arrival. Details will be sent to your devices now. Is that understood?"

"Yes."

He felt his phone vibrate in his hand and saw he had a notification of new documents to open.

"That will be all Agent Red. Thank you for your service."

The phone line went dead. Taylor tapped his phone, and when the green padlock appeared, he opened the documents and started reading.

42

Meanwhile...

It had been another long night for Jane. She had taken
the Volvo and left the house once she had cleaned up
and had a quick nap to refresh herself. This entailed
another nightmare, but this one didn't affect her as
much. Yes, the shadow man was there, and this time he
was chasing her, but while it was uncomfortable, she
had managed to always keep in front of him. She had
once again woken in sweat and discomfort, but it was
as deep inside her as it had been before.

She knew that with two people – and the soldiers –
dead, it wouldn't be long before she would be out of
time.

Once they knew what she was doing, they would scatter
the people she wanted to find and send others to find
her. She couldn't risk using the Ford Ranger again as
they may track it down. They could even have a tracker
on it, so she stuck with the Volvo for now.

She wasn't sure what resources they had and if they
would be able to find a way of finding her through the
vehicle – if they realised she had taken it at all – but it
was her best bet for now.

She had driven out of Willow Creek and followed the
directions to the next nearest name on the list, it wasn't
a long drive, and she soon found herself cruising on
Route 36 at a steady speed, making sure she followed

the rules of the road so as not to draw any unwanted attention.

The next name on her list was *Doctor David Jenkins.* He had an address in Bird City, and he had arrived just as the sun was beginning to set.

It was called 'City', but in reality, it was a small town. She had parked once again a short way down the street from his house. This little town wasn't much bigger than Willow Creek, and most houses were single-storey units, set far back from the road by long paths and distanced far enough apart to fit at least another house in-between them. He lived down the street from *First National Bank,* so she had factored in the possibility of the bank having cameras when she planned her approach/extraction.

She had seen movement in the windows and knew he was there. Jenkins had a wife and child, but she hadn't seen them.

Maybe they were out?

Maybe they were there, and she just couldn't see them?

He had been moving around with vigour, and as soon as she saw him load up a suitcase into the car, she knew he was running.

Less than thirty minutes later, Doctor David Jenkins was secured to a chair at the rear of his house. His wife and child were locked in a closet in the master bedroom. They had been crying but seemed to have stopped now.

Jane sat across from Jenkins, just as she had with Reece. She took a moment and realised how she must look in the fading light with the dried blood all over her clothes. Jenkins had wet himself when he had seen her walk through the open backdoor, and at one point, had even tried to put his wife between them as a shield.

Poor excuse for a husband.

There was nowhere for him to go now, though.

Jenkins had blurted out everything he knew – or said he knew as soon as he had been forced into the chair, he hadn't stopped talking for a few minutes straight.

"…That's everything, I swear to you." He ended. He had tears streaming down his face, his nose was running, and he was shaking. The fact she was there was more than enough torture for him.

"The thing is," she sighed, "I don't care."

"W-What?" He stammered.

"I really couldn't care less. At this point, I don't care why or anything like that. I don't want to hear your sorry, or you had no idea what was going to happen..." She rose from her chair and leaned down, placed her hands on the arms of the chair Jenkins was sitting in and moved in close to his face. He tried to pull his head away as much as possible.

"… Because you did." She whispered in his ear, "you knew exactly what was going to happen. You all did. You all knew that you were going to kill us, just like all the others."

"That's not true," he sobbed, "it was Conners. It was his idea to kill you. I- I- I wanted to keep you guys on, most of us did, but Conners, Conners said you couldn't be trusted, you couldn't be trained, you weren't good enough. He said you would be a liability to the programme, especially after you failed that test in the run house. He said, he said, said you were not good enough. You had reached your potential and needed to be replaced so that the programme could carry on and make better soldiers – that's what he said, not me. Obviously, I wanted to – a lot of us wanted to keep you guys. You two were special, by far the best we had ever had. But he's senior, and he had the final say."

Jane had stood and looked into his eyes as he blubbed his way through his plea.

"It's that easy, is it?" She asked, pulling away and sitting down again. She knew this was scarier, more painful to him than breaking his fingers. She knew his weak point. "Because I gotta say, if you're lying to me, I won't be angry at you. I'll just be…disappointed. And it's Ok. It really is, because I won't take my disappointment out on you…I'll take it out on your wife."

She had been expecting a reaction, a plea for his wife's safety, maybe even a fire in his eye and a last-ditch attempt at defiance. But there was nothing. Plan B then: "Or your kid." She added.

"Ok, I understand," was all he mumbled.

Jane was aware she had limited memory, but she was pretty sure she had never seen someone so easily throw their family as a shield against their potential harm. She wasn't sure why exactly, but this made her even madder. She had undertaken this revenge against a large group of people she deemed responsible – even if only by proxy – for the death of a loved one. But this

203

guy, this guy would happily have her hurt his wife and child over hurting him.

"Tell me, have you always been such a spineless piece of crap?"

"I- er- I'm, what?"

"You would have me kill your wife and child over hurting you. That's a kind of cold-heartedness that is evil, even to me."

"I, I'm telling you the truth. Please, Conners is the one you want."

"I'll get to Conners, but right now, I'm trying to work out what to do with you. I'm not sure I believe everything you're saying. While I agree that Conners is definitely someone I will be seeking to talk to, and soon, I just need to figure out what to do with you. Would you die to protect them?"

Jenkins hesitated. "Yes."

"I don't believe you. I think you'll do anything to protect yourself, even at the cost of those you claim to love. Or should at least. You're a whole different kind of monster, aren't you, Doctor Jenkins?"

"Conners is the one you want," he wept.

"You know, I've decided. I'm going to be kind."

"Thank you, thank you so much," Jenkins sighed with relief.

"…to your wife and child. They deserve better."

Jenkins' eyes widened as she stood up, drawing the Sig Sauer from the small of her back, bringing it round and firing twice into his heart. He died before his plea could leave his lips.

She went out of the room, took the sheet from the master bed, and used it to cover him over, blood-soaked and spread through the white linen. She went back to the bedroom and knocked on the door.

"I'm going to unlock the door now. Leave it another thirty minutes before you come out and call the police. OK?"

A whimpering voice replied, "OK."

"What's the boy's name?"

"Randy."

"Ok, don't let Randy into the back room. It's not appropriate."

"Why?"

"Trust me; this is better than how he would have had it happen."

Jane left, got back in the car, and drove off.

Once she was back on the highway, she drove for a short while, it was dark now, and she liked that. She felt invisible. She was just another car driving home.

43

She pulled in a few miles down the road at a rest stop and fired up the laptop. She had left it plugged in the aux socket in the car – she needed to make sure it kept its charge.

She opened the file on *Doctor Richard Conners*. The next one on the list.

She was locating his house, not far from her, as it made sense that you wouldn't want to live much more than a couple of hours away from work.

She programmed it in and started driving; he would be crossed off by morning with a bit of luck.

It was about a twenty-minute drive to Conners house in St Francis, but what struck her most as she drove was just how open and baron everywhere seemed to be. She could drive for hours and barely see a soul.

That's probably why there's a secret military testing facility hidden out here, she thought.

She hadn't been able to find Willow Creek on any map. When she had put the directions up, they had just said she was in the middle of nowhere.

She carried on driving towards St Francis.

44

She arrived at his house on Whittier Avenue and parked up. There were no lights on, but it was late, so it could be that they were in bed. The streets were laid out similar to Bird City, but some houses had been converted to two-storey buildings. Conners was one of them.

She waited for a short while, seeing if anybody came out or if there was any movement inside. There wasn't. She climbed out of the car and closed the door quietly behind her. She moved up to the house. Her bag rustled as it moved against her back, but she was comforted by the fact that she could take more things with her and get to whatever she needed quickly enough.

She was looking forward to this one. According to Jenkins, Doctor Conners was the one that had sealed their fate, and while she was sceptical about the accuracy of what Jenkins had said, it would be nice to find out.

They all had to die anyway; it didn't matter the order. She stalked up the side of the house and around to the back. The lights in the neighbouring houses were also off, so there was little chance of her being seen.

But don't get complacent. Jane reminded herself.

She was able to pick the lock easily enough and went inside. She crept, careful not to wake any of the occupants, scanning the rooms as she went. The ground floor was clear and had nothing exciting to offer. It was a generic ground floor layout, a living room and a kitchen.

The living room floor was littered with kids toys and fluffy teddies. The kitchen had a couple of plates next to the sink, ready to be washed up, and there was a downstairs bathroom. It looked like during the conversion, they had had the kitchen and living areas extended. They were large rooms and looked to have been knocked through to where the bedrooms were once situated.

She went upstairs.

She drew her Sig Sauer, held it close in a tight two-handed grip, close to her chest, the barrel facing slightly down.

She didn't expect much resistance; only Doctor Simms had put up a fight, she had caught Jane off guard, and she wasn't going to let that happen again. She searched the top floor rooms. There were three bedrooms and a bathroom. All were empty. The middle-sized room was for the child *Elise*, according to the file. It was pink. Very pink. But Elise wasn't in bed. The covers lay on the mattress in a disturbed pile.

She moved to the master bedroom. It, too, was empty. The bed was made up, and as she looked around, she noticed the open, empty drawers of clothes and in the top of the wardrobe where suitcases were situated, a gap that looked like a large suitcase should have been there.

Running, she thought as she rifled through the drawers, *maybe Jenkins was right; Conners knows I would be*

208

coming for him if he ordered our executions and is
trying to get away.

She finished her search, went back to Elise's room. She had some empty drawers too, and the remaining clothes were a mess, like they had been missed when someone was quickly scooping them up and forcing them into a case.

She looked through the third room; it was used as a home office. There was a desk with a monitor on top and a lamp. There was a bookshelf against the wall and a filing cabinet next to it.

She looked through the cabinet, there were gaps, and it looked like he had taken anything to do with The Phoenix Initiative with him. She did find a copy of vehicle registration documents in the top draw, along with details of the bills and other payments for the house.

She put the vehicle documents in her bag and kept searching.

Once she had finished searching, she stood in the living room, turned in a small circle, and looked to make sure she hadn't missed anything.

She felt disappointed. She had come here expecting to cross another name off her list, possibly a big one, but she had been left wanting.

Her body was now tired, and she needed sleep. She knew they had run, and she would get on their trail in the morning, but she needed to be on her game; she couldn't mess this up by being impatient.

There was a guest house a few streets down, and she drove round and checked in.

It was late, and the lady looked her up and down, paying particular attention to the blood-stained clothes, but eventually, she allowed her to stay. The guest house seemed to be a large house that had been converted into separate rooms. She had a room painted baby blue with a double bed covered in white sheets, an en-suite shower and a toilet. Once in the room, she took a shower – there was soap provided. She reflected it might be the best experience of her life, a hot, soapy shower.

Once showered, she used the toilet and then Jane laid on the bed, an actual bed. It felt like a long time since she had been taken out in her sleep to be killed. So much had happened in what was, in reality, a short space of time.

Her mind wondered, and eventually, down her minds path, she found John. She turned her head in instinct at where his bed would have been in the facility, and for a brief moment, she expected to see him sitting on it, saying something annoying.

The sadness hit her like a train as the realisation of reality set back in. A tear ran down her cheek.

"Oorah, Yank," she whispered to an empty room.

45

The following morning Jane went shopping. She had had another nightmare, this time, the shadow man was carrying Doctor Conners, and no matter how much she chased him, she couldn't catch up. The nightmare hadn't lasted as long this time, though, and once she woke up, shuffled about, and went back to sleep, she didn't dream of him again.

She had found a small amount of money in the bedside draw at Conners house, and she still had the $200 she had already acquired. She needed new clothes.

She ate breakfast at the guest house, thanked the woman for her hospitality, and allowed her to stay at such short notice. She was wearing the dress again, she still wasn't keen on it, but it blended in better than the blood-stained t-shirt and cargo trousers.

There was a shop on Washington Street, and that was her first stop. It wasn't really what she was looking for, she liked combat style, practical clothing, but most of this was cowboy style. She did, however, manage to find a pair of jeans that would do, they were cut to fit the body tight, but she brought a size too big, which allowed her a bit more manoeuvrability. She also grabbed a plain grey t-shirt and went to the checkout.

"Love that dress," the young woman behind the counter said as she put the new clothes on the checkout.

"Thanks," Jane said.

"It looks posh alright, like a night dress."

"I suppose so."

"Did you have a good night?" The young woman asked, her tone suggestive.

"Not as nice as I would have liked," she said.

"Oh, well, his loss."

"Or a lucky escape," Jane admitted.

After paying for the clothes, she walked to the hardware store. Inside there were locks of various sizes in the corner, and next to the bolt cutters was what she was looking for - lock picks. Actual lock picks! She picked up the best set and went to pay.

"That's an unusual purchase," the man puzzled. He was a rounded man, with a chequered shirt held up by suspenders.

"Is it?" She asked, "why?"

"I only really stock them for heavy-duty use," he said. "If you have a lock that you've lost the key for, your best bet would be to break it open and buy a new lock," he pointed to the bolt cutters, "…or call a locksmith, maybe?"

"Is there one round here?"

"Hm, what?"

"A locksmith?"

"Erm…No, no, I don't think there is."

"Then these will be fine."

"Ok," he scanned the barcode, "that's a lovely dress, by the way, if you mind my saying so."

"It does seem very popular today. It's not my favourite. I can barely keep myself in it half the time."

"Hm, yes, I…" he cleared his throat, "…I hadn't noticed that. I just, I just like the colour is all."

"Cheers," she said, holding her hand out for her change. The man snapped back to earth and cleared his throat again.

"You have a lovely day, miss."

As Jane left the shop, she thanked him.

She walked back to the Volvo and got changed in the back seat. She was still parked at the guest house and had logged on to their Wi-Fi.

Once changed into the new clothes, she got back in the front and started looking. She was a competent hacker, she knew enough to use in the field, and as before, most of it seemed to be muscle memory. She didn't have the skills to hack into anything too advanced; she wouldn't try to access anything military or anything highly secure. The DMV, however, was easy.

A few keystrokes later and she was in the Department of Motor Vehicles.

She typed in the cars the Conners had and used a backdoor into the camera systems to search for their licence plates. It took a bit of time, but she found them. They weren't together, though, so she decided to take a punt on his car first. It was logical they would stay in their own cars.

Conners Citroën was showing as being parked at a hotel in Denver. He had a few hours head start on her. But he didn't know she knew where he was. She had the advantage.

She started up the Volvo, topped it up with fuel at the station on the outskirts of town. There was a cheap store near it, and she grabbed a couple more pairs of jeans, t-shirts, and a brown leather jacket. They all cost less than the single outfit from the cowboy store, and she wished she had known about it before.

She got back on Route 36 and put her foot down.

46

Mister Knight walked into his office to find a man sitting in his chair with his feet up on his desk.

He felt himself go red with rage at the sheer audacity of someone who had the nerve to do this. He had never seen this man before, and he was about to let him know what a huge mistake he had made.

"Who the fu-" was all he got to say.

The man raised his hand, and Knight stopped mid-sentence. It was partly due to surprise, but there was something else behind it, an air of authority that was even more of a surprise to him.

The man was wearing a brown suit with an alligator print tie and cowboy boots.

"Mister Knight," he said with a southern accent. His voice was smooth as he spoke. "I presume."

Knight nodded, "yes," then got some of his confidence back, "and this is my office!"

"It's mighty nice." The man acknowledged as he looked around. He remained seated.

"You're in my chair," Knight stated.

"Yes, I suppose I am, and what a chair it is, it's very comfy."

The man rose from Knight's chair and stepped out from behind the desk. Knight circled around the other side and sat down.

He was now in his chair. At his desk. In his office. And yet…how did this man seem to still be in control?

"Who are you?" Knight demanded.

"You can call me Leo."

"Who the fu…"

Leo raised his hand and cut him off again.

"Now, now, Sir, there's no need for that kinda language, is there? We're all friends here."

"The hell we are!"

"Now, Sir, there's no need to speak like that."

"What are you doing in my office? I should beat the living sh…"

"Enough." Leo interrupted. Knight stopped.

"Have you listened to yourself? The way you talk to people. I'm sure your mamma taught you better than that Sir…" Leo was still standing, and he had taken to pacing slowly around the room with his hands cupped behind his back. He looked like the most relaxed man in the world. It was unnerving. "…I have been sent here," he continued, "because you made a call about a problem y'all have. I have had to fly out here at short notice, and I'm trying to deal with said arisen situation. However, if you continue to go down the path y'all currently walking, I am more than happy to make a call of my own and say that you don't want my help, and then maybe they can call you, and you can explain your…unique style of hospitality and see where we go from there. How does that sound?"

The penny dropped. Knight went white.

"No, no, of course not, that won't be necessary, please, have a seat," he rose, gesturing to the chair.

"That's very kind of you." Leo said, sitting.

"I'm sorry fo…"

"I don't want your forced apology," Leo uttered, "I'm not interested in it. Tell me about your problem."

"O – Ok. Well, a few days ago, we were disposing of test subjects for the programme."

"This Phoenix Initiative?"

"Yes, and they escaped…but we have caught and killed one already."

"But you said you were disposing of them?"

"Correct."

"So, shouldn't they already be dead?"

Knight hesitated, "we usually kill them at the grave site."

"Why?"

"It's just what the containment unit does. It's up to them how they do it."

"Well," Leo sucked his teeth, "maybe that should change. It makes no sense to me," he raised his hands, "but what do I know, ay? So, they escape, one is killed, and one is still in play? I'm assuming nothing has changed in that regard?"

"Correct, and she has taken out a team already. She seems to be killing members of the team that worked on them."

"Well, I gotta say, I'm not surprised. From what I've read, I'd be a bit ticked too."

"It should be easy once we have found her. It's just a girl."

"Now hold on one escaped super-soldiering minute there, *just a girl*? Sir, I'll have you know that some of the most dangerous human beings I have ever hunted or crossed swords with – metaphorically speaking, although there was that one time in Japan – have been of the fairer sex. They are not to be taken lightly."

"My team can find her; I was just letting the investors know because I felt they should be aware."

"That's mighty kind of ya, and they felt, with this information, that I should be sent here, to the middle of nowhere to see if I can't help y'all out." He beamed, "now, tell me what you know."

Knight wiped the sweat beads from his brow, it wasn't an overly hot day, but this conversation made him uncomfortable.

"Ok," he began, "after the escape, we moved to the backup site; we are back in the primary now. Obviously, while we were away, she broke in. We don't know what she took, though - if anything. We have limited cameras in the admin areas, and that's the only place we don't have eyes on her, but all we otherwise see is just her walking around."

"Where is she now?"

"I don't know."

"Why?"

"We lost her."

"Ok," Leo sighed, getting up from his chair, then he leaned down, placed his palms on the desk, "get me everything you have on her."

47

It was a lovely morning as the flight touched down at Denver International Airport. Taylor disembarked in the steady flow of passengers, and once he had collected his luggage, he made his way outside.

With his phone off of aeroplane mode, he had messages. One stated his car had been delivered to the car rental place with a code. Another saying to meet the client at a Motel 6, with an address. It was a hot day, and he regretted his choice of colours in his outfit. He was wearing a black three-piece suit, with a black shirt, black leather Converse hi-tops and a red tie. It was a lot of black, and even the few minutes he stood waiting in the sun were causing him to begin to perspire.

It was a nice day, though, and even though all he could smell was jet fuel and the other passengers' sweat, he was happy. He had never been to Denver before, and a part of him relished working in a new location. He was UK based, so it was nice to go international sometimes. *Even better when I don't have to spend all the time in a casino.*

He used the park and ride shuttle to get to the car rental place and walked inside. The air conditioner was on and gave a slight hum as it tried to cool the room. There was a queue, understandably, and the staff behind the counters wore branded uniforms and jackets.

At first, Taylor thought it was too hot for jackets, but then he realised they lived here, their bodies were acclimatised to this weather, his wasn't.

He reached the front of the queue. The man lazily looked up and asked, "How can I help you?"

I'm pretty sure that's obvious, he thought, but instead just showed the man the code.

"Cool," he typed before looking up again, "the car is in the lot, space thirty-four. Have a nice day." The whole interaction was monotone; his voice barely changed octave. Taylor just smiled, thanked him, headed through the side door under the sign directing him to the lot and found space thirty-four.

Parked in the space was a Ford Mustang Shelby GT350. It was grey with two black stripes down the bonnet, roof, and boot. On the outer edge of each stripe was a thin red stripe. He couldn't help but smile when he saw it and wondered if it was ironically given to him.

It didn't matter. It would do the job.

He put his luggage in the boot. There was already a care package in there waiting for him. He unzipped it and glimpsed the weapons inside before closing it back up. He climbed in and started the engine.

The 5.2 litre V8 burbled into life, the deep rumble sending vibrations through the seat.

It wasn't his Jaguar, but it would be fun for a few days.

He pulled up into the Motel 6. From above, the building was shaped like someone had written two capital letter

T's on the ground and joined the top lines together. The building was cream white, the room doors were blue, and each room had one window facing the parking area. The rooms on the top floor were identical to the ones on the bottom from the outside. The doors mirrored each other on both floors.

He had parked next to Conners Citroën. He had the description from the information he was given, and he knew which room Conners was in; it was the one right in front of where he had parked.

He killed the Mustang's engine and climbed out. The air-conditioning had been on in the car, and as soon as he got out, the humidity hit him again. He was wearing sunglasses to shield his eyes, and he made a mental note if he ever came back for another assignment not to wear all black.

He knocked on the door. No answer.

He knocked again, listened, and heard movement inside.

He knocked again.

"Doctor Conners, I'm Agent Red. You should be expecting me."

He heard the chain pull back, and the door opened. Taylor walked inside. It was bigger than he imagined it would be, there was a short corridor into the room, the first room was a living style area, with a sofa and a tv, to the right was a kitchen dining area, this was small, and the table was almost touching the cupboard space. Further down was the bedroom with the bathroom attached. He was expecting something similar to the hotel chains in England, but this explained why there were only three or four doors on each level. For what it was, it was nice. The décor, however, was very grey. The walls were the same cream white as the exterior, the sofa and chairs in the living area were a light grey coloured material. The chairs in the dining space were basic wooden items, as was the table. They matched the wardrobes and furniture in the bedroom. The bedsheets were almost the same grey as the sofa, and the bathroom was a toilet, a sink, and a small walk-in shower cubicle.

"First things first," Taylor said, "are you Doctor Conners?"

"I am," Conners said, retreating back into the room. Taylor closed the door behind him and put the chain across.

"Second thing, don't ever unlock the door without authenticating the visitor."

Fear entered Conners' eyes, "so, you're not Agent Red?"

"Oh, I am, but if I weren't, you would have just let me in."

"How do I know you're you?"

"Because if I were here to kill you, by now, you'd be dead, and I'd be halfway back home."

Conners nodded, "Ok."

Doctor Richard Conners was an average looking man. He was of average height, brown hair, brown eyes, and he wore glasses. He was wearing a white shirt and black trousers. He was very… average.

"Who knows you're here?" Taylor asked as he searched the rooms, checking the bathroom, the cupboards and fittings for any traps or devices.

"No one."

"You have a family?"

"Yeah, why?"

"They know where you are?"

"No."

"Good."

"They're with family."

"Ok."

"But I'm safe now you're here, right?"

"I'm only temporary. Another Agent will relieve me once he gets here, then he will take over."

"Oh - OK."

Taylor finished his sweep; he found nothing. He stood in the middle of the room and looked at Conners, who sat in a chair. Conners looked back after a moment. Then a confused expression spread across his face.

"What?" He asked.

"You still haven't asked for any form of verification."

"I believe you."

"Then you're a fool, but whatever."

"You haven't asked me for any either."

"Yes," Taylor agreed, "but one, I have a file on you, and it has your picture, and two…" he pulled out Conners wallet and threw it on the table. "…I lifted this from your jacket on the back of the chair while I was securing your room."

"Oh."

There was a long silence that hung in the air, Taylor broke it:

"Put the TV on if you want. We're here for a while."

"Are we stay- staying here?"

Taylor sat on the sofa. "It's as good a place as any short term. Once Agent Orange arrives, I believe he has set up a longer-term option, but for now, this is fine. Just stay away from the windows. No one knows you're here, and as long as you haven't told anybody, no one will be looking for you here."

48

A short while later, Taylor was sat in one of the chairs at the table. He had brought one of his weapons in and a change of clothes for tomorrow. He had opted for one of his more relaxed outfits – a white t-shirt and blue lightweight chinos. He had left his other suits in their bags in his luggage.

Conners said he had felt uncomfortable around guns and had asked Taylor to leave them in the car. He had refused, but they had compromised on him having his Glock 17. Taylor wasn't happy about it, but he reasoned that one was better than none, and if Conners had been truthful and not told anyone of his destination, it was unlikely he would need any weapons. But he felt comforted with it.

He was in the process of cleaning it. It wasn't his original weapon, his was still in his apartment in England, and it was a habit that had been drilled into him always to clean a fresh weapon. You never knew when it was last fired or how well it had been maintained. He knew the Company wouldn't provide bad quality, but it was a habit. And habits die hard.

He had stripped and cleaned it and was almost finished putting it back together when Conners walked through from the bedroom. They glanced at each other as he passed and went and sat on the sofa.

Taylor knew not to ask questions; he had learned that lesson many times over in this line of work.

The truth was, they didn't matter. He wasn't about saving the world or stopping the 'bad guys'. That wasn't what he was hired for, and as far as he was concerned, as long as Conners was alive when Agent Orange turned up, he had done his job.

It shouldn't matter to him who's coming to kill this guy or why.

But he wasn't naive, and as he had once been told:

Information is intelligence.

So, he got up, walked over, and sat in the chair next to Conners, facing him.

"What's this about?" Taylor asked.

"Sorry?"

"All this, what's it about?"

"I- I don't follow."

"Look, you're obviously a clever man, and I know you don't live here, so why are you here, why is your family staying with other family, but more importantly – and this is the part I need to know – who is coming to get you?"

"I can't say."

"You ca…you can't say?"

"Yes,"

"Why?"

"I can't. I signed an agreement. An NDA."

"Ok," Taylor muttered as he rose from the chair. "Ok, just so you know, your NDA isn't going to save your life when someone points a gun at you. You came to us, a third party, not the authorities like most people would, so clearly you have – or know, stuff you don't want getting out. I'll be frank with you; I couldn't care less about all that. My job is to keep you alive, and if you hired someone like me – us, then you must be scared, and someone that puts the fear of God in you must be on your heels. That's someone I need to know about… Stab in the dark here, but I'm guessing whatever you do – whomever you work for, has security and protocols, and from what I can gather from the little bits I have available, I'm guessing they're not mall cops. And yet still, you contacted us to keep you alive. So, this could be serious, and if someone is going to burst down that door and come in here all guns blazing after your head, I need to know what to expect in order to make sure that doesn't happen. Understand? I don't know if someone wants to kidnap you, kill you, both or neither, but don't, for one second, treat me like an idiot."

Conners nodded, "ok, wha…"

"Sshh," Taylor breathed, raising his finger to his lips and looking at the entranceway.

"Bu…" Conners started before the look Taylor shot him stopped him mid-word.

Taylor could hear a light scratching, but almost as soon as it started, it stopped. He glanced down the short entrance at the door, but there was nothing there. He walked back to the seating area.

"Sorry about that," he apologised, "you were saying?"

Conners looked like he had seen a ghost. His gaze was fixed over Taylor's shoulder, and then he felt it; the realisation shivered down his spine as it settled in.

He had missed something.
What?
He glanced down.
The carpet!
It can mask footsteps if someone knows what they're doing...
He turned and saw the woman standing in the entranceway. She was the most beautiful woman he had ever seen. She looked to be in her mid-thirties, her hair was tied up in a ponytail, and she had a backpack on. She was wearing jeans that looked a size too big for her, a plain grey t-shirt, and combat boots. Her stance signified her intent. She was stood relaxed yet poised, her feet slightly apart and elbows slightly bent. It wasn't much, but it screamed at Taylor.
There was a split second when both the woman and Taylor looked at each other. Neither was expecting the other to be in that room.

Taylor's brain fired through options, none of them good. She wasn't carrying a weapon, but that didn't mean she didn't have one.
Good job I do, he thought, then he glanced at the table. At his half-assembled weapon.
Shit.
Her eyes followed his, she was between him and his gun, but if she was who he thought she was, he was between her and her target.
Keep it that way.

All this had taken place in the space of a second or so. Taylor knew he would have to stop her. He moved towards her, and she came at him.

49

Taylor knew he had to get the attacker off balance. She was just not expecting him, and he needed to make that work.

He covered the distance between them fast and used the momentum to swing a punch.

But she was fast. Faster than Taylor was expecting. She blocked, grabbed his wrist, and punched him in his side. He gasped but stayed on his feet and pulled his arm free. She launched a knee strike, but he used the palms of his hands to block and push it down, used his momentum and fired a punch into her stomach, she swung a hook, but he was able to push it wide and then landed an uppercut under her chin.

He expected her to rock back and fall over. She rocked back but stayed on her feet.

She shook off the blow and got herself in a stance for another attack. She struck out with a kick, but as he went to block, he realised too late it was a feint, and she punched him across the face.

It sent Taylor's world spinning, he stumbled back, using the fittings in the room to support him, and he was able to stay up, but she had taken her chance and was on him. He blocked the left punch. Then the right, but he missed the kick to the back of his leg, and he dropped to one knee. The woman punched his face again. He was able to block the follow-up, but she was relentless, and the blows just kept coming. Taylor tasted blood. He had been able to block a few attacks and knew he had to counter-attack. Soon. She tried to repeat, but he blocked, grabbed her knee, and twisted, trying to break the kneecap, but she moved with the turn and struck him in the eye with her other knee as she twisted. They both went to the floor.

Taylor managed to get himself up. He felt the blood run down into his eye. He wiped away what he could. She was up on her feet again. The fight had moved away from the seating area, and they were nearly in the bedroom. They were evenly matched, but he had the feeling she was better. However, he was still between her and Conners.

The woman lunged again. There was an anger in her eyes, a single-mindedness that he knew all too well. She swung a punch, but Taylor grabbed her wrist and twisted it hard. He expected it to break, but instead, she leaned in with it, moving in a way he had never seen other than the movies and now he was holding her wrist, but her other hand was on the floor like she was doing a one-handed handstand, and her legs were clamped around him.

She twisted, and Taylor felt the force spin him across the room. He crashed into the kitchen cupboards and fell to the floor.

His head was numb and painful at the same time, there was a ringing in his ears, and time felt slow in his mind. He tried to concentrate, bringing his view into focus. She was now coming at him; he knew she would kill him first now – he was a threat and needed to be neutralised so she could deal with Conners.

He kicked the chair at her with all the force he could. There was no way around it in the small space, and it hit her, causing her to stumble. Taylor scrambled up. As he did so, his fingers found the kettle on the side. He grabbed it and threw it at her. The cord ripped from the wall, and the kettle hit her in the shoulder as she was trying to steady herself.

Taylor had an advantage, the first one since they had engaged each other. He knew he had to press it home. He moved in fast, punched the woman across the face, tried to follow it up, but she had regained her composure and countered his attack and punched him in the stomach.

The wind was knocked out of him. For a moment, he was vulnerable – and she knew it. She moved in behind him, kicked him in the back of his knee, causing him to lean back and grabbed him in a choke hold.

He knew he didn't have long. He threw himself backwards into the wall, but she hung on, applying pressure. He was becoming lightheaded and could feel his vision closing in, the blackness at the edge, threatening to seep in and put him to sleep, or worse. He moved his hand up to the wrist of the arm around his neck - her right, and clawed his fingers around it, then he twisted it with all his strength – she was strong, but he was able just to break the pressure. He stamped on her foot as hard as he could, hoping to break it, but she was wearing combat boots, and he was wearing canvas trainers.

That'll teach you. His brain teased him.

He struck out into her shin with his heel, dragging the back of his foot down; it was enough to cause her to shift her footing and give him his opening. He swung his elbow into her ribs, turning at the same time. He tried to tuck his leg behind hers and force her down, but she had seen it coming and moved away. It was enough for her to have released the pressure entirely now, and he grabbed her wrist and flipped her over his side. She hit the floor and rolled, rising once again to her feet. With what little his body had left, he lunged and tackled her, and they both fell into the bedroom. Taylor was on top of her and tried to use it, but she struck him in the ribs she had kicked earlier. It hurt like hell, but he didn't feel anything break. It gave the woman an opening, though, and she punched his throat. He felt the force like a train and instinctively reached his hands up. He coughed, spluttered, trying to get air into his system, he gulped in what air he could, and she punched him just under his ribs, winding him.

He felt like he was going to choke. He was winded, and his throat was swollen and closing up. He couldn't draw breath in. She easily forced him off her, then pushed him into the bathroom, he stumbled into the shower cubicle, and as he tried to stand, his leg gave out and, still coughing, he slipped and fell.

His body wouldn't move. He wanted to, he really did, he willed it to, but it was like it knew she would probably kill him if he went again.
You have a job to do.

Taylor gasped air into his lungs and forced his body to cooperate. He slowly climbed up and stumbled back to the main area, gripping the door frames for support.

The woman was over Conners. She was unarmed, but she clearly didn't need a weapon. She was a weapon. *Weapon.*

Taylor glanced at the table, his gun had been disturbed during the fight, but the parts were still there.

He stumbled over as quickly as he could. He was recovering slightly, making sure he kept focus.

Adrenaline was helping, his breathing was better, but he rasped as he inhaled. His vision was still a little blurry, and his movements were rigid.

He reached the table. The woman looked back at him and then at the gun. She knew what he was going to try. She started moving towards him.

All he needed to do was the final stage. He fumbled for the slide. His fingers felt numb; he couldn't coordinate himself properly but managed to line it up and slide it back. There was a satisfying click. Now just the magazine.

Where's the magazine!

It was too late. The woman kicked him hard in the chest, and he crumbled to the floor, groaning. He moved his head and saw the magazine was on the floor. It was within reach. He just needed a moment. He lashed out with his foot at her knee; it was weak, but if she hadn't have moved at the last second, it would have broken her kneecap, but it became a glancing blow to the shin.

It was enough, though.

He reached, grabbed the magazine, slid it in the Glock, chambered the first round and fired.

It was a blind shot in her direction. Taylor's vision was still blurred, partly from the choke hold, partly from the lack of oxygen to his brain and partly from the blood in his eye from the cut just above it.

He missed, but it was enough to cause her to move. He knew he had enough rounds to kill her. He got to his knee, fired again.

She wasn't close enough to disarm him without getting shot, so she ran as he fired, the bullet shattering the window at the rear; she used it and jumped through.

Taylor wasted no time; he knew she would be back at any second. Chances were she had a gun in the backpack, and it wouldn't take her long to return fire.

"Move!" He tried to shout, but it came out as a dry croak. He coughed as he grabbed Conners arm and hauled him up, dragging him through the entrance.

"Get in!" He wheezed, rubbing his throat. He unlocked the Mustang and climbed in.

"Are you able to drive?" Conners asked.

"You want to stay here and wait for round two?" Taylor coughed.

"No."

"Good choice. Me neither."

He slammed the Mustang into reverse and pulled out, then he put it in gear and put his foot down. There was a moment when the car only spun its wheels, then it found traction and launched out of the car park.

50

Taylor kept his foot down until he was far enough away and was sure she wasn't following him.

He was coughing and weaving around the road, his vision was clearing slowly, but he wasn't in the best condition to drive. His phone linked up to the Mustang's Bluetooth, and he called Carol. An operator called Edgar answered the phone.

"Well, well, well…" he said in his best villain voice, "Look wh…"

"Edgar," Taylor growled. "Not the time."

"Ok." His voice changed; he was now all business. "What do you need?"

"The safehouse Agent Orange set up for this protection assignment. Where is it?"

"I don't know; I'm not on the op with him. I can try and find out, though."

"Don't try. Find out. Fast."

"Ok, hold the line, caller."

The line went silent, and Taylor just carried on driving. The growl of the Mustangs engine rumbled through the cabin. The occupants were silent as they drove. A moment later, Edgar's voice filled the car:

"Ok, I have the address. I'll send it to you."

"Thanks. Hey, Conners, grab my phone and direct me in."

"Ok, sure," Conners said, picking the phone from the centre console.

"What? No, I've sent it to the cars sat nav man. Get with the times."

"Why don't you ever do that to the Alfa?"

"Because the Jags personal, you're in a Company car now."

The sat nav beeped a notification, there was an address, and a message asked if they would like to set as the destination. He pressed yes, and the route appeared. If he weren't in so much pain, he would have been impressed.

"Thanks, Edgar, oh, where's Carol?"

"Reassigned, of course. I'm only temping right now; Gary is Orange's techie on this, so he will take over soon.

"OK. Thank you, Edgar."

"No problem, my good man. Enjoy the Americana sunshine." The light heartedness had returned to his voice.

Taylor hung up and followed the navigation.

The safehouse wasn't a house. It was an apartment building called *Springwater Forum* situated on 14th Street. It looked nice enough from the outside. It reminded him of a holiday complex. There was a big pool with seating around it at intervals. The water looked cool and clear. He felt like just falling in and letting the water surround him.

They parked up, and he checked his phone then got out. He left the bags in the boot and made sure his Glock was concealed.

They walked into the foyer, it was grand, with high ceilings and good lighting, and there was a seating area in the corner. They walked up to the desk, the woman behind it looked up, and her face twitched when she saw him. Taylor was walking with a slight limp, he had hurt his leg in the fight, and he was hunched slightly. He had taken a beating but was trying to hide it. Obviously badly.

He smiled at her, and she hesitated before returning it.

"Can I have my key please?" Taylor asked.

"Yes, of course, Sir, have you lost one?"

He grunted as he stood up straight, winced and said, "It's been a rough day. I don't have the key on me. Can you please give me the spare?"

"Yes, Sir, of course. Are – are you OK?"

"I'm fine; nothing a nice bath and a glass of wine won't fix."

"Would you like me to call an ambulance?"

"I'm fine." He insisted, then nodded to Conners, "I asked my friend to keep an eye on me tonight. If anything happens, he'll look after me."

The woman looked to Conners, back at Taylor, then back and forth for a moment before conceding.

"Ok, Sir. If you're sure. What number is it?"

"37."

"Ok, and if I can just check the name."

"Richards, Keith."

"OK," the woman was typing as they talked. She looked up, "Do you have any ID?"

Taylor raised his eyebrow. It hurt, but it made his point.

"Oh, of course," she said. "That's – that's no problem."
She finished typing and bent down behind the counter,
re-emerging with a key on a fob.

"Would you like me to organise a replacement for
you?"

"That won't be necessary. Thank you." He said as he
took the key and moved to the lifts.

It was in the lift that he caught the first glimpse of what
he looked like. The lift was nice, it had mirrors all the
way around and a brass rail to hold onto.

The mirrors revealed Taylor's face to him. He knew he
didn't look great; he could tell from how he was
feeling, but it was worse than he thought.

He had blood around his mouth, from his nose and the
cut above his eye. He was battered and bruised, and
blood stained his clothes – thankfully, the black hid it
well. He was pale, and his head still hurt. He looked at
himself and decided he looked like a black and white
photo, with only the colour red enhanced.

"I'm here to look after you if anything happens?"
Conners said, "I thought that's what *your* job was."

"You're still alive, aren't you?" Taylor responded.

They arrived, and the lift opened, welcoming them to
the floor. Taylor looked down the corridor, there
weren't many doors, and he found thirty-seven easy
enough.

He turned the key, heard the lock disengage. He turned
back to Conners.

"Stay here." He said softly. Then he drew his gun and
went inside.

51

She had been unable to get to them in time before they escaped after she had jumped through the shattered window. Jane hadn't expected there to be another man in the room.

Amateur. I won't make that mistake again.

Whoever the man was, he was well trained, but now she knew that Conners had hired protection, she would account for it. She wouldn't let him get away twice.

If he's hired protection, maybe he is what Jenkins said he was, perhaps he was right, and he knew I would be coming for him, so he thought this guy – whoever he is, will be able to stop me.

She had made it round to the front of the hotel in time to see the Mustang that was parked next to Conners Citroën speed out of the car park.

She was grateful she had taken down the license plates of the cars in the lot.

52

Leo arrived on the scene after the party had finished. A crowd gathered around, and police had taped off the motel room and put a taped barrier to stop people from getting close. Officers were standing around the door, but it was closed, and he wondered if anyone was inside.

He had made his way here after leaving Knight's office in Willow Creek. He had taken the information Knight had given him and called a couple of contacts he had in places that don't exist to the public. They had been able to find her on traffic cameras using a facial recognition system and had been directing him in real-time as he drove towards her.

It had been a few hours since he had hit the road, but he knew, standing in that parking lot, that he wasn't far behind her.

The facial tracking had lost her near the motel, but when they had told him of the disturbance, he knew it was her. He had driven to the scene and was now stood, in the crowd of on-lookers, trying to assess if there was anything useful to be gained from the location.

He walked away from the small group and around the back of the room. There was shattered glass all over the grass under the window at the back and a single strip of the same '*Do Not Cross*' tape that was at the front.

He peered inside, looked for movement, but there wasn't any. The tape was easy to get around, and he was soon inside.

He looked around, but there wasn't much that was of any use to him at this point. The place was a mess, and it was apparent a fight had taken place, things were everywhere, and it looked like a tornado had torn through the place.

He did a second scan but didn't find anything to give him any leads to where his prey had gone to.

Who had she fought with here?

What was she even doing here?

Leo had been given files on the people Knight believed she was hunting, and none lived in Denver.

He kicked and picked his way through the rooms, but again, nothing presented itself. He decided it was a dead end.

After climbing back through the window, he walked around the front for one more pass, and then, just as he was about to turn and walk away, a car caught his eye.

It was the car in front of the motel room that was taped off, it was an older model Citroën, nothing special, but it connected something in his mind. He took a photo of the registration plate.

Once back in his car - a black BMW M5, he pulled the files out again and started flicking through.

It took a moment, but he found it.

Doctor Richard Conners drove a Citroën, same model and year, and the plates matched.

Conners was her target.

If he could find Conners, he would find his Jane Doe.

53

Apartment Thirty-Seven had been clear, and once he was happy, Taylor had told Conners to go inside while he went down and got the bags from the Mustang. The apartment was a great space. As you entered, you were greeted by the kitchen area. The entrance opened up, and the appliances were down the left-hand side wall; only the cooker was in a little nook on the right. Before that was a coat cupboard, with a little rack for shoes incorporated in. On the other side of the alcove containing the cooker was a small table with a chair at each end. The entire kitchen surfaces and fittings were finished in a brushed stainless-steel effect. Taylor liked it. The floor was wood effect all through, and there were controls for the underfloor heating on the wall. Through the kitchen area was the living space. A large TV was on the wall to the left, and there was an 'L' shaped sofa in front that also acted as a barrier from the living space to the kitchen area. On the back wall were the double doors that led to the balcony, and the balcony overlooked the large pool at the back of the complex. To the left of the living space were the bedroom, bathroom, and a walk-in closet. The bed was king-size, with white sheets and a small bedside table on each side that matched the kitchen's décor. The bathroom was white and tiled, with a toilet, sink and a shower over the bath.

It reminded him of a scaled-down version of his apartment at home.

Taylor brought the bags in and put them on the bed. He drew the blinds and secured the door. Only then did he begin to relax. Conners was stood awkwardly in the corner of the room, like a child who didn't know where to sit or what to do.

Now he had had a moment to secure the situation, Taylor nodded to the table and instructed him to sit down.

"Is it safe here?" Conners murmured.

"Yes. Well, it should be. But then, I was under the impression the motel would be safer for longer than it was," Taylor nodded towards the table again. "Sit." Conners shuffled over and sat nervously.

"I'm going to wash the blood from my face," Taylor said, "…and then, you're going to tell me what the hell just happened."

54

Even with the blood cleaned up, Taylor looked like he had just done ten rounds in a boxing ring. His face was bruised, and the cuts were visible. He knew he got lucky.

He was sat at the table opposite Conners now, his Glock, freshly cleaned again - and fully reassembled, sat on the tabletop, next to his resting hand.

Conners took a deep breath and began. "I don't know where to start. So, I suppose the beginning would be the best place. The U.S has been in a race with Russia and China, amongst others, for decades, trying to build the best soldiers. Potential soldiers get recruited and then trained. The ones that pass join the military and go on to serve. That's how it works…but what if you could take it further? That's the goal. We wanted to take soldiers, the best soldiers, and make them better. Smarter, faster, braver, stronger, help make it so that they could excel in the weak areas. Make sense?"

"So far," said Taylor, "I've seen the films."

"Well, we were hired for a new programme, and for almost a decade now we have been working on developing the subjects, little by little, each group are getting better. Taking what we learn from the previous ones and using that as ground zero for the next, and so on and so forth. The end game is to create the best soldiers ever to step foot on a battlefield, the kind of soldiers you can send to do any mission, and they would succeed."

"What you're talking about sounds a lot like 'super-soldiers."

"Close, but no, that's science fiction. They will, of course, be better than the average. They will be the evolution of soldiers. Keeping America safe at home and overseas. I dream that once we have been able to perfect it, we are still a long way off, but we will be able to use it for military applications and doctors and nurses, fire fighters, and police. We could use it to make ourselves safer, maintaining order and saving more lives than we could possibly have hoped for." There was a tone of hope, optimism in Conners voice. He honestly believed in what he was saying.

"So," Taylor nodded, "how did we end up here?"

"Well, we ask for volunteers for the programme, and in order for the total commitment, we need the best, but we need a blank slate. We need them only to have their muscle memory of certain things, no bias towards anything…" Conners hesitated, swallowed before carrying on, "…so we wipe their minds."

"You what? You wipe their minds?" Taylor frowned.

"Yes, but it's for the greater good," Conners elaborated. "They need to be truly impartial. We inform them of the things they need to know, but not much else."

"What do you tell them?"

"Their old units and things, things that will help them understand what they are doing, why they chose to join the programme."

"Ok, that's not as bad as I thought. I thought you took their identities from them."

"We kinda…did." Conners sagged. "We gave them names, it was always two, a male and female, and they were told their names were now Jane and John Doe."

Taylor leaned back in his chair; he couldn't believe what he was hearing. "You basically named them after unidentifiable corpses?"

"Unidentifiable people. Not just bodies."

"You honestly think that helps your argument?" Taylor shot.

"It's for their own good."

A thought came to him, "how many of these have you done?" He asked.

"A lot."

"How many is a lot?"

"I don't know exactly, I'm not consulting on all of them, but most subjects last a couple of weeks, maybe a month or two."

"How long's the programme been running?"

"I have been with it just over five years, but it's been running over seven."

Taylor leaned forward, put his hands together on the table, "Jesus," he whispered. "Why this one? Why is she trying to kill you? What did you do to her?"

"We use an array of different techniques, medication of various sorts, reconditioning, brain surgery…"

"Brain surgery?" Taylor interjected. "What the fuck?"

"It's very effective," Conners defended, "but when subjects are no longer viable, they are removed from the programme so we can get new ones in."

"Removed?"

"Yes, they are taken out and disposed of. Both Jane and John escaped, though. I believe John was killed, but they haven't caught Jane yet. But it's only a matter of time before she is caught, or killed though, and then this will all be over."

"Are you serious?" Taylor demanded as he rose from his chair and turned away.

He turned back; he was angry. "So, let me get this straight," he began, "you take a 'volunteer' and tell them you are going to wipe their brain a…"

"Oh, no, we don't tell them that; they are told it's reconditioning their mind."

"You're unbelievable. You get them in, then wipe their minds, then you perform brain surgery, and other God knows what on them in order to make them the 'perfect soldier', making them – at that point – the best there is, and then, when you're done with them you just throw them away like stale food. And now one has escaped your little play and death loop, and you think whoever is involved will be able to stop her? You've trained her to be fucking unstoppable, you idiot!" Taylor's voice had risen as he had got angrier. "So basically, I'm protecting you from G.I Jane on steroids."

"They're not steroids," Conners pointed out.

"I know they're not steroids. I was making a point," Taylor retorted. He shook his head, "Jesus, this is insane. Did you honestly think this would never happen? You told The Company a highly skilled and trained operative – or words to that effect."

"She is," Conners reasoned.

"I'm a highly skilled and trained operative." Taylor said, pointing to himself, "she, she is Captain America out for revenge on the people who experimented on her and then tried to have her killed! And by all accounts, given you wiped her mind, you killed the only person she 'knows'."

"You can keep me safe, though, can't you? The Company I mean, I have paid what you asked, and my family is safe, and it's only a short while, maybe a couple of weeks. Then it will be OK."

"Maybe the rest of your life. Which, given what I have seen from her, may not be long." Taylor paused, took a deep breath, "I will do whatever it takes to keep you safe, but we barely made it out of that motel room. She is like no one I have fought before. She knew my moves before I made them. She threw me around like a doll. She won't be easy to keep at bay."

"You don't understand…"

"No, you don't," Taylor cut in, "you were basically playing God. You have no right to do what you did to her, to any of them. What was the end game? Remove their free will as well so that they become the 'perfect' soldiers. Soldiers you could just point at, shoot at, whatever you want doing, and they would just do it, no morals, no compunction, just mindless slaves."

"Isn't that what soldiers are asked to do?"

"They have the ability to refuse. There are consequences, of course, but they can also leave. I'm guessing you weren't going to programme an exit in for them, were you?"

"I hadn't thought about that."

Taylor shook his head. "It's always the same. We never learn. Well, it looks like Jane Doe has decided on her own exit plan, and it involves removing any players that may come after her. As I say, I'll do what I can, and I know Agent Orange will as well, but if I were you, I'd make peace with my maker. Because she sure as hell is pissed with hers."

The look on Conners' face told Taylor this didn't reassure him.

"Ok," was all he said.

Taylor went for a shower to freshen up and clear his head. He needed it; he could hardly believe what Conners had told him. It was like a plot from a film. Only he wasn't sure how this one was going to end. He felt like he was one of the characters that would get killed off trying to protect the protagonist.

He decided he would call The Administrator after his wash and inform her of the developments. He couldn't shake the feeling he was outclassed.

He got out of the shower and was drying off when he heard a knock on the door. Conners ran in, fear in his eyes, shaking. Taylor wrapped the towel around his waist and grabbed his gun for the side.

"Get in the wardrobe," he instructed, "don't come out until I say so."

He nodded, ran past and into the wardrobe, closing the door behind him.

Taylor chambered a round, made sure his Glock was ready to go. He was prepared this time. He crouched down behind the bedroom doorway. It was parallel to the door, so all he had to do was lean one hundred and eighty degrees around it and fire. It was the best cover from the door.

Another knock.

Was it her?

She didn't knock last time.

Was she testing each room, seeing who was in?

A key entered the lock, and the handle turned. The door opened slowly. Taylor used the reflections of the surfaces like a mirror, so he wasn't exposed as he watched a man enter. He had his weapon drawn and moved carefully and efficiently.

The man was white; he had a strong jaw line, a cropped haircut, and a black suit with an orange tie.

Taylor moved out and around, facing the intruder. They both froze, weapons trained on the other. Water was still dripping from his hair and body; it was the only noise as the drops fell and tapped onto the floor.

The downside to an organisation that the operatives rarely meet is that no one knows who the other is. Also, they live in a dangerous world, and the agent wearing a colour one meeting may not be the same one wearing it the next. It was a high turnover industry.

"Lovely weather we're having for the time of year," Taylor said, his finger poised to pull the trigger. What the intruder said next would depend on if he would live. Taylor's eyes locked with the intruders.

"I prefer the rain," the man said, "it means I can use my favourite umbrella."

It was a code, and they both said their part correctly. It was Agent Orange.

They both lowered their guns.

Orange looked him up and down, beaten and bruised, dripping wet with just a towel on. "Did I come at a bad time?" He asked.

55

Agent Orange sat and listened as Conners repeated what he had told Taylor. His reaction was much the same.

"She did that?" Orange said, pointing at Taylor's face.

"Yeah, and that's just what you can see. Don't underestimate her."

"Noted."

Taylor had dressed in a white t-shirt and blue chino trousers. He was sat on the sofa; the others occupied the chairs.

"I knew it was a bad idea," Conners hung his head low and breathed deep, "but I honestly did it for the right reasons."

"That path paved with good intentions and all that," Orange said.

Conners just sagged. He was defeated.

Taylor's phone beeped. It was his travel plans and the order that he was relieved.

"That's me, guys. He's all yours." Taylor said. As he passed to the bedroom, he patted Orange on the shoulder.

"Where are you staying until your flight?"

"It's this evening; I'll head to the airport and wait around for a bit."

"You're welcome to stay here," Orange suggested.

"Thank you, that's very kind, but it's OK. Got a thing about punctuality, and if I'm at the airport, nothing can stop me from missing my flight," he laughed.

He came back out, put his bags down and shook Orange's hand, "Pleasure meeting you. Agent Orange"

"You too, Agent Red," Orange said.

He looked to Conners and then back, "and good luck."

"Thanks. Enjoy England."

Taylor smiled and left. He went back to check-in and handed the spare key back.

Then he left *Springwater Forum*, into the dry heat of the day and drove back to the airport, recalling what a day it had been.

56

Jane had been camped out down the street. She had
tracked them down following the Mustang, just as she
had the Citroën and had found it parked in the
apartment complex. She didn't know which room it
was, and she didn't have time to try them all. If
someone got suspicious and word got around before she
found it, she would blow her element of surprise.
She watched him leave, and she was glad she had done
as much damage to him as he had to her. She had been
cut and bruised from her fight with him. He was the
best she had gone against, after John.
He got lucky. It won't happen again. She told herself.
The man was alone, so it looked like he felt safe and
had left Conners in an apartment while he went out.
If she was quick, she could get in, find out if Jenkins
was right, and kill him before the man got back.
Jane knew she could move on to the next name and
come back to him, but she had the bit between her
teeth, and she hated the feeling of being bested.
She had a plan.

57

After waiting a few more minutes, ensuring it wasn't a short recon trip the man was making, Jane left the Volvo and walked down the street and into the *Springwater Forum.*

It was a lovely building, but she didn't stop to admire the décor; she just walked straight up to the reception desk.

"Hi," Jane said in her sweetest voice.

"Hi, how can I help?" The woman behind the desk asked as she looked up and looked over her face.

"Yeah, hi, so, my boyfriend came back earlier; we were mugged this morning."

"Oh my god, did they catch the guy who did it? Yes, Mister Richards, number Thirty-Seven, he came in earlier, and he looked in a lot of pain. Positively awful."

Internally, she smiled.

"Yes, he took me to the hospital, but then came back here, you know men, always trying to be macho and tough. But I talked him into going to the hospital, but he left some of his medication here. I don't suppose you have a spare key I could use to pop up and grab it for him?"

"I'm sorry, I can only give out the key to the residents, its policy. I just can't."

"Really?" She sagged, "but he's on his way to the hospital now to get checked over, and I know if he comes back, he'll decide it's not worth it. Please, I'm really worried about him."

"I'm sorry, I just can't."

Jane sagged her shoulders, put a defeated look on her face.

"Ok. Thank you."

"His friend may still be up there, though, the one who was looking after him. I don't recall seeing him leave."

"That's great," Jane smiled, "hopefully, he's still there and can let me in. Thank you."

"You're welcome." The woman looked pleased with herself; she had managed to help but wasn't going to get in trouble.

Jane moved to the elevators. She didn't need the key; the conversation was done the second she found out the occupant's name and number. She just needed to keep it going long enough not to look suspicious.

She entered and selected the third floor.

58

Jane walked down the third-floor corridor, looking at the apartment numbers until she found thirty-seven. She placed her ear up against the door and listened. There was movement and muffled noises coming from inside.

Was someone else in there with him?

Maybe it was just the TV.

She considered her options, running them through her head.

He would have been told not to open the door to anybody. Knocking will put him on alert, and if there is, someone else will get them a chance to prepare.

Quiet entry, then.

She took her lock picks out.

59

Agent Orange's name was Gabriel Caine. He had dirty blonde hair, dark brown eyes, was cleanly shaven and was a born and raised American.

The Company was a global unit and had the resources to operate in every country, each with its own support team and safehouses. Most of the agents had a pool of support that they were assigned, so more often than not, any help would come from their base country even when an agent was international. This was sometimes a hindrance due to the time difference and other elements, but it had never been a significant problem.

Caine was sat at the table with Conners. He was going over all the usual details and the protocols when involved with protection.

They had set up a rendezvous should anything happen, and they got separated. Conners also had an emergency contact number should he need it. Caine was just finishing up the details when he heard a faint noise outside the room.

He picked up his weapon, an M45 MEU (SOC) semi-automatic, as favoured from his time in Force Recon.

"Get in the wardrobe, stay there." He whispered, ushering Conners up from his seat and past him through the bedroom. He took position behind the wall leading to the bedroom, the same he imagined Agent Red had done when he had arrived.

He thought it could be Red, but then realised he would have knocked or given them notice of his return. He hadn't been gone long.

Caine braced, peered around the corner, then saw he could use the reflections from the kitchen.

The door handle turned. He took a breath. He always felt just before a confrontation that time seemed to slow in the few seconds leading up to it – the anticipation.

The door opened.

60

A woman entered the room. She was quiet. There was only the faintest tap of her boots on the wooden floor. Within a second, Caine knew who and why she was here. Her body position screamed it; she held her weapon out and scanned the space efficiently.

Not housekeeping, then.

He leaned around the door frame and opened fire. The apartment had been quiet until the bark of the Colt erupted. She was fast, though; she had seen the threat and had dived from his line of sight and retreated through the door, firing as she did so, shattering the glass to the balcony and lodging bullets in the walls. They traded a couple of rounds of fire each from their respective covers, hoping to catch the other one out, but Caine knew his ammo was getting low.

He moved around, keeping his sights on the doorway, his finger ready. He moved through the space and crouched by the opening to the apartment. There was a short walk into the main room, and he crouched by the kitchen cupboards, hoping to catch the attacker as she came in. There was a moment of silence, and Caine heard her too late; she was in front of him, her aim was high, and he was crouched. He pushed himself up and forced his shoulder into her, knocking her off balance and releasing the gun from her grip. She hit the wall and came at him again. He raised his gun to her, but she slapped his hand wide and struck with her palm to his face. His head rocked back, and his gun slipped from his grip. She punched, but he blocked, forcing it wide, moving around behind her, and getting her in a chokehold.

He applied pressure, and she weakened her resistance. "How this goes is up to you," Caine said.

"You think you can stop me?" She gargled.

"If I have to. I won't even think about it. I'll just get it done."

"So will I." She said as he realised she had faked being weakened. She dragged her heel down his shin, he shifted his body weight against the pain, and she fired her elbow into his side, grabbed his wrist as his grip loosened, twisted it, turned her body, and threw him over her hip to the floor. She tried to punch him in the face, but he was able to block. Caine punched her in the face, tucked his foot up against her stomach and pushed her off.

The woman got up before he could, grabbed onto the chair and swung it. He was able to raise his arms to block, but the force sent him reeling. He looked up and saw her coming at him, she punched him across the face, and he felt his tooth dislodge as blood filled his mouth.

He was still on his feet, though, but then he looked over her shoulder to see Conners in the bedroom doorway. She caught his eye and turned.

She wasn't arrogant, though. She knew she still had to deal with Caine before she could get to Conners, so she turned back as Caine tackled her, lifting her off the floor and slamming her down onto the ground. She blocked his punch, lashed a knee into his side, then punched him, rolling him off her.

As she went to get up, Caine swept his leg and kicked hers out from under her.

"RUN!" He shouted at Conners.

Conners froze to the spot.

"RUN!" Caine bellowed again, louder.

Conners moved, running for the door and disappearing down the hallway.

The woman growled her anger and kicked him in the face; he was lucky she hadn't broken his nose.

She was up and moving. He got up; his body felt exhausted. She was fast, strong, and motivated. A bad combination to be up against.

He dived at her from behind, and they tumbled into the hallway. She rolled and got up. He did the same.

Caine moved in to punch her, but she grabbed his wrist, jabbed him in the ribs, kneed him in the groin, swept her leg behind him and pushed him down, rolling him over, so he was on his front, his arm outstretched behind him. She was about to break it.

Caine twisted his body, put his other hand on his shoulder, forced his body and dislocated it. He cried out in pain.

This took the woman by surprise, and she let go of his hand. He twisted, kicking her in the leg, and she dropped, then he push kicked her in the face, and she fell backwards.

Caine scrambled up and ran for the stairs.
She was on his heels.

He pushed the door open and started racing down them. Every movement sent a new agony up his arm. He had lost a tooth, his head ached, and his ribs felt like a bat had hit them – they were definitely bruised, possibly worse, but the adrenaline was masking that for now. He could hear her following him. He never ran from a fight, but she was good, and his job was keeping Conners alive. She had him at a disadvantage.

She crashed into the back of him, forcing him against the wall. He turned, and she punched him across the face, and again, then in the side, then kicked his leg, and when he dropped, she punched him again.

They were still two flights of stairs up, and Caine couldn't beat her. He summoned all he had left, forced himself into her, pushing her against the railing, then he uppercut punched her and pushed her over the rail. She hit her head on the handrail and she turned and fell to the ground below. It wasn't a long drop, but she landed in a heap and didn't move.

Caine hobbled down the rest of the stairs, breathing heavy and deep, each time causing his ribs to hurt more. His body was broken, and he had lost count of the places it hurt. He grabbed his wrist and pulled his arm straight and forward; he felt the ball of his arm pop back into his shoulder. He cursed at the pain, but a bruised and swollen arm was better than a broken one. She was still alive, so he moved over to her body, placed his knee on her back, grabbed her head and was about to snap Jane Doe's neck when the door to the lobby in front of him opened and a lady in her sixties walked in, looked at the scene before her.

"What the devil?" Was all she said. She was holding the door open, and now people in the lobby could see him. He knew The Company would protect him from law enforcement, but it would be hard to get rid of a murder with this many witnesses.

"Fuck." Caine muttered under his breath. He got up and pushed through the gathering crowd, through the lobby, and into the sunbathed car park.

He climbed in the Black Jeep Cherokee Trackhawk and started it up. The fob for the keyless system had been cracked, but the sender-receiver still worked, and the car fired up.

It was more than could be said for his phone. The screen was like spiderwebs crisscrossing the entire screen. But it still paired to his car, so it was still operational. He used the cars onboard screen to call in. Conners was a block away, heading towards the rendezvous when Caine caught up. He pulled over, and Conners climbed in.

The face he pulled as he did so told Caine everything about his appearance. He knew he had had a rough fight; he could see his white shirt and orange tie were stained in red, and he had lost his weapon. It had not gone well.

However, the client was still alive, so that meant it wasn't a total failure.

61

The conversation had been brief. Caine had called in, spoke to his operator Gary, and informed him the *Forum* had been compromised. He needed a backup location and medical assistance.

He had told Gary what had happened and had been told The Company would deal with the Denver police and given a location for backup and assistance.

Caine was given an address on W 84th Avenue. It was a lodge of apartments; he was told assistance would be waiting for him in lodge seven.

Caine pulled the Jeep into the car park.

"Stay here and keep your head down until I come and get you. Got it?"

"Ok," Conners said. He was looking pale; it had been a very emotional day for him.

He climbed out, wincing as he moved. He opened the bag in the boot, got out a Baretta M9 pistol, checked the magazine, and ensured there was a round in the chamber and the safety was off. He went to lodge seven.

He opened the door – it was unlocked and went inside. There was a man in a doctor's uniform waiting for him, he had a bag with him, and Caine made him show there were no weapons. Once he was satisfied, he brought Conners in.

The lodge was basic and minimal, it was decorated and furnished on a budget, but it was clean and would do the job.

"Sit down." The doctor told him. "I need to have a look at you."

Caine did as he instructed. He was exhausted; he wanted to sleep.

62

It seems all I have to do is follow the trail of destruction. Leo mused to himself as he stood next to a crime scene tape for the second time that day.

He had been trying to find a lead on either Conners or Doe since leaving the Motel 6, but there wasn't a lot of camera coverage in Denver - not as much as he would have liked anyway.

Then he had been told about a fight and the attempted murder of a woman in a luxury apartment complex, and it seemed too coincidental to be anything else.

He had gathered what he could from talking to the crowd gathered around, but as with many groups where no one really knows anything concrete, it was all Chinese whispers.

He knew he wouldn't be able to pull the same trick of getting in and out as he had with the Motel.

Leo had contacted his contacts, but for now, it seemed the trail had gone cold. This was frustrating but happened more than you might realise. Sooner or later, though, he knew he would pick up the trail. He wasn't far behind; all he needed was the next direction of where to step.

63

Taylor was at the airport. He was sat in a comfy chair, with a book he had brought from a shop in the terminal and a can of coke in his other hand.

He was relaxed. He knew he had two debriefings when he got home, one for the Mei Zhen assignment and one for the stand-in of Agent Orange's, but for now, he could just relax. He still had a few hours to wait, but the airport was quiet, and he took the time to calm his body and enjoy the moment.

Then his phone rang.

64

The following morning.

Caine woke with a start. He jolted and sat upright in the bed. It was a single bed with a loose sheet covering him.

He tracked back through his thoughts of what happened the previous day, and once he had his bearings, he got up.

He was in number seven of lodge apartments, he was on a protection detail, and he could hear voices from the other room.

He got up. He had no weapons with him, so he got dressed in his trousers and shirt and carefully walked through to the living area.

Conners was sitting on the brown sofa. Agent Red was standing in the room talking to him. He had a couple of days of stubble on his face and was wearing a black three-piece suit – the jacket was hanging over the back of a chair, a black shirt, and a red tie. He was wearing black leather Converse high tops. The bruises on his face were more apparent now, and the cuts still looked sore.

It was a simple room, small TV in the corner on a stand, grey carpets. Not much else.

"Morning," Agent Red greeted him as he walked in. Caine's shoulder still hurt, and he had a headache. His body felt slow and heavy and sore.

"How long was I out?" He asked.

"All evening and night," Red answered. "It's now…" he checked his watch – it looked expensive, "…just gone 8 am."

"Where's the doctor?"

"Gone. Did what he could and then had to go back to work. I got a call to come and assist until you were able to get back at it."

"I'm fine." Caine shot. He felt a stab of annoyance that Red had been called back to help.

"Ok, fair enough," Red said, raising his hands in defence. "But seeing as how I missed my flight by many hours now, how about I stick around for a bit and see if I can help? I've had a run-in with her too."

Caine thought it through. He didn't want to admit that help would be useful. Since joining The Company, he had always worked alone. But he was a realist, and that woman was brutal. Two might be better than one if she came at them again.

"Ok, sure, pal." Caine shrugged. He tested his shoulder. It hurt.

"Ice packs in the freezer."

"Thanks." He opened the freezer and took one out, pressed it against his shoulder. It was cold, but it was nice. He turned back to the room, looked at Conners sitting on the sofa.

"You OK?" Caine asked.

"Yeah," Conners replied, "I just didn't sleep well. I kept thinking that Jane was going to show up, and it scared the hell out of me."

"Well, I threw her down two flights of stairs, and she was barely breathing when I got down there, so maybe she didn't make it."

"Maybe," Conners said, his eyes were glazed over, and he was looking into the distance.

"Did the doctor leave anything for me? My head's killing; it feels like a jackhammer."

"Sure," Red said, walking over to the kitchen counter, he tossed a small box to Caine, and he read the label. "Paracetamol."

"Yep, only the best."

"Nothing stronger?"

"Not if you want to work."

Caine nodded, "great."

"Get dressed," Red said, "we need to restock and then figure out what we're going to do with him." He pointed at Conners.

"Sure," he said, putting a couple of pills in his mouth and swallowing them.

"…and take a shower first," Red added.

Caine used the bathroom and then took a shower. He let the steam fill the room and breathed it in. His nose was sore, but the steam helped. He slowly moved his shoulder as he didn't want it to get stiff. He knew he was supposed to have it in a sling for the next few weeks to allow the soft tissue to rest and heal, but he needed to be mobile, just in case.

After his shower, Caine dressed in a new black two-piece suit, white shirt with an orange tie, it was a deeper shade than before, and it looked like a burnt orange tone.

He walked back through to the seating area. It looked like Conners hadn't moved. Red was in the kitchenette.

"How's he been?" Caine asked, nodding to Conners.

"I think he is worn out now. He barely slept. He's on edge, barely spoke a word all night. I think he's running on empty."

Caine nodded. Then a moment of silence.

"Next time you're in England," Red said as he looked at him, "let me know. I'll introduce you to my tailor."

"What do you mean? Nothing wrong with this. Does the job." He said as he looked down at his suit.

"Ok, your call."

"If you're buying, pal, then I'm there, though." He chuckled, took a sip of the coffee, and walked back to Conners.

"Load up, time to go," he said.

"Yeah, yeah, Ok. Sure." Conners mumbled as he got up. Caine put his hand on his shoulder and looked into his eyes.

"Conners, are you sure you're Ok?" Caine asked, looking at his pupils.

"Yeah, yeah, fine," he replied, "just tired."

He hesitated, "Ok, get your things, man."

Conners nodded and went to the back room.

Caine looked at Red, who just raised his eyebrow and shrugged. Clearly, they both had the same worry.

65

Meanwhile…

Jane woke up slowly. Her body was taking a moment to boot itself up. She felt groggy and sluggish. Her head hurt, her legs hurt, her arm hurt…she hurt.
She couldn't remember if she had dreamt, but if she had, she hadn't had a nightmare. That was fortunate. What was better was that she was alive, but as she became more aware of her surroundings, she realised she was in a hospital. This wasn't good.
She knew if they delved into her too much, they may find something that they shouldn't. She remembered when she was being trained; they were told that they could only go to a public hospital as a last resort in one of their sessions.
How long have I been here?
I need to leave.
She was in a room, and the door was closed. How long before someone comes back in? She was about to start pulling the lines out of her arm when the door opened, and a nurse walked in.
Jane closed her eyes and groaned, showing the nurse she still wasn't entirely lucid.
The nurse leaned in, whispered, "Hello, hey, can you hear me?"
She opened her eyes a little.

"Hey," the nurse smiled, "it's OK, you're safe now. How do you feel?"

She moaned and coughed.

"Take your time. We're still running tests to make sure everything's OK. And when you're ready, there are some officers here to talk to you about your attack. But only when you're ready."

The nurse smiled and turned to leave the room. Jane sat up, grabbed her and choked her unconscious. It had taken longer than expected; she was weak and tired, the short rush of panic and adrenaline helped, but the nurse hadn't put up much fight.

She took the lines out, turned the monitors off, dragged the woman into the bathroom, undressed her, and put her uniform on. She took her phone and belongings and closed the door.

The uniform was a little big – it hung from her, but it was enough. She grabbed her bag of things from the corner of the room, and keeping her head down, she passed the police officers in the waiting area, headed down the stairs, through the hospital and towards the main entrance, her head low and her body movements purposeful – she was just a busy nurse doing busy nurse things. The hospital was a blur, her vision was a little cloudy, and everything was white: walls, floor, and ceiling. She had followed the signs as she weaved through the busy people scurrying around working and visiting loved ones.

No-one stopped her.

As she walked through the main door, a man was walking in. He was wearing a brown suit with a strange tie and cowboy boots. This was odd, but she didn't dwell on it. She needed to get out as soon as possible. Once outside, she hailed a cab and sat in silence in the back as it drove her to the *Springwater Forum.* She paid, hurried over to the Volvo, and got in.

There was police tape across the entrance, and a few police officers were coming and going. A small crowd were still gathered around, trying to get the gossip, and as people walked past, they craned their necks to get a view of the excitement.

Jane was angry at herself; she had been bested twice now.

Why was there another man in that room?

Who were these guys?

She tried to figure it out, but her head hurt. She needed to get some painkillers and change her clothes.

She searched for nearby pharmacies and found one only a few blocks away in a shopping complex. She drove carefully, making sure not to draw attention. It was another hot day, and the sun was making her head worse, but finally, she made it. In the back of the car, she got changed into another pair of jeans and a black t-shirt, grabbed her boots from her bag of possessions and slipped them on.

When she returned to the car, she had got what she needed and disposed of the uniform in a bin. She took a couple of tablets and downed them with a bottle of water. Her throat was dry, and she didn't realise how thirsty she was until she started drinking. She

swallowed the first bottle and half of the second before
she stopped.

Think.

How do I get to this guy?

I need to get whoever these guys are away from him…

Then a thought struck her, and she cursed herself for
not thinking of it sooner.

No, I don't!

She grabbed the laptop and fired it up.

66

Caine, Red and Conners drove in Caine's Jeep to a nearby climbing wall centre.

They walked in and looked around. There was a reception desk and a rack of leaflets and paraphernalia about the different kinds of walls and the different kinds of events they did. Everyone was dressed in tank tops and shorts, with harnesses around them and helmets on as they looked around. In suits, they could not have looked more out of place if they tried. Conners was the closest, now wearing jeans and a shirt, but he looked more like a bank manager on his day off.

Red turned to Caine, keeping his voice low. "You been here before?"

"No, can't say I have. I'm normally based in New York when I'm here, so this is all new to me," he muttered back.

"Ok, here goes," Red said, walking up to the counter.

"Stay with him," Caine instructed Conners and walked off towards a door at the far end.

All the climbers were instructed to go down a tunnel on the right side of the desk once they had checked in, but there was a door to the far end of the room on the right side.

As he followed it round, Caine came to another desk, almost hidden from view from the entrance. The sign said:

A man sat behind it. He was wearing a black shirt and trousers with a white tie.

Company man.

He approached the desk.

"Hi," he said.

"Welcome," the man said, "do you have your membership?"

Caine nodded, putting his card on the table. It was a simple card and had an electronic chip in the corner on the front with the words:

Agent Orange

On the back, it had a gold letter 'C' logo embellished with a mandala pattern around the edge. The card was white and had no other information.

The man took it, scanned it in a hidden scanner under the desk, and returned it.

"Welcome, Agent Orange." He greeted him as he pressed a button under the desk, and the door behind him buzzed and popped off the lock.

Caine turned to see Red and Conners walk up behind him.

"Welcome," the man said again, "do you have your membership?"

Red smiled and took out an identical card, only with:

Agent Red

On the front.

"Welcome, Agent Red. Pleased to have you both with us today." He looked at Conners. "Your guest will have to stay with me, though, don't worry, he will be safe."

Conners looked worried. He looked from Caine to Red and back again.

"You'll be fine." The man reassured. "I will protect you with my life."

"We won't be long," Caine said, nodded to Red, and they both went through the door.

"Please, sit," the man said to Conners, gesturing to the vacant chair next to him.

Conners stood for a moment, not sure what to do. Eventually, he shuffled around and sat down.

Caine and Red followed the tunnel and walked down the flight of stairs at the end to what looked like a large storage area. It was simple. There were racks of weapons, medical supplies, grenades, phones, and a whole manner of other things neatly arranged.

There was an office walled off at the back, and a woman came out to meet them.

She looked in her early twenties; she was curvy with a soft face, brown hair and was wearing a black t-shirt with a cartoon on it, black jeans, and a white tie as her belt.

"Well, this is a treat. I don't see an agent for what, two years? And now I get two. You guys are like busses."

Caine and Red both stood there, not sure what to say.

"Not a talkative couple either, are ya?" She continued. She was moving her hands as she talked and didn't seem able to stand still. "But then," she continued, "you both look like you just had your asses handed to ya, so I probably wouldn't want to talk about it either."

"We're here for a resupply," Red said.

"Oh-la-la, he speaks," she smiled. "So, what can I get for ya? Have a look around." She turned and walked back to her office, came back a moment later with a giant drink in the kind of cup with a straw you get at the cinema, but it was huge.

"I need an M45 MEU SOC spec. And clips." Caine said.

"Sure, military man, I see…Or was. Recon by any chance?" She raised her eyebrow as she asked.

"And an M4 carbine as well, please."

"Not too talkative are ya? That's a shame. I don't get much company down here a lot of the time…All the time actually, and that's Ok, because you gotta be happy in your own company before you're happy in someone else's hey." She paused to take a deep gulp of her drink. "What about you? Where's that accent from? Europe, I'm betting…England…am I right?"

"You are." Red smiled.

"Yes!" She exclaimed, thrusting her hands into the air. "I'm right, I'm always right."

"Congratulations," Red said.

"Where'd you come from? Give me a clue, your English, so were you a spy or something? You were a spy, weren't you."

"No, not me."

"Gimme a clue then."

"We don't have time for this," Caine said.

"C'mon, I never get to see people," she took another deep drink.

"What's in that?" He asked.

"Caffeine, mostly," she admitted, "I drink a lot. It gets me through the day…I do need to pee a lot, though." She turned back to Red, "So c'mon, give me a clue."

"Ok, what sort would you like?"

"Commendations? Awards? Employee of the month, anything to help me narrow it down."

Red thought for a moment. "Ok," he said, "I have been awarded the DCM, and I have a Victoria cross. That help?"

The woman's face dropped. She put her cup on the side and saluted him. "I am so sorry for my rudeness," she breathed, "so, so sorry."

"It's fine," he said, "and put your hand down."

"I'm sorry," Caine cut in. "Have I missed something?"

"Nothing important," Red said.

"Nothing important, are you crazy, he…" The woman began.

"It's nothing that can't wait," Red said.

"Ok, yes, Sir," she said. "Just know it's an honour, Sir."

"Thank you."

"What can I get you?"

"C8 Carbine and Glock 17 ammo would be great, please."

"Coming right up."

"How come she's like that with you?" Caine asked.

"Because she recognised talent." Red smiled back.

"Yeah, that must be it."

They had everything they needed a short while later, and it was bagged and ready to go.

"Thank you," Red said, "I didn't catch your name."

"Oh, right, people call me Chickpea."

He frowned, "why?"

"Dunno, they just always have. 'Cause I'm small, I guess."

"And you like that?"

"I don't mind it."

"Want me to call you it?"

Her eyes lit up, and she gained a smile that would make a Cheshire cat jealous.

"Oh, my god. Yes!"

"Well then, thank you, Chickpea."

Somehow her smile got wider.

"You're welcome, Agent." She saluted, turned, picked up her drink and slurped more as she danced back to her office.

"What was that about?" Caine asked.

"No idea," Red admitted, "but I like her." He said as they walked back through to the main reception.

Conners was waiting for them; they loaded up the Jeep and drove back to the Lodge.

67

Once Leo had confirmed that a woman matching Jane's description had been taken to one of the Denver hospitals, he made his way there. He was annoyed he was so far behind now; he had lost almost a day. But he was told she was out cold, so now he had her where he wanted her. As he walked in, he passed a nurse carrying a bag walking out the front entrance and out of view. She was clearly in a hurry, and nearly shoulder barged him as she passed.

He made his way to the ward she was on, told staff she was his sister, and he was worried sick – there's a lot of that in hospitals, and they are all so busy they rarely have the time to check everything. He found the ward, and two police detectives were waiting to speak with her in the seated area. Leo assumed it was her; it made sense. He knew they were police due to the cheap, ill-fitting suits; the biggest giveaway was their shields attached to their belts that were on display every time they raised their arms or shuffled in their seats.

"Hi there," Leo integrated himself into their conversation.

"Hi." They both said.

"What brings you here?" He asked, "I hope an officer isn't in here?"

"No, Sir, we are just here waiting to interview a victim," one said.

"You want a coffee?" His partner asked.

"No thanks," the detective said. He got up, started walking away, then turned, looked at Leo, and asked, "would you like a coffee?"

"Well, that's mighty kind of y'all, but I'm OK, thank you kindly."

"Sure." He said and walked off down the corridor.

"So, what happened, detective…?"

"Shaw," he answered, "and I'm afraid I can't discuss an ongoing investigation."

"Oh, why sure, course not. I just watch a lot of cop shows, love all that stuff."

"Well, it's not as fun as the shows make it out to be." Leo chuckled and then took a deep breath. "It is dull, just waiting. Been here long?"

"Long enough. But it's rewarding when it all comes together."

"Yeah, I bet." Leo rose from his chair, "Well, a pleasure to meet you, and good luck."

He walked off towards Jane's room, looked through the glass panel in the wooden door, but couldn't see the head of the bed as the wall for the toilet blocked it. He glanced back, waited until Detective Shaw wasn't looking, then he slipped inside.

The room was empty.

God damn it.

The monitors were off, and the tubes for her fluids were on the bed, the liquid slowly seeping into the bedspread.

He looked around, found nothing of use until he opened the bathroom door and saw the nurse in a heap on the floor.

The woman at the door.

Leo left the room and kept a steady pace as he walked past the detectives – Shaw's friend had returned – he gave a polite nod as he did so, but as soon as he was out of their sight, he sprinted through the corridors back towards the main entrance. He ran out into the sun, the sudden change causing him to squint, but as he looked around, he knew he had lost her.

He made a call.

"Tell me ya got summit?" He said before the recipient had even said hello. He heard typing.

"Still no hit on Conners. How about Doctor Reece?"

"Doctor Reece is dead, has been for a few days now."

"Then why has his car gone through a camera?"

"Probably his wife."

"From what I can see, he doesn't have one."

"Well, now, that is strange." Leo thought out loud.

"Where is it?" He asked.

"I'll send you the markers and real-time updates."

Leo hung up and made another call.

"Put me through." He said when it was answered.

There was a slight pause, and then he heard The Chairman's voice.

"Yes?"

"I'm closing in on her. It won't be long now," Leo said.

"Have you seen the news?"

"No, why?"

"Because I have. Denver is very popular on it. I want this dealt with and contained now. There are already too many people asking questions, and this was supposed to be handled quietly."

"Yes, Sir."

"Kill the girl, kill the scientist."

"The scientist?"

"It's time for a clean-up, and I'm told he is the one she is hunting, the one you are using to find her. This is a representation of you. Don't make me regret it."

"Correct, Sir, and I won't, Sir."

There was a long pause before The Chairman spoke again. "No loose ends now."

"Yes, Sir. It will be done."

The chairman hung up, and Leo realised how tense he had been. Now it was killing the girl and the scientist. No problem. But a bit of backup wouldn't go a miss.

68

It had been a few hours since Caine, Agent Red and Conners had got back to the Lodge room. They had set up cameras on the approach, gone over new extraction protocols and backups, and were now sitting in the room.

Red was sat at the table. He had moved one of the chairs to face the door. His Glock was sat next to his hand. He had barely moved.

Caine and Conners were sat on the sofa. The TV was on, but the volume was low, barely audible.

"What's your plan after this?" Caine asked, turning to face Conners.

He frowned, "I don't know." Then he thought for a moment, "obviously I'm leaving the programme, this has been the worse few days of my life, I'm a wreck, jumping at every noise, I think every second that at any moment she will turn up, and we will all die. I honestly don't think she'll stop."

"Why haven't your employers taken you in, given you protection?"

"There are a few of us in each team, and we're just one team. I know of dozens of tests like ours going on, and that's just in this country. We are in a race for global supremacy, and we have to beat China, Russia, Korea, all of them, because if they do it before we do, then our country's safety is at stake. The moon landing race, the cold war, this is just the next one, and whoever wins takes the first step to basically being unstoppable – in the wrong hands."

"Are there right hands for things like that?" Asked Caine.

"He's an idealist," Red remarked. "He wanted to heal the country."

"Oh." Caine sighed.

"That was my dream, a safer world. But I've learnt this isn't the way. Doing this to people – even people that volunteer for it is soul-destroying. Every time we would hit a dead end and move on, I felt like a piece of me went with them, and I justified it all with being for the greater good. But this Jane, the Jane that is now hunting me down, and the John, they were the best we had. They showed few side effects; they never received the nightmares, or the muscular defects, nothing."

"Defects?" Caine frowned.

"Some of the subjects didn't respond well to some of the substances we injected them with. It started as slight muscular tremors, and then it could amplify to muscle spasms, and even cause the arm – or leg to have major involuntary movements."

"Not ideal when aiming a gun or fighting," Red said.

"Yes," Conners nodded. "I've learnt it's better to surround yourself with ideals and goals that don't have a face. They are easier to betray and won't break your heart nearly as much." Conners leaned back on the sofa as a tear ran down his cheek.

"I think, if I survive this, I'll become a whistleblower." He said after a few minutes.

Caine rolled his eyes, "well, that would make all this redundant," he said. "They'd kill you before you opened your mouth."

"Accountability, I suppose," he wondered. "Maybe if I can raise enough attention, they'll have to close it all down."

"What about the whole 'keeping America safe thing'? And the 'real-world applications you dreamed of'?" Red quipped.

"What was the programme?" Caine asked.

"It was called The Phoenix Initiative," Conners began, "it was about taking remarkable soldiers, stripping them down and allowing them to rise from the ashes of their former selves and being better than they were before. The absolute best."

"Cheesy."

"I'm doing it to keep my daughter safe. But there's no point in any of it if I'm not there to see her be happy. Selfish, I suppose."

"No, a dad wanting to see his daughter happy, that's something I can relate to," Caine said.

They sat for a while longer, and then Conners asked, "what time is it?"

Red looked down at his watch, "five – seventeen," he answered.

"Think I could give them a call?"

"It's not safe." Red asserted.

"Just for a minute?" He pleaded.

Caine looked at Red. Red looked back, raised his eyebrow, and shrugged, "He's your assignment. I'm just the backup."

Caine looked over, "one minute," he said.

Conners turned his phone on to see he had seventeen missed calls. He called Molly.
"Doctor Conners. I have your family." A calm, steady voice answered. "If you want to see them alive again, you better meet me. Alone."
Conners' face dropped. He felt cold as the colour drained from his face, and fear gripped his heart like a vice. He couldn't breathe. He started hyperventilating.

It was Jane's voice.

PART THREE

69

Jane took more tablets. They didn't seem to help, though. Her head still hurt, and her body was still weak, sore, and beaten. Her logical brain said she still needed medical attention. She recalled hitting her head as she fell and wasn't sure what damage it had done. She couldn't feel anything – other than the headache, the dull pain behind her eyes, but that in itself could be a problem.

Her arms and legs hurt, they were covered in bruises that were turning more purple, but everything still worked. In the back of her mind was still the voice telling her she wasn't operationally fit.

It didn't matter, though. She could get help after the job was done.

Jane had driven straight from Denver to find Conners' wife and child. It was easy enough to do, she had managed to track the car, and it hadn't taken her long to find it once she was in the vicinity.

It had been easy enough to coerce them to come with her. All it had taken was a few threats, and they yielded and got in the car.

She had suffered a few setbacks the last day or so, but this put Jane back in charge, and there would be no way that he would not come, not now she had her leverage.

They had driven in near silence. The child was whimpering in the back seat, and the mother had her arms around her, trying to console her and telling her it would all be alright.

Once they were secure, she started calling Conners. It took a while – his phone was off, but eventually, he called her back.

70

Conners put the phone down and just stared at the wall. Unable to speak. Unable to move.

"Hey, you alright?" Caine asked.

"I have to go," Conners mumbled, not really sure what he was saying. He just stood, swaying slightly, shocked by the call.

"What is it?" Red asked as he got up from the chair, moving over to where the others were standing.

"My family…she has my family." His voice sounded distant, quiet, barely audible.

"Shit." Red breathed.

"I have to go," Conners repeated, then he seemed to snap back into his body, and his movements became fast and erratic. He didn't know where to start.

"You need to take me back to my car!" He settled on.

"No. Can't do that, you can't go. She will kill you." Caine said as he put his hands on Conners' shoulders, trying to calm him.

"Take a breath," Caine instructed.

"Can't. Have to get back, have to help them."

"You'll be no help to them dead," Red said. "Think it through, they're bait, they're safe, she wouldn't hurt them, hurting them hurts her chances of getting you."

"I don't care!" Conners erupted, "I have to do something, let go of me!" He shouted as he pulled away from Caine. He moved to the door, but Red blocked his path.

"Move." Conners commanded.

"Sure, make me," Red responded.

"You don't understand. It'll be my fault if something happens to them. You don't understand!"

"I don't understand," Red said. "I don…we don't understand? Can you hear yourself? Do you think we've never lost anybody? Seriously? You think we live in this bubble, and no one gets hurt. I feel like every time I take an assignment; someone gets hurt or killed. People die; it's a fact of life, but your family needs help, and how are *you* going to help them if you're dead?"

"What…this is different, this is my family!" Conners countered.

"We'll help you," Caine reassured him.

"Absolutely." Red agreed.

"No, no, no, no, I can't risk it, please, just move."

"I can't let you." Caine sighed, "I have to keep you safe."

"Why?" Conners spat angrily.

Caine frowned, "you hired me to."

"Yeah, well, that doesn't mean squat now, does it? It's done. Thank you for everything, but I really need to go. Consider yourself relieved, or completed, or, or whatever you want to call it…"

He was becoming more erratic. He was pacing, he was flailing his arms around as he spoke, and his voice was getting louder and his speech faster. He was spiralling. Understandable.

"No." Caine stated.

"What do you mean, no?" Conners questioned, his face not able to comprehend the response. "Just go, let me go." He begged.

"No." Caine repeated. "You want to go, fine. We'll go. But you're not going on your own."

"She said 'come alone', that's what she said, and she said it, so that's what I'm going to do." Conners sobbed. He was moving through emotions and had now broken down and started to cry.

"I can't lose them," he wept.

"You won't," Caine promised. "And you'll have a better chance with help."

Conners relented and nodded. He had lost the will to fight.

"You really going to do this?" Red asked, coming away from the door. Conners had sloughed onto the sofa, resigned to not being able to leave.

"Yes." Caine nodded. "If it were my daughter, I'd destroy cities to get to her."

Red lowered his voice. "Yeah, but you would have a shot at making that happen, he…" he pointed over his shoulder to Conners, "doesn't." Red then looked around, making sure Conners couldn't hear him before he continued, "look, we both know the probability of this working. There is every chance she will just kill them all. And you."

"I'm tougher than I look," Caine assured him.

"Yeah, and you look like you just went ten rounds in a ring," he looked down, "with a dislocated shoulder," he added.

"I can't turn my back on him, Red. You have family?"

"Not the one you're speaking of, no."

"Then you don't get it."

"The hell I don't. I get it. I get the fighting for a loved one thing perfectly."

"Yeah, I heard about the Carson incident," Caine said.

"That was just me, though," Red shot. "I wasn't carrying around a dead weight with delusions of rescue. I'm telling you, we go in that room. We don't all walk out."

"We?"

"Yeah, we."

There was a moment's silence between them.

"You don't think I'm going to let you go in there by yourself, do you?" Red said.

"This isn't your assignment. No hard feelings if you want to pass. I get it."

Red shook his head.

"You can get on your white stallion and try to ride to the rescue all you want, but it's not just you on the line; it's him and his family. I doubt she'll think twice about killing them all when she's done."

"Look," Caine said, "the best chance – the only chance we have of ending this in a way that it can't come back, is to remove her from the board. If we can do that, then it's done."

"Risky, R.O.E's are specific. It could cost you if you break them."

"I get it, but the rules of engagement state that if she tries to kill him, I can take her out. It's the logical move."

"There's only a small window between 'trying' to kill him and 'killing' him." Red pointed out.

"That's why I'm hoping you still think this is a 'we' thing." Caine smiled.

71

For a while, Leo thought Jane had eluded him. This was a problem as he didn't want to report that to The Chairman, but he was back on track. He had tried to close the gap, but just when he thought she was going one way, he was told she had stopped, and then shortly after started again and was moving in a completely different one. He was closing on her, though.

He ended up in the town that reminded him of an old TV show, and it wasn't on any of the maps he could find. He had been told she was somewhere in that town. He was driving down what looked like the main street. There was a convenience store, along with a charity shop, a vet, and a diner, amongst others. He drove around the back streets for a while, but there was too much ground to cover even though it was a small town. He knew where he was, though. He had started here.

He pulled back onto the main road and decided that if anyone knew anything, it would be a town gossip, and a local store is a perfect place for gossip.

He parked the BMW up and got out. He let the sun warm him for a moment as he looked up and down the street. It wasn't overly busy, but a few people were coming and going.

He walked into the store.

Inside there was a short queue, as he wondered about, scanning the shelves and eventually opened the fridge, took a bottle of water, and joined the line.

It took him a few minutes to reach the front – evidently, he was right about the gossip part. There was a lady behind the counter with a round face and a smile that came out at every opportunity.

"Howdy," he greeted her when he reached the front.

"Well, howdy to you too, stranger, say, you're not from around here, are you? No way no how. I never heard anyone talk like you do, have I? No, I haven't."

"It's surely a pleasure to be your first ma'am."

She giggled.

"Say, I dunno if y'all can help me, I'm looking for a friend of mine, new to town, she said I should come up and see this place, but I don't rightly know where she is, an' my phone died."

"Oh well, she was right to say to come and see it. Willow Creek is the most beautiful place on God's given earth; it's like our own slice of heaven."

"I can't argue with that," Leo smiled.

"But the only new person I know of is the lady, and that's not to say I gossip, of course, I like to keep myself to myself, I think that's the way it should be, not like certain others I could mention," she chuckled. "The only place she could be in is the place for sale at the edge of town, near the farm, that's it. Other than ol' Doc Simms place of course, I mean a terrible shame what happened to it, what happened you ask, well I didn't see anything, but I was told that there was a gun shooting fight thing in the house. I mean, Lord only knows why, or what the dickens happened, but that happened after she came to town, I believe. So, I would say yes, it wouldn't be Doc Simms old place."

"Thank you, ma'am, that's mighty helpful."

"You are welcome. I mean, the only other empty place in town is the old office building, but that's been vacant for a long time now, but no one would live there, it's not a house. What kind of person would do that? Not a right one, that's what I say. Anything else for you love? Or just the water?"

Leo smiled. "Just the water, if you may."

He paid and left, opened the bottle, and took a mouthful.

"What kind of person indeed?" He said to himself.

He took a moment, then drove to the edge of town and looked for the farm. It took some time, but eventually, he found it, and then a short while later, he was able to find the vacant house. There was a hole in the lawn where a sign had been, and he had peeked through the windows to find it empty.

Just because you can't see someone; doesn't mean they're not there.

Leo made a note of the address and went in search of the office building. He found it easy enough, but there were blinds down on all the windows. He tried to look in but couldn't see anything.

When Leo got back in the car, the black leather was hot to the touch from the sun. He set the air-con and made a call.

"Mister Knight," he said when it was answered.

"What do you want?" Mister Knights voice demanded. "I'm going to be needing a group of your finest soldiers, if y'all be so kind."

72

It had been a long drive. In the hours they were in the car, Conners barely spoke. He just sat in the back and looked out the window. The Jeep was a nice ride, it took bumps well, and the supercharger on the V8 whined like a jet engine whenever it accelerated. Caine had his foot to the floor, and the Jeep covered ground at an alarming rate. He knew he had passed several speed cameras but didn't care. He knew he would never see the tickets.

The night drew in as they drove, and it was almost midnight by the time they reached Willow Creek. Conners had been given the address Jane had provided – it was a vacant office building.

They pulled up around the back. The door looked like it had already been broken and quickly repaired.

"You ready for this?" Caine asked Conners, looking at him in the rear-view mirror.

Conners just nodded slowly.

"Stay calm when you're in there. It will all be fine."

"Ok."

Caine looked to Red, "you ready?"

"As I'm going to be."

"Let's go."

They opened the doors and stepped out into the night. It was cool now, the heat from the day's sun had gone, and it was a pleasant temperature. As they walked around the front of the building, he could hear crickets and insects clicking and chirping in the silence of the night.

He tested his shoulder, it was still sore, but he figured it would still be useable if the meeting went sideways – of which he had no doubt it would.

They reached the door, and Caine took point, slowly turning the handle, checking for any trip wires or catches. He didn't find any, he opened the door, and they went inside.

73

Inside the office building was quiet. There was no furniture in the front area; it was just cream walls and a grey carpet.

Caine and Red both had their weapons drawn, but they were angled down behind their backs. She would know they had them, but it was a show of faith that they weren't raised.

They heard movement.

Red raised his Glock and aimed at the doorway to what looked like a back room as the woman walked through.

"Jane," Conners breathed.

She just stood there, a Sig Sauer in her hand, raised at him.

"I told you to come alone." She said through gritted teeth.

"They wouldn't let me."

Caine and Red slowly closed up to shield Conners.

Red's weapon was raised, Caine put his away in his holster under his left arm.

"We don't want to fight." He assured her, raising his hands from bent elbows. This showed he was now unarmed and not a threat – but also meant Caine could draw his M45 at a second's notice.

"What would I want to talk with you about? Who are you people anyway?" Jane paused, "actually, it doesn't matter. Just leave. Conners is the one I want."

"I have to protect him," Caine said.

"Protect him? You can't protect him, not forever."

"You're the only one hunting him," Red said, his Glock still raised in the stalemate with Jane.

"It doesn't matter if there's only one predator out there." She countered, "as long as there is, the prey will never be safe…Imagine – if you can – how safe the sheep would be if there were no more wolves." Her face twisted with anger and her lip curled, "but there's still a wolf left, and I will hunt you down, and every single one of the others – all of them. You are not safe. You have nowhere to hide. I will find them all; no matter who they hire as fodder, I will find them. I am coming for them, and there is nothing you can do about it. So stay out of my way."

"Jane," Conners said as he pushed through the agents, "I'm so, so sorry."

"You are now, but you didn't hesitate to try and have us killed."

"I did, I hesitated. I was one of the few that did…I, I know it's no excuse, but I had no idea what this was doing to you. If I had known, I would have tried to end it years ago."

"Bullshit. If we hadn't woken up and fought our way out, we would be in a shallow grave in those woods over there now, and you would just be carrying on, like nothing had happened, with whoever you picked next." Jane growled, hatred in her words.

"I…I have nothing to say to defend myself. The work I was doing, I…we…were doing it to try and make the world a safer place."

"No, you were doing it to make soldiers. That's what we were before we came here, so that's what this *Phoenix Initiative* is all about. War. Only," she raised her voice. "It's not so easy when it's at your own door, is it?!"

Caine drew his weapon and aimed; Red hadn't moved, his eyes and sights still firmly on her.

"This doesn't have to end in death." Caine said, trying to calm the situation, "just lower your gun, let his family go."

"It's always going to end in death," she said, "everything does. But this, this started in death, when they tried to kill us…when they killed John."

"I'm sorry for your loss," said Caine.

"I…I tried so hard to fight Jenkins, and Francis, and all the others that wanted you gone," Conners pleaded, "you were the most remarkable couple we had ever worked with. You were strong, fast, smart, and above all, you both showed compassion towards each other. It was more than just two people training; you bonded, much more than any had before you. And you were both so strong. You had none of the side effects that impacted the others. You see, some of them couldn't take it, and the medication had bad reactions. Yes, I agreed that some of the participants needed to be removed, but by that time, it was for their own good. And they knew failure meant they wouldn't be allowed to re-enter society."

Jane frowned, "What? They knew they couldn't re-enter society?"

Conners hesitated, "Yes, it was part of the volunteering process. It was agreed if they couldn't do it, they would be killed in order for the next to proceed. Everyone signed...including you."

Jane faltered, "why would we do that?"

"To try and make the country a safer place."

"Phoenix," she whispered.

Red spoke, "taking soldiers and stripping them down, and then from the ashes rising to be better, that's what you said doctor...but only it's not, is it? It's taking what you do with one, and then from the ashes of that 'failure', you rise the next one, bigger and better."

Conners swallowed, "if you want to look at it that way, though I never did." Conners looked at Jane. "...But you were perfect, untainted and showed the most improvement we had ever seen."

"Untainted?" Jane asked, "what side effects?"

"The muscle twitches, numbness, nightmares, th..."

"Nightmares?" Jane interjected, "what nightmares?"

"On some of the 'medication', some of the participants would have nightmares, mostly it seemed about parts of their old life – memories, that would seep through, but with dark twists."

"So, the little boy and girl? They could be real," she said to herself more than the room.

"You...you've been having nightmares? What about the muscle twitches? Why wasn't it reported?"

"I haven't had any of the muscle stuff. I got the first nightmare the night before you tried to kill me, I hadn't had an eval since the dream and my execution attempt," she muttered.

"I, I…look, I didn't try to have you killed, it wasn't my…"

"That's not what I was told." She snapped, back in focus again now.

"Ask Jenkins, please."

"Jenkins is the one who told me."

"And you believed him?"

"No, not completely, that's why we're talking now, and I didn't just kill you and move on. But then you hired protection," Jane nodded to the agents who were standing behind Conners, weapons still raised. "So, my suspicions grew. What are you hiding?"

"Nothing, I promise," Conners' hands were up, trying to reassure her. "I just wanted to keep my family safe and stay alive long enough to see Elise grow up." He tried to look around her, "where…where are they?" He asked, panic growing in his voice.

"Upstairs." She gestured. "Safe for now."

Conners took a step towards her.

"Doctor," Caine said. "Don't."

"It's OK," he whispered, "it's OK. It's what needs to be done. I have been thinking about this for a while now, and I think Jane is right. I think it's my time." He looked up into her eyes, "but you, you sp…spare my fam…fam…family though. OK?" He was crying, choked up, and he was struggling to get his words out. "Please."

She nodded. "Agreed."

Caine frowned; his grip tightened. "Doctor, stop walking. Now."

Conners was almost at Jane. He sank to his knees on the dirty grey carpet, and his head was down.

"I can't let you do that!" Caine demanded as he took a step forward, and Jane adjusted her stance. For a second, Caine thought she was going to fire. But she didn't.

Red moved around, his sights trained on her. They were now stood like a triangle, with Conners on his knees in the middle.

"Doctor, come back. Now." Caine commanded.

"Do it, Doc." Red supported.

Conners slowly reached in and took out his phone, powered it up, it seemed to take forever, and the tension in the air was suffocating. It wouldn't be long before a trigger got pulled. It was a testament to the level of those involved that one already hadn't been.

Conners tapped his phone and then made a call.

"Hello," he said when it was answered. "Yes, I'd like to change my contract to complete, or accomplished, or done, or whatever it needs to be. I have transferred the remaining money I have to you."

He hung up.

Caine's phone beeped. He looked at Red, who nodded, so he knew he was covered, and then he took one hand from his M45 and took his phone from his inside jacket pocket. There was a message that read:

Contract Complete.
Report back for debrief.

He looked back at Red. "It's done."

Red lowered his weapon. Caine did the same. Jane lowered hers slightly, but she wasn't an idiot; she kept it ready in case it was a trap.

"Can I see them before it ends, please?" Conners asked. Jane looked at him for a minute, then at the agents, she was still weary, but the look in his eye told her he was resigned to his fate.

"Ok," she said.

"Thank you," Conners said as he rose, "make sure it's not in vain, get everyone, all the people higher up in the programme, don't give them a chance to re-start this." He was walking past her as he spoke. She put her hand on his shoulder and stopped him, and he turned around.

"Higher up?" she questioned.

"Yeah, the ones above me."

"My file shows you're the highest, you and a Francis."

"Of the group, yes, but not of the programme. There are many levels higher up than in pretty much any file they will allow access to."

Jane took her hand from his shoulder, and he ran upstairs.

Upstairs was much the same as downstairs, except there was still a couple of desks and cabinets in the room, there was a window at the front overlooking the street and a small one at the back overlooking the alleyway. It wouldn't have provided a lot of light, but some is better than none. The most significant difference, though, was Molly and Elise huddled next to a desk in the middle of the room. Zip-ties bound their hands and feet. They were on tight but not tight enough to bite into their skin.

She had only put them on as a precaution.

"Daddy! Daddy!" Elise screamed with joy as he walked in. He ran to them, dropped to his knees, and held her as tight as he could. He breathed her in and gripped her so hard as he never wanted to let her go. She started crying.

He started again.

He let her go and looked over to Molly. She looked unharmed, her mascara had run from tears, but she looked ok other than that. He cupped his hands around her face and kissed her firmly on her lips, and then he brought her into an embrace just as tight as the one he had given Elise.

He felt a weight lift from him as the relief washed through his body. He was so relieved they were safe.

"Are you OK?" Molly asked him.

"I'm fine, how, how are you? Are you both OK? Did she hurt you?"

"No, no, we're OK. I was just so worried about you." She said as she kissed him again, and he stroked the back of her head, placing his forehead to hers.

"It's all going to be OK. I promise."

"I'm sorry," she sobbed.

"Don't, don't you apologise, it's me, my fault, but I promise nothing will happen to either of you. I promise." He looked to Elise. "I'll get you out of this," he smiled.

She was smiling now, a big smile, and her eyes were happy.

"Elise said you were coming," Molly said, "she kept saying, 'daddy will come, he will save us'" she gave a little laugh through the tears, "she said you wouldn't let us down."

"I won't. You will both get out of here. I promise."

"What about you?"

"I have to go now," he said, getting up, "just know that I love you both so, so much. You are the best things that have ever happened to me, and I hope you remember me as the man I tried to be. I know you'll do an amazing job with this one."

He knelt back next to Elise and held her close, kissing her head a few times.

"You be good now," Conners whispered; speaking was hard as he was choked up. He tried to release his grip but couldn't. He took a deep breath, kissed her once more and stood up.

"What, what are you saying, what are y…why are you talking like that?" Molly stammered. She tried to get up, but the zip-tie caught, and she dropped down to her knees.

"What are you doing?" Molly asked again.

But she knew. Tears ran down her face, and as Conners looked into Molly's eyes, his heart broke.

"I love you." Conners choked. He couldn't stop the tears as he turned and walked out of the room.

The last thing he heard as he closed the door was:

"No, Rich, please don't!"

Followed by:

"Daddy?

74

Leo had watched from across the street. He wasn't sure which of the units she would be in, but the office was the last he had checked, so he had set up shop and waited there. Half the team had been sent to the house to see which one it was before they planned their attack.

He had watched the black Jeep drive past and pull in down the alley around the back of the office. Then a moment later, three men had rounded the corner, one in a black suit, white shirt and orange tie, one in a full black three-piece suit, black shirt and red tie, and one in casual jeans and a shirt.

Leo recognised Conners.

He took photos of the others, sent them for identification.

The night was cooler but not cold, so the wait hadn't been unpleasant, he had just been looking at the stars, listening to the insects and planning his attacks for each residence, but now he knew where they were.

Surely, they must be going to meet her.

Two targets in the same place. Things were finally looking up for him.

He called Wells.

"Hello," Wells' deep voice answered.

"They're at the office, get y'all selves over here and let's end this."

"Copy that."

A short while later, Leo, Wells and a ten-strong unit were ready to attack.

"Everyone clear on what y'all doing?" Leo checked.

Everyone agreed.

"Then why don' we all get in positions, and let's do it."

Almost silently, the men got into position. Wells and Leo stayed back by the truck. There would be five spaced out at the front windows, five at the rear: all wielding Heckler and Koch HK416 rifles.

"Everyone ready?" Wells said into the radio.

"In position, ready to go, over."

"Copy that." Wells looked to Leo. "Ready when you are."

Leo ran his tongue over his bottom lip and smiled.

75

Conners walked back down the stairs. Caine, Red and Jane were in the room.

"You don't have to do this," Caine said.

"Me for them," Conners said.

Caine could see his whole-body language was defeated. His head down, his shoulders slumped, he shuffled as he walked back into the front office.

The three of them had stood quiet while he was upstairs, keeping an eye on each other. No one relaxed; everyone was ready to raise their weapons at a millisecond's notice. It was like an old western shootout, but it was two against one.

"It's OK." Conners said, "you can go now."

Caine and Red stayed where they were.

"It's not necessary," he assured them.

"Just a head's up," Red said. "Once you pull that trigger, you better turn it on me quick."

Caine looked over, surprised at what Red had said, but he felt the same. They weren't all leaving that room tonight.

Jane moved her eyes from Red to Caine, back and forth a few times.

"I have an alternative," she said eventually.

Conners looked up, confused.

"I want everyone on that list. I won't deny that. I made a promise, and I intend to keep it. But I believed you in what you said. And if you're right, there are people above you that need to answer as well. So, I propose a truce. I won't kill you."

Conners' eyes widened. He looked tired, but there was a hint of hope.

"If," Jane continued, "you help me dismantle the rest of it."

"Ok," Conners exclaimed before she had even finished the sentence.

"It will mean me killing people, you know. And if you try to stop me, try to dissuade me, it's off, and I kill you."

Conners frowned and stood for a moment. He was thinking it through. Caine and Red looked at each other.

"I understand," said Conners finally. "It wasn't long ago I was saying I would try and bring it down anyway, that has consequences for those involved, including me, but if I can redeem myself, I will do what I can. But I can't be there when you, you know, do the killing stuff."

"What's my name?" She asked, "and not the given one."

Conners panicked, "I honestly don't know. We don't get told that. It's to try and keep us disassociated from you. But I will help you find it, I promise. Please."

"Ok. I agree to this deal. You tell me everything and help me when I need it, you're not there when I catch up to them, and you help me find out my name, John's, and the names of everyone else they have done this to."

"And we can help the others?" He asked.

"Others?"

"The others, like you, in the other facilities around the country, the world."

"How many are there?"

"I don't know exactly, most of it's compartmentalised, but occasionally we would get status and stats from other groups and teams in the programme so that we could compare and correlate."

Jane nodded slowly. "We take it all down," she said. Conners nodded.

She walked up to him and held out her hand. He hesitated, went to shake a couple of times, and stopped. He was scared it was a trap. He looked up into her eyes. She looked into his. Conners relaxed, and they shook.

Caine had been watching the interaction like a hawk, expecting a surprise attack, but none came. When she initiated the handshake, he thought that was it, and he prepared, gripping his weapon tighter, the safety was off. He expected Red was doing the same.

Everyone relaxed.

Then the world around them exploded.

76

Bullets shattered the windows, piercing the night and peppering the walls of the office. Red and Jane dropped the second the first rounds were fired, Conners hesitated, and Caine leapt and tackled him to the ground, covering him.

The firing was relentless. It fanned across the space from left to right and then back, repeating the pattern a few times; glass and chunks of the wall covered the floor and the bodies of the people lying on it, curled up, trying to make themselves as small as possible.

The noise echoed. There were light thuds as the bullets found the walls and dug in, making it look like a cheese grater.

Nobody spoke.

Nobody moved.

If any of them had tried to get up, they would have been killed almost instantly.

The gunfire continued. It seemed like it would never stop. Caine's ears rang. He glanced up; the walls were destroyed, some of the stud wall sections had fallen off, and he could see through to the back room through them. There was glass everywhere, and the blinds were shredded. It looked like a warzone, and they hadn't even been able to fire a single shot.

Caine realised through the ringing in his ears that the guns had stopped, and it was just the sound in his head. He took stock, looked around;

"Everyone OK?" He asked. He actually shouted, trying to speak over the ringing. He saw everyone nod and heard a muffled "yes" from Red and Jane.

He looked down at Conners.

Conners hadn't moved since Caine had tackled him. It was then he realised why. There was a puddle of blood underneath him, and his eyes were wide open but not moving.

Caine quickly checked himself, in case it was his, and the adrenaline was masking it, but he seemed in one piece physically. He lifted himself up from Conners to a knelt position next to him, checked for a pulse. Nothing.

Caine then rolled him from his side and saw two bullet entry wounds to his chest. His shirt was soaked in blood and getting redder at each passing second. He looked up at Red, at Jane, both looked taken aback, and Jane looked sad – he was surprised by that. Everything seemed to slow down, like his brain couldn't accept what was happening, so it had slowed his perception so it could try and catch up, try, and understand what was happening. But his moment was cut short by the sound of metal hitting the pavement outside through the ringing.

Reloading.

Caine had to move. There was nothing more he could do for Conners now.

"They're about to breach!" He shouted – probably loud enough for those outside to hear, but he didn't care. Caine drew his M45, seamlessly made sure it was ready. This would not go unpunished.

He glanced at Red; he also had his Glock drawn and was already moving to the front door. Jane had her Sig Sauer in her hands and was moving to the door to the backroom.

Caine wished he had brought more than just his side-arm. All the other weapons were in the boot of the Jeep, and that may as well be a hundred miles away now.

"I'm going for the rifles." He declared as he got up and moved to go past Jane, but the back door opened, and a grenade rolled in as he did so.

Caine spun and dove back through as it detonated. He was lucky it hadn't travelled far, but the explosion forced Jane to the ground. They got up, Jane braced by the door, and Caine took the hole in the wall, and as the soldiers breached through the back door, they fired.

77

Taylor had been first up after the onslaught of fire through the office had ceased.

Caine had made the check. He was ok.

Then he saw Conners had been hit, and Orange was knelt over him. This was bad; he had thought for a moment that this would have a happy ending, Jane seemed to accept his apology, and they would help each other take down *The Phoenix Initiative,* but now Conners was gone, and a wave of frustration, annoyance and anger came over him, one Taylor hadn't felt in about a year. He pushed himself and moved to the front of the office, using the wall next to the door for cover.

Taylor peered through the window and saw three men outside in uniforms and body armour. They were finishing reloading and looked like they were moving to breach – but there may have been more he couldn't see.

His head was sore, and he had a loud ringing in his ears, but he ignored it; the ringing would go away.

If he survived long enough.

"At least three," Taylor said, but wasn't sure if he was heard.

Then the door opened, and a grenade rolled inside.

It rolled past him, but he dived and scooped it up, he wanted to throw it out the door, but it would have taken too long and detonated, so in reaction, he tossed it through one of the windowless frames. It exploded outside, but Taylor still felt the heat and the force of the blast through the windows. At the same time, an explosion came from the back room, and he saw Orange and Jane clamber up and take position.

They're coming from both sides, Taylor thought, *boxing us in.*

The smell of smoke and gunpowder filled his nostrils, his throat felt dry, and his hearing was still partially impaired, but he scrambled up and prepared for the assault.

78

The first soldier appeared through the door. He entered carefully but with too much haste. There was no cover in the openness of the first room, so Taylor had to press himself against the wall next to the entrance to keep out of sight.

As the first man entered, Taylor raised his Glock 17, aimed as best he could through the darkness and the smoke and fired twice.

The body dropped to the floor.

He was ready for the next one, and sure enough, he saw a head and the barrel of what he believed was an HK416 rifle. The angle was difficult for the soldier, and he stepped over his fallen teammate into the room, but he swept left when he should have swept right, and Taylor fired another two rounds at his head.

He, too, dropped to the floor.

Taylor used the split second he had to crawl across the floor and pick up the rifle. He was right; it was an HK416. Taylor quickly checked the magazine and made sure it was ready to go. He could hear the unrelenting fire over his shoulder, part of his brain wanted him to look around, make sure everything was ok, but he knew if there were a problem, he would know about it. They would tell him, or the bullet that would kill him from behind would resolve the issue anyway.

So, Taylor focused, he used the fallen bodies like a makeshift sandbag wall for cover and leaned up enough to see through into the night. He saw figures at the back but couldn't make them out well enough. His focus was taken with the three soldiers still stacked up and ready to enter. Taylor unleashed the rifle in short bursts, managing to kill a third before they retreated. They were firing at him, and he felt the bullets hit the wall around him, felt small parts flake off and fall on him like dust. He could feel the bodies he was using as a protection move as the force of the bullets hit them, narrowly missing him, but he couldn't move back; he had to hold the line. He fired again, and again, but failed to land any more hits.

Taylor saw one of the men at the edge move forward and leave his view. He wondered where he had gone. Wherever it was, it wouldn't be good.

He braced and waited for an enemy combatant to enter his field of view or hear instructions from Jane or Orange to move. He held his position; all Taylor could do now was wait and hope they were doing as well as he had.

79

Caine and Jane waited. It seemed at the same time that they came through the front; they breached the back. They were lucky however, it was a small narrow single door, so they had to go through single file.

As the first soldier presented himself, they both fired. His vest took a lot of the hits, knocking him to the floor.

Another soldier grabbed him and tried to drag him back through the door, but as he lifted him up under his arms, Jane was able to get a clear shot and didn't waste it. She hit him with a clean headshot, and his body went limp. The soldier dragged it out anyway. Then came through himself. He made it halfway across the room before the wall of bullets felled him.

The next round of fire came from around the door. It seemed they had realised walking in was too risky and were using what cover they had, leaning around and firing. The bullets thudded into the walls, and Caine had to take cover as he was only protected by a stud wall, and some of the rounds ripped straight through it. Caine and Jane returned fire but were caught in a stalemate. Caine was also thinking about Conners' family on the second floor; if they panicked and came down, they would be cut to ribbons.

He glanced over his shoulder, Red was on watch at the front, using a human sandbag wall, and he thought if he could get the family down, then they could get out.

"I'm going upstairs!" Caine shouted over the volley of gunfire.

Jane looked at him. She hadn't heard him properly. He signed him going upstairs, and she nodded.

When there was a moment's break in the barrage of bullets, he cried, "cover me!" and broke cover, running past Jane, through the door and up the stairs.

He heard her firing, forcing the soldiers to stay in cover until he was clear.

Caine burst through the door, found a woman and young girl quivering on the floor. The mother was cuddling the daughter, trying to protect her. They were in roughly the middle of the room, nearer the front than the back, and had their hands and feet loosely bound by zip-ties.

He took a second to assess the situation. He realised the woman thought he was there to kill them and raised his hands.

"It's OK. I'm a friendly." Caine assured her, moving past her to the rear window.

"Wh…what's happening? What…what's going on? Is, I…Is Rich OK?" The woman asked, holding the child closer. She was shaking, this wasn't Caine's first gunfight, but he knew it was probably hers, and if they couldn't fight them off, then there was a chance this woman and child would be killed, just by proxy of being in the building and bearing witness. He didn't have the heart to tell her of Conners' death, so he didn't say anything. He crouched by the window at the rear of the office. He could see the men in the street below, ready to go in once they had suppressed Jane. It was only a matter of time before the Soldiers overpowered them.

They hadn't seen him, though, so Caine leaned out the window and started firing.

There were five in his view. He fired, some of the bullets only wounded, but he was able to kill two more before he ran out of ammunition and his gun dry fired. They realised what was happening and started firing towards the window as Caine ducked back in, looked defeatedly at his M45, and tossed it away.

He could still get Conners wife and girl out though.

He moved over to them, knelt down, "it's OK, I'll get you out of here."

"Her first," the woman said, nodding to the young girl, "save Elise."

He leant down and broke the cable ties on Elise's hands and ankles and was about to release the mother, when a grenade came in through the back window and rolled – in what seemed like slow motion, across the floor towards them.

80

There's always that moment when you have options of what to do. Sometimes you have time to decide, but this time Caine didn't.

The grenade rolled menacingly across the floor.

I could try and get to it and throw it out the window, but his head had done the calculation and knew it was too far down the countdown for that to work.

I could throw myself onto it, but in a room this small, it wouldn't make much difference; they would all die.

Caine ran these options through in a millisecond and then let his reactions decide.

He knew he couldn't save them.

But he could save one of them.

He grabbed Elise, and she screamed as he sprinted the short distance to the front-facing window and jumped, just as the blast erupted behind them and the heat hit them as the force pushed them through.

They were falling. The air raced past them as they plummeted. It was a long drop, but the anticipation of the floor felt like it took forever.

Caine gripped her as close as he could, protecting her head as best as he could, having nothing left to help his own landing.

They hit the floor.

Caine landed hard. He felt like he had shattered his shoulder and cried out. He hit his head, but not too hard; he was able to stay conscious. His legs hurt, his back hurt, he was a heap on the floor. He slowly managed to open his arms. He could still hear gunfire from inside. He felt he had burnt some of his face; he couldn't talk, his throat was dry and coarse. He couldn't see; his vision was blurry and coming in and out of focus, and all he could smell was smoke and gunpowder, even out in the open air, his system was clogged.

He couldn't hear much. Everything sounded muffled, but Caine realised the muffled sound wasn't just the gunfight; it was the girl in his arms, screaming and crying.

She had been hurt in the fall. But she was alive.

As Caine tried to focus, he saw a man walk over. He was wearing a brown suit with a patterned tie.

For a moment, he was relieved someone had come to help, but then he realised that that wasn't the man's intention. Caine was hazy, and he kept coming in and out of focus. The man in the brown suit said something. It took Caine's muddled brain a moment to process it. The man had said: "No witnesses."

Caine saw the gun rise from his side, pointed one-handed at his face.

The last thing Caine saw was the flash as the man fired.

81

Meanwhile…

After the one with the orange tie had gone upstairs, Jane was left to defend by herself. The one with the waistcoat and red tie was positioned by the front door. Jane knew she was in danger of losing her position; she was running low on ammo and needed a new weapon.

"Hey, waistcoat!" Jane shouted over her shoulder.

"Me!" He shouted back.

"I don't see anyone else down here at the minute looking like they're going to a wedding, do you?" She replied, "I'm almost out."

A moment later, waistcoat and red tie was where orange tie had been, and he threw her the HK416 from the other downed soldier at the front door.

"Hello, baby," she smiled as she opened a burst of fire towards the door.

Gunpowder and sweat filled her nostrils; she had to admit, she liked it.

They exchanged fire, and after a few minutes' waistcoat guy turned and looked towards the door. As he turned back, a grenade was thrown in through the back door, it didn't reach their position, but he was oblivious to it. Jane launched herself and dived onto him, pushing him aside, and there was a sound of an explosion above before it detonated.

She was on top of him, more of the stud wall had come down, and now there was barely any left. She looked down at him. He was looking up at her.

He was a handsome man. He was the most attractive man she had ever seen – but that wasn't saying much in her state.

"You alive, waistcoat?" She asked.

"Yeah," he said, "fine, thanks, and call me Red."

There was a moment between them, but then she snapped out of it.

"Yeah, sure, whatever," she groaned at her pain as she rolled off him and fired at the soldier that came through the door. First at his knees, and when he dropped, she landed the kill shot. The last thing Jane needed was to be diving on people, she had had a rough few days, and her body was not in the right state for this, but the adrenaline and her sheer bloody-minded determination would not allow her to die until she had fulfilled her promise.

"Right. Yes. Good." She heard Red say as he got up. He was moving back to position.

She glanced over at him but then shook it off and retook her cover point.

There was dust lightly falling from the ceiling. There had been the sound before the explosion in front of them.

"Go check!" Jane instructed. "I'll cover you!"

He nodded but then turned and looked out the front door. Then he ducked low and ran towards it.

"What the fu-" she mumbled to herself and then fired at the soldier coming through.

82

Taylor was about to make the run for the stairs when he heard a thud and a cry from outside. He changed his plan, ducked low and ran for the front door.

He drew his Glock – having left his rifle on the floor after Jane had tackled him. He reached the door and saw Orange lying on the floor, it was hard to know as he couldn't see him completely, but he looked to be holding someone. Taylor started to climb over the bodies and then heard a voice say, *"No witnesses"*. Then he heard a gunshot ring out – somehow, it was louder and more prominent than the others of the night. Taylor moved around, and the man came into view, he was still climbing and off-balance, but he saw the man in the brown suit move the sights of his gun at whoever was in Orange's arms. Taylor knew what was coming, but he wasn't in the position to stop it.

Move! Taylor's mind screamed at him.

He rushed to clear the body he was climbing over. His feet were still off-balance, but instinct told him he had to try and stop whatever was happening, urgency took precedent over control, and he fired a shot.

The man was standing side on to him, and the bullet passed through his neck, he fell to the floor.

Taylor ran to Orange, but it was too late. There was a bullet wound in his head.

He opened his arms up and saw the girl buried into him, crying – *Conners' daughter.*

Then Taylor looked up to the second floor. The window was destroyed, and smoke was coming from the windows.

He knew two people had been up there, and now Orange was lying on the floor with one in his arms. His heartfelt heavy. He never got used to it.

He was brought back to reality as the sounds of Jane still fighting entered his ears, bringing him round. Taylor turned to go back inside but saw a man walking away at a fast pace, he was wearing the same clothes as the soldiers, but he didn't have armour on. He was moving towards a Ford Ranger that was parked down the street. Taylor picked up his gun and fired twice. The first missed, but the second hit him in the back, and he fell forward.

He started walking over to him, and as he walked past the shop, he realised he could finish off whoever was there.

They had tried to kill a child was all that went through Taylor's mind, and he walked around the back of the office building. He saw the Jeep, still parked where they had left it, but it had had its tyres slashed so that it couldn't be used as a getaway car.

Taylor could see two men. He walked up behind the first one, rammed his heel in the back of his knee and as he leaned back, Taylor grabbed his head, pulled it back, jammed the barrel under his chin and pulled the trigger.

There was one more; he was in front of Taylor and hadn't noticed what had happened behind him. As Taylor walked up behind him, he must have sensed something because he started to turn. Taylor kicked the rifle from his hands, grabbed him by his armour and forced him up against the outside wall.

"This is for Orange," Taylor said as he pulled his helmet off, forced his gun up under the vest, and looked him dead in the eye as he fired twice at his heart. He became dead weight, and Taylor watched as the life left the soldiers eyes.

Jane came out a moment later, her H&K levelled to her eye, looking for a trap.

"One left." Red coughed as he turned and walked over to the man he had shot in the back.

They had been lucky – the ones that had survived, neither had taken any damage that couldn't be walked off, which was good considering how much they had taken fighting each other the day before.

"I know him." Jane snarled as they reached the man. He was still breathing, and he rolled over.

"You. I'm glad I get to kill you. There was a time you stood over my grave. I'm glad I get to send you to yours." She said as she raised her gun to him.

The man said nothing. He just looked defiantly at her.

"He may be of use to you," Taylor suggested, then he looked down at the man on the floor. "I bet he knows all sorts of things that'll help you."

Jane's eyes narrowed, "Nothing that I'd trust."

"He's all yours." Taylor said as he turned and walked away.

"Wait!" He heard a deep, base filled voice plead, but then the final shot of the night rang out into the settling stillness.

Taylor knelt by Orange, touched the girl on the shoulder. She whimpered and tried to hide herself. She didn't seem to notice the man she was cuddling into couldn't hold her back.

"I'm here to help." Taylor said softly, "I will make sure you're safe."

83

The next day…

Taylor had called The Company as soon as he was sure it was safe. He had stayed with the child, Elise, while Jane went back inside, she came out and shook her head. He suspected it, but she confirmed the mother was gone.

They moved the bodies inside, cleared the weapons and bags from the boot of the Jeep and into the Volvo's. They put Elise in the car. She was reluctant, but after a short struggle, she conceded.

Taylor took one last look at the wreck that was the old office building, the shattered windows, bullet-ridden walls and wondered how it – and they – were still standing.

The three of them drove in near silence through the night and eventually arrived at the house Jane had taken Elise and her mother from.

The woman opened the door and almost cried when she saw him standing there with her – Jane was waiting in the car, they decided it was best. The woman did cry when he told her of the day's events, and she held Elise tight.

Taylor left shortly afterwards and got back in the Volvo.

"How'd that go?" Jane asked.

"As expected," Taylor replied.

"What now?"

"Now, I go home. There's nothing left for me to do here, the office is being dealt with, and the contract is done. So, now I try and get my head around the last few days events and then go home and try to explain it."

"What about your friend?" She asked.

"What about him?"

"Will there be a service? A memorial? Did he have family?"

Taylor nodded, "I think so, but I don't know. I'll probably never know; I didn't even know his name."

There was a silence between them. Jane started the engine and pulled off down the street.

Taylor looked over, "what about you?" He asked, a few minutes into the journey.

"I'm not done yet," she said, "I still have much work to do. Starting with Doctor Francis. I'm looking forward to meeting her." She smiled to herself.

"And then what?"

"What do you mean?"

"After this? After everyone is dead, and you have your revenge, closure, justice – whatever you want to call it. What will you do?"

Jane paused a moment, staring out the windscreen as she drove, "I don't know," she said.

He watched her, the light dancing across her face as the car passed under streetlamps. There was a sadness in her eyes, an emptiness that saddened him.

The rest of the journey was spent in silence.

Taylor hadn't realised how tired he was, and he couldn't wait to stop. He knew he would sleep on the plane. He had another flight booked, and he wouldn't have to wait long once he was at the airport.

They arrived in plenty of time, and he looked over at Jane; she glanced at him but then looked straight ahead again.

"Thanks for the ride," he said.

"You're welcome," she replied, "you sure you want me to drop your bag off at the climbing wall place?"

Taylor smiled, "Yeah, they'll know how to get it back in the right hands."

"Ok," she shrugged.

"Thank you. Hey, listen," Taylor said, "If you need anything, just give me a call." He gave her the contact number, "they'll know how to get hold of me."

"Ok." She said flatly. Then, her body relaxed, her shoulders dropped, and she sighed. "Thank you," she smiled weakly.

"Any time."

Taylor climbed out of the Volvo, glanced back, met her eyes, smiled, and closed the door. He took his luggage bag from the boot and then watched her as she drove away.

"Good luck," he said to the air as he watched her drive away.

Then he went into the airport.

84

The Chairman was sitting in his office. He had the door closed and the blinds down across the internal windows. The room was all chrome fittings with black glass tabletops, black sofas, a TV on the wall with the news on in silence, and a grey floor. It was morning now, and he had recently learnt of Leo's death. He was not happy about it. In the last year or so now, he had lost two of his members. He could replace them – and would with the right people, but he was still angry that he had been inconvenienced twice now, twice his plans had been interrupted. And Jane Doe was still on the loose.

He was looking at a photo that Leo had sent shortly before losing contact. It showed three men walking into a building. Two were in suits, and despite the low light and the angle, one of them looked remarkably like the one Gemini had reported back a year or so before. The same man that Aries has been working to track down.

So, who are you?

"It's time for a new plan," he said aloud to himself, then he picked up his phone and called Aries.

"He's been in America." The Chairman said.

"Then what am I doing getting drowned in the rain here for then?" Aries replied, "I'll be on the next flight; where is he?"

"He was in Denver, in Willow Creek, he somehow got involved – with another man, in the Phoenix affair."

"How?"

"I assume it was the same circumstances that Gemini encountered, only this time, we didn't play the hand."

"Ok, Sir, what's the plan?" Aries asked.

"Leo is dead." The Chairman said matter-of-factly.

"By his hand?"

"It's not confirmed, but I suspect yes."

"Sir, we need to end this!" Aries said, his tone becoming angry.

"I agree, but that is why I sent you a year ago to deal with this. So be careful who you raise your voice to."

"Sir, I'm sorry, I have been tracking him, but I have never come across a group this hard to dissect. Even with all our resources, I'm struggling to pin him down."

"Then it's time to change how we approach this."

"Yes, Sir, what do you want me to do?" Aries asked.

"We're going to stop chasing. And bring him to us…"

85

The flight from Denver to London was almost nine hours. Taylor slept most of it. He needed it.

He was still sore, still aching from his encounter with Jane at the Motel 6, even though it seemed like it happened a long time ago now. His face was still bruised – they were a lovely shade of purple now, but at least the cuts were stinging less.

He had a new bruise on his thigh from where Jane had dug her knee in when she had dived on him in the office confrontation. He rubbed it and smiled as his mind wandered to her.

Once he landed, he collected his car from the rental place with his code sent to his phone. He walked out and found the blue Jaguar XFR-S. He put his bag in the boot and climbed in.

He drove, and halfway back, it started raining.

Welcome home, he smiled to himself.

He went straight to *Craftsman Bespoke Tattooing*, an unassuming building on an unassuming street. This was his base for The Company. He parked in the car park around the corner, walked around, heard the reassuring swing of the studio sign in the breeze and entered. Its familiarity welcomed him as he walked in; the layout, the smell, it was comforting. He walked straight through and through the door at the back marked 'PRIVATE'.

He went up the flight of stairs, past the large office through the door – that was where Carol and Edgar had been while they were his support. He continued up the next flight and came to a locked door. Taylor entered the code, and a little light on top went from red to green, and the audible sound of a lock disengaging was heard. He pushed down on the handle and went inside. As he did so, the green light above the door turned red. Inside was nice, simply decorated with lots of wood. It was the main office area, and a woman was waiting for him; she was wearing a white blouse and a black knee-length skirt, her tattoos were visible down her leg.

"Good afternoon, Administrator." Taylor smiled as he walked to the seat.

"Good afternoon, Agent Red," she welcomed, "I trust you had a safe flight."

"I did, thank you," Taylor said as he sat.

The administrator tapped the tablet she was holding, and the large screen came to life.

A voice filled the room, a woman's voice, with a metallic sound, the same he had heard through the phone at the airport when he was first planning to fly home.

"Good afternoon, Agent Red," she said. A line was reminiscent of a heartbeat monitor along part of the screen; it spiked as she spoke. "Welcome back."

"Thank you. Before we debrief, I wish to offer my condolences on Agent Orange. He was brave and saved a child's life."

"Noted, Agent," she said. "The child will be seen to."

Taylor nodded. He expected there were many cameras in this room, and the owner of the voice could see him perfectly.

"Shall we begin the debrief?" The Administrator said.

"Yes, let's." The voice agreed.

"Very well." Taylor nodded, "where should I start?"

86

Nine days later…

Daniel Knight power-walked down the hallway and stomped into his outer office; his receptionist jumped as he slammed the door.

"What is it?" Knight demanded. He had walked fast, and sweat was running down his face, and he had patches forming under his arms in his suit.

"Sir, it's Doctor Francis. She was killed a few hours ago."

"This is preposterous. The programme was shut down. Everything was destroyed, erased. Wha…why is this still happening, and how is it still happening?"

"I don't know, Sir. I just thought you should know. I didn't know you were working this late."

"Well, it seems I have to; people keep dying!" He pointed out, "the investors have completely abandoned us, bloody wiped their hands of us, so I'll have to put a stop to this one, once and for all."

"Anything I can do to help?" She asked.

"Nothing, what can you do? What, what can you do that I can't?"

"Nothing Sir, I, I just…"

"Well, don't 'just'," Knight boomed as he turned and walked into his office and slammed the door.

It was dark, almost midnight, and he was getting less and less sleep. He was agitated.

"Stupid woman," Knight grumbled to himself, taking his jacket off as he walked to his chair. "What does a woman think she can do that I can't? Stupid. Pointless. Women." He continued muttering under his breath as he sat down. It was then that he glanced up and realised one of his chairs from behind his desk was missing. He looked around, confused, but the room was in darkness, and his eyes hadn't adjusted yet from coming in from the light of the corridor and outer office to the gloom inside.

Then the lamp in the corner of the room clicked on and illuminated the woman sitting in the chair beneath it. She was wearing blue cargo trousers, a grey t-shirt, and a brown leather jacket. In her hand was a Sig Sauer P226 resting on her leg and pointed straight at him.

"You really shouldn't talk like that," The woman said. "Women can do so much more than a man of your narrow mindedness can comprehend."

Knight swallowed hard; he recognised the woman. He realised at that moment how much trouble he was in.

"Mister Knight." She smiled. "We need to talk. And what you say will depend on how this night ends for you."

The End.

The Company will be issuing a new assignment soon.

About The Author

Mark Reddan was inspired during the Covid-19 lockdown of 2021 when he woke up one morning with the idea for Agent Red, and The Company fully formed in his mind and decided to write the story down. It took just over two weeks for the first draft of his first novel – 'Agent Red' to be completed. There were no ambitions to make it available to the public – it was just for him and him alone, but when he shared it with his wife, she soon had a social media presence and a website in development to help him reach an audience.

Upon release, his First novel 'Agent Red' landed in the top ten in its category and reached an international audience.
He currently lives in the Southwest of England with his wife Sarah and writes around working as a tattoo artist.

www.markreddan.co.uk

Printed in Great Britain
by Amazon